YOU KNOW WHO I AM

Diane Patterson

Want to get an email when my next book is released?

Sign up here: http://eepurl.com/uP4yD

To Darin.
Like there was any doubt.

CHAPTER ONE

MY FIRST CLUE THAT COLIN was somewhat angrier than he had let on came when the Bowie knife landed next to my right ear. The Bowie was the first knife in our magic act, and it was supposed to land over my head. Colin didn't miss a beat while he continued the patter about how the knife-throwing act was our version of couple's therapy. I hoped it wasn't turning into his version of divorce.

The Bowie popped one of the small bags of red dye and corn syrup under the top sheet of the vertical wheel I was currently strapped to. As Colin spoke, my ear started "bleeding." A couple at a table in the front row leaned forward, as if trying to see if he had really hit me, or even if he was truly throwing the knives.

Colin outlined my left arm with stilettos. "Marriage is a bond until death do us part," he yelled—a complete ad-lib on his part. He grabbed the edge of the wheel and started it spinning.

Mystery solved: Colin wasn't angry at me. Oh, no. He was furious. And I was handcuffed and legcuffed to the wheel while he worked through it.

Colin furious was Colin unpredictable. And he was throwing knives at me.

The wheel spun and the bloody goo ran into my ear and hair. Every single night, the stage blood found new places to leak into. I hated cleaning up from this part of our magic show, but the blood was a wonderful stage effect. As long as it was fake. I did not want to clean up the real stuff. Particularly if it was going to be mine.

When my head reached twelve o'clock, I glared at him. "Honey! Let's talk! Drinks?"

The audience laughed. Colin didn't. Without a word, he threw three more times. His throws were in perfect sync with the turning wheel. The silver knives sailed through the air, making a little whispery "snick" sound as they dug into the backboard. The cold metal outlined my arm much closer to the skin than I was prepared for. And we had prepared a lot. The audience gasped at Colin's precision. So did I. I shouldn't have been that surprised: he was the three-time winner of the Eastern Canada Knife Throwing Championship, and he'd thrown more knives than most toddlers have thrown fits. But still. Everyone thinks the knife-throwing act is a sham and the backboard is gaffed and the knives actually come from the back. Perhaps some magicians take that route. But not all of them. Certainly not the one in front of me.

"I have you insured against the most horrible accidents," he said.

He was lying. Colin didn't have a spare sou to spend on anything like life insurance.

My husband's dimples were quite pronounced as he talked.

Most nights that meant he'd spotted a hottie in a sequined mini-dress somewhere in the audience. Tonight, though…he bounced his eyebrows suggestively at me. Damn, I was married to a handsome SOB, and didn't he know it.

He could flirt even while threatening to skewer me. Up until this moment, I hadn't believed Colin would hurt me during the show. Being angry at me was one thing. Being angry at me with knives in his hands was quite another. This wasn't Colin overacting; this was Colin on a dangerous mood swing. I wanted off this wheel, and I wanted off now.

My peripheral vision is excellent, so I could see Kristin on the far side of the stage. Kristin Blake was the blonde in the show. During the knife segment, she operated the controls for the wheel. All she had to do was move the speed dial to the notch marked by a silver marker. As she watched us, she smoked, which was forbidden in this part of the casino, but no one ever said anything. She gave me a little wave of her cigarette, her way of saying everything looked good from where she was standing.

No help from that quarter.

I smiled, as wide as I could, especially under the circumstances. "Colin, sweetie, let's do this somewhere else."

He picked up a few more daggers. "No, here and now is good. You. Are. Not. Going. Anywhere." He punctuated each word with a throw, and a line of knives kissed the insides of my legs, including the one that made everyone gasp, the one right by my crotch. I always held my breath a little during that throw, too. If I held my breath any more tonight, I'd pass out from asphyxiation. I had no idea what he was capable of.

Perhaps right before showtime had been the wrong moment to say I was leaving Las Vegas, the show, and him.

I hadn't meant I was leaving right that moment. Although that looked like a better plan all the time.

I started to pull against the straps holding me to this wheel. Maybe I'd get lucky and one would be loose. No, they were all fastened tightly. "Colin, stop! Please!" I yelled. If the audience figured out things had gone wrong, so much the better.

I tried getting Kristin's attention again.

But Vin Behar was looming over her. Usually a fate worse than death for any girl, except at the moment I could honestly say I had that one beat. Vin was the head of security for the Marrakesh Casino. Why he had his doughy, greasy arse here, watching our show, I had no idea. But because of him, Kristin was not watching the stage.

The wheel sped up. For a second time. I looked over to see what was going on.

Kristin was shaking her head at Vin, who had probably made some icky, lewd proposition at her. He had also maneuvered her away from the control box. Which meant he was the one changing the speed of the wheel. And Vin Behar didn't like me much.

Oh, hell.

We'd only rehearsed with one speed increase. A second increase changed the dynamic a thousand-fold. And Colin wasn't aware anything had changed.

He whipped around to face me and threw a knife in one seamless balletic movement. It was supposed to land near my foot. It sank into the platform by my left cheek.

Damn it, that knife felt cold on my face. I strained away from it as much as I could.

Colin's eyes widened a bit as he realized that something was very, very wrong here.

"Please, Colin!" I improvised. I should note I wasn't hired for my acting ability.

He glanced over at the wings, where Behar was standing, arms folded. Colin raised his hands, probably at Kristin. I didn't try to look over because the speed was beginning to make me dizzy, and it was everything I could do to avoid vomiting on myself right then and there.

"Well, I'm glad we've worked all of our problems out," Colin stammered.

Oh, thank you, Zeus. He was cutting the rest of the act. Only three knives left—not many. Stopping now was good.

Then Colin surprised me. And not in a good way. Despite the change in the speed and the lack of rehearsal and everything else going wrong, he threw the remaining knives. I didn't even have a chance to scream.

Pop. Pop. Pop.

One, two, three—they came flying at me. I closed my eyes. Which was kind of foolish, because all darkness does is make you focus on the coming pain.

From the sound of the first two knives hitting the platform, they'd landed far to the right of my right side. So he'd aimed away. Good. The last one, though…the last one ended up right against my right wrist.

The underside of my right wrist, next to the bone.

A second later, my wrist started to sting. And then to burn. Which meant he'd hit me.

Colin was about to find out what furious really was.

The wheel slowed to a crawl. Then it stopped, leaving me upside down and spread-eagled. Colin came over and rotated me right-side-up. As soon as he freed my left hand, I reached down and pulled the knife by my right wrist out. I clenched my teeth to avoid screaming. The last knife had left a clean thin line down the side of my wrist, and it was starting to bleed.

Not that a minor thing like *having stabbed me* dissuaded him from finishing in character. "Darling," he said, "are you all right? More importantly, are you going to sue?"

I glared at him, debating whether or not to snap his neck. In return, he gave me a little grin. Colin and I may not have been married in the conventional sense—money had changed hands for a green card, to be precise—but he couldn't help himself. He flirted with every woman he'd ever met. Even the one who wanted to leave him. Even the one he'd just cut.

My wrist hurt.

He put his arm around my waist and we took our bow. And on cue, I took a small step backward and slipped on some of the fake blood that had dripped off the wheel. Colin caught me and pulled me into a dip, whereupon he laid a warm kiss on my lips.

"My lovely assistant, Drusilla Thorne," Colin said as he pulled me upright. "Drusilla Thorne Abbott," he said, emphasizing his own last name. And he kissed my hand. The right one. Very close to the cut.

I looked up and down my body at all the fake blood decorating my outfit and steadfastly avoided looking at my hand.

"I'm going to kill him," I wailed.

Now that the audience was in the spirit of things, with gore and violence and mayhem aplenty, they found that line hysterically funny. As usual, we got a lot of applause as Colin locked our hands and dragged me off into the wings as Sam and Q, the stagehands and guys-of-all-work, came out to mop up the blood.

Once we were off-stage, I pulled away from him. "What the hell were you thinking?" I demanded.

"Christ, I'm so sorry, love." His Australian accent came out with a vengeance. That was a good sign. When he was upset, he couldn't maintain the Canadian accent he used on-stage.

"*Sorry*? Sorry doesn't cut it."

"I lost my head."

"I could have lost a fuckload more than that, you idiot."

He clenched his lips and lifted my hand. His fingers flicked the clasp to my bracelet and the strand of blocky platinum links fell into his hand. I always had to fiddle with the thing for thirty seconds, but not Colin. No, those magic fingers of his could work any clasp. Lots of women liked what he could do with those hands.

Whatever he was going to say, Kristin came running over with the first aid kit. "Oh, Dru, are you all right?"

"When you're backstage, pay attention," Colin growled at her. Then he pulled the blue-and-white kit open and took out disinfectant, gauze, tape, and a scissors.

She twisted her hands together, and then reached up to fiddle with her hair. How like Kristin, messing with her hair, right before she was going on. I wasn't the professional showgirl, she was, and she still did nonsense like that. "I know," she stammered.

Of course she knew. Kristin screwed up all the time, which was part of the reason Colin had needed a second assistant—me—in the act. He would have gotten rid of her altogether, but she was a very young twenty-four-year old, this was her first major job, and she was also ten thousand miles away from her home back in London. He felt responsible for her. Fine. She was solely his problem now.

He sprayed disinfectant on the cut. I counted backwards from a thousand by thirteens. Stevie had taught me that one: give your brain a problem to focus on other than the pain. I'd worked in restaurant kitchens, and there you have to saw your own hand off before anyone might okay your seeing a doctor.

He held a layer of gauze to my wrist. "Hold that."

Kristin reached forward, but I put my hand on the edge first.

He glanced at her. "Get out there and start setting up."

She vanished.

"You could have killed me, you son of a bitch," I told him.

He shrugged but he couldn't look me in the eye. "Dru, listen —"

"You listen. Our deal for four more weeks? Is off."

He wrapped the tape around the gauze, packing it tightly. "Drusilla, I need you."

He did, didn't he? Too fucking bad. That ship had sailed. "Why in the hell would I ever go out there again with you?"

"Because we're good together."

"Colin. You kept throwing the knives. That changes a girl's attitude."

He slammed the roll of tape on the counter. "You're leaving me. Changes a man's attitude."

"When a man shows up, do let me know." I waited for him to begin to snarl and I cut him off. "You're unpredictable and you're unprofessional. It's like waiting for Vesuvius to blow. I don't love you, remember? We'll figure out the INS thing. I will pay you your money back. And I'm sure you can talk someone else into marrying you. You're good at talking." I held up my left wrist. "You'd better do this one, too."

He shook his head.

"Matching wristbands?" I said. "Don't want your handiwork to be too obvious."

He wound tape around my other wrist too. "You're going to finish the show?"

"Nothing in the rest of the show can literally kill me, so yes."

Then he kissed me lightly on the lips. "Thank you. We'll talk after the show, okay? It won't happen again."

"You're damned right it won't."

He looked at me again, all regrets and apologies and contrition. "I'm so sorry, Dru." He kissed my cheek.

Son of a bitch. How did I find all of these charming, handsome bastards?

"The music's starting. Get going."

It wasn't until he was on-stage again that I realized he must have slipped my bracelet in his pocket. Not having that bracelet made me nervous. Even more nervous than an irate husband throwing sharp knives at me.

The bracelet wasn't valuable. Well, it was made of platinum, so it was worth something. No, the valuable part was the engraving on the inside. The words had been worn down until they were almost unreadable. The engraving said IN CASE OF EMERGENCY CALL and a phone number. A phone number I knew by heart. A phone number I would never ever call again. The last time I'd called it was eleven years ago, when I was sixteen. I'd had the kind of emergency that the word "emergency" was dreamed up to describe.

I'd killed someone. A man whose death people were going to notice. And that death screwed up my father's business something dreadful, to the point where I knew I needed protection from his wrath and whoever he sent after me.

I called my mother to plead for her help, and she said no.

The bracelet was the reminder I was truly on my own—well, on my own with Stevie, at any rate. Which is why I kept it close at hand and on my wrist.

I didn't need anyone else paying too much attention to that bracelet or its owner. I had to get it back from Colin before the evening was over.

After the water cabinet trick, in which Kristin had to escape before drowning and the body switching (Colin beheaded Kristin and me and then refastened each head on the other's body, a minor acrobatic feat involving new costumes and wigs) came my solo turn in the show. I went on-stage as he set up backstage.

I drifted out into the audience and shaded my eyes with my hand. "We have a minute. Would anyone care for a quick psychic reading?"

A woman raised her hand.

Lovely, a volunteer. Without one, I'd have to scan through the tables and find the woman who appeared the most interested. And who sat in the lighted section of the audience, because I couldn't see a damn person in the dark areas. I always aimed for having a woman as the first volunteer, because starting with a man appeared too much like a come-on.

Of course, everything with men is a come-on. Which is one of their better traits, true, but not in the middle of a magic show.

I sized up my volunteer. I'm not bragging when I say I have exceptional eyesight. It's a simple statistical fact. My eyesight is off the charts. I see better at twenty feet than a normal person does at maybe five or six. One of the things it allows me to do is examine people in tight close-up, notice little things about them that normal vision would miss. This woman was in her early forties, perhaps: fine crow's feet developing; her mouth framed by light lines starting to set in; the skin on her hands beginning to dry and wrinkle. Stocky. Nice clothing, nothing Wal-Martish—I could tell by the stitching. Quality shoes, a tad too practical. She needed them for more than holidays in Vegas. She was a trifle embarrassed but laughing, looking to have fun. Not seasoned with speaking in front of a crowd. She and her male companion both wore wedding rings that had the same style and lost their initial luster, so they'd been married a while. He had a redder face than his wife did and had crossed his arms over his chest.

"Do you have a specific question?" I asked her.

She shrugged and shook her head. "Didn't think you were going to pick me." Then she giggled again.

Southern accent. Sounded…Texan. East Texas, possibly Houston.

Here's what I did: I picked the topic. Then, a few possible angles, all of them light-hearted. Never anything heavy, like divorce. Every time I got a hit off the person, some sign that what I'd said registered, I got a new direction to go in. It was sort of like one of those "pick the adventure you want!" stories my sister Stevie loved so much when she started reading. Granted, she was eighteen months old at the time, and she was over them by the time she was three, when she'd moved on to reading Dumas. In French.

Colin and I had added mind-reading to the act five months ago. We did twelve shows a week, two mind-readings per show for twenty weeks, and in all that time I'd had one person say that I was wrong. All the rest were amazed, confounded, excited by what I said. More than a few people, women and men both, had made their way to the dressing room afterwards, asking for a longer reading. Yes, periodically I did it, because it was an easy way to pick up some extra cash, and a nicer way than half of the showgirls in town earned extra money in their dressing rooms.

I took the woman's hand and asked her name. Rebecca.

"You're a Becky, aren't you?" I said.

She giggled again and nodded.

I took her hand, damp and cold from her drink and trembling with stage fright, and closed my eyes. What would a woman in her early forties who had a comfortable marriage ask questions about? It was either her job or her kids. Job it was. I stay away from doing readings about kids. Too much chance to hit a deep nerve.

"You don't want to know about your job, do you?" Starting out with a question like this was a win-win—if the person said yes, then I get points for bringing up the topic, and if she said no, then I get points for having dismissed the idea.

Becky's hand clutched mine a little and she nodded.

"You work in—" Good comfortable shoes, an amiable demeanor, easy with people. Health care or teaching? "—the medical field."

Becky gasped.

"You're a nurse?"

She nodded.

"You've been overworked lately, haven't you?" The least psychic thing I could have said: nurses everywhere were overworked. "You're wondering if you should change positions?" A tiny flex in the hand. "You heard about a new position opening up and you're wondering if you should move to it."

Becky shrieked as she pulled her hand away from me and clenched her fists. She was smiling though, which was a good sign.

"Becky, I think you know exactly what you need to do. You

need to trust yourself more that you can do what's right for you and your family." After a second's pause, I grinned at her. "Would you mind telling the audience how well I did?"

I tilted the microphone toward her and Becky said, "That was amazing! That's what's been on my mind! We've been talking about it every minute we've been here!" She grabbed me and hugged me, which caused a minor bit of feedback over the sound system.

When she let go, I asked for the second and final volunteer, and a lot more hands went up.

I glanced over at the side of the stage. Colin was leaning against the pole, his arms folded across his chest. He was smiling. Stupid bastard. I picked a second volunteer.

⁂

After I finished, the music for the final illusion started. The house lights dimmed and I went backstage to get into position. Colin came up behind me and put his hands around my waist and his cheek against my head. "They love you." He kissed my hair. "Don't leave." He interlaced our fingers.

Fabulous. Now he was lovey-dovey Colin. Up mood, down mood. I was tired of babysitting him, just as I was tired of babysitting my sister Stevie, but she came much higher on the priority list than he did. Colin didn't know that, because he'd never even heard the name Stevie, let alone met my younger sister. Six months into our stage partnership and sham marriage was not the time to mention her existence. Or the fact she lived in a small one-room apartment in a run-down building a few miles off the Strip. He had never asked where I went when I wasn't with him, and I never volunteered that information. "Colin, don't do this."

"At least tell me where you're headed."

"I have to get on-stage."

When Colin's mood was up, he was fun, he was exciting, he was supportive. Those times I actually looked forward to doing the show—well, if not the actual show, then the rehearsals and the kidding around and going out together afterwards. Bad Colin made things unpleasant.

I remembered what Bad Colin had just done, and I reached into his pocket. No bracelet.

My hand moved to his right pocket but he smacked it away. "Yes, I'm irresistible. Save it for later." He grinned and pulled the curtain aside. "Your cue."

I headed out.

The finale was an over-the-top spectacular of blood, gore, and exceptional deftness with capes. Or, in some cases, dropcloths stained pink from all the stage blood that had been dropped on them during previous shows.

At the end, Colin merrily lopped parts off Kristin while I ran around reattaching them. It was all very Sweeney Todd and the audience enjoyed it, finally getting into the blood and gore of the Grand Guignol. Then Colin eluded both of his assistants, vowed to return, and then disappeared.

In sync, Kristin and I both looked up at the large sheet-covered mass hanging from the stage ceiling. It had hung up there the entire finale, of course, but no one would have looked at it with all the antics on-stage. And a bloody stain began to spread from where the cable disappeared into the sheet.

"You don't think—"

Kristin said, "Isn't he afraid of heights?"

"Isn't he afraid of hooks?" I always got a laugh with that one.

I shimmied out of my heels and lifted my foot. After waiting a moment, I wiggled my toes. "Oh!" Kristin said, late on the mark as usual. Then she wove her fingers together to form a platform for me. I stepped on her hand, she boosted me up, and I jumped to snatch the sheet off Colin.

I landed on the ground, bloody sheet in hand. And nothing happened. The audience was supposed to gasp at the sight of Colin, impaled on a meathook, before he raised his golden head and winked at them. But as I stood there with the sheet, the audience sat there, silent. Waiting.

Kristin stared up at Colin. Then she looked at me, widening her eyes a little to signal me that something was wrong.

I looked up. The round, smiling plastic mannequin's face of the practice dummy beamed down at me. The blood pack leaked dark red corn syrup. And the dummy wore a square piece of paper pinned to his chest.

Right on cue, as though the show was continuing as usual, the meathook began to lower. At the point where Kristin and I would help Colin off, to fervent applause, we unhooked the dummy to silence broken only by ice in glasses and a few murmurs here and there.

Kristin took the note off the dummy's chest. "Sorry, have to go," she read. She looked at me. "What does that mean?"

The audience seemed to get the idea that something had gone terribly wrong, because the murmurs graduated to talking at full volume.

I put my hand on Kristin's shoulder. "Stay here," I whispered. I ran backstage, to where Sam and Q waited by the curtains. "Where is he?"

Q shrugged at me. Sam said, "He went around to stage left. Said he had a new end tonight."

Sam, darling Sam. So good with the mechanical things, and so much slower with others. I ran behind the fire curtain to the other side of the stage: no Colin.

I dashed to the back door of the stage, which emptied out into the employee parking area. When we arrived at the casino for our little talk, Colin had taken the space right by the fire door, and I parked next to him. I pushed open the fire door into a cool Las Vegas night. The Strip lit up the heavens two miles away. The halogen light near the fire door showed me the parking space was empty.

Colin Abbott had abandoned his own show.

I stood in the entrance of the fire door for a millennia or two, trying to understand this. I could sooner believe Colin would literally saw me in two—or three, or more—than I could wrap my mind around him leaving his magic show.

I thought of the note. *Sorry, have to go.*

He'd left before I could.

"Filth-swilling whoremonger of Babylon," I muttered before slamming the door shut. Q slouched nearby. "Give me your phone." He handed over his mobile without so much as a peep. Smart boy. I called Colin's cell.

It rang. And rang.

He was gone. And he'd taken my bracelet with him. My stupid goddamned bracelet.

"Where is he?" The voice was oily and loathsome, and that was the best part of the man.

When I turned around, I found Barry Coffey glaring at me. Barry Coffey was short, round, balding, and the producer of our show for the casino. He had thick, stubby fingers and his suit—I think he had only the one—stunk of cigars. He'd hated me since I arrived, because I'd told him, rather forcefully and a mite shy of breaking a digit, that I was not open for business. He'd tried again when Colin had proposed the Grand Guignol theme. Colin explained that it would be messy, but a great selling point. Coffey's response? She gives me a blowjob, you can have your show. Without missing a beat, Colin mentioned that not one but two other casinos had contacted us, and we'd tank every show from here on out if we needed to. Coffey caved, but he never forgave us. Didn't send us a wedding gift either. Told us to be at the theater at the regular time that night.

Colin had shown some real pendulous testicles with his shove-back at Coffey, because in reality no other casino was interested in us. I admired him for that. It wasn't like he'd done it out of love.

Behind Coffey was his main goon, Vin Behar. If Coffey was my number-one *bete noire*, Behar was not far behind. Of course, Behar had nearly gotten me killed tonight, so he was moving up the list fast.

"I'd like to know where he is as much as you would," I told them.

"You would, huh? So would I. That's my money." Coffey waved his cigar around. He grabbed my arm, his fingers digging into my bicep, and he leaned in close. Ugly cigar smell, masking something…uglier. "Where is he?"

I looked him right in the eye. "I recommend taking your hands off me."

Coffey grinned at me as he let go. "You're his wife. So until I find him, I'm keeping your ass under hard surveillance." A nasty grin, his gaze fixed on my tits. A grin that meant that one way or another, I was on that hook Colin had disappeared off of.

He was kidding himself if he thought he'd get anywhere with

me without some part of his body snapping off. Any part. I wouldn't be particular.

"Find him. And you're not going anywhere, until I get my money back. One way or another." In case I didn't get his meaning, he stuck his cigar back in his mouth. The man had all the subtlety of the rhino he resembled.

I grabbed his hand and twisted his arm behind his back, and then kicked the back of his knee. He was face-down on the ground, lighted end of the cigar dangerously close to his cheek. "Don't touch me. Or next time I'm going to break this. Slowly. And with a great deal of pleasure." And I yanked his arm up a tiny bit more before letting it drop.

Which I would. I'd done much worse than break someone's arm when they hurt me. The first time you hurt someone, it's the worst thing in the world. After that, it gets easier. I have learned my lesson over the years: I don't make threats. I make promises I am absolutely willing to keep. It helps to make everyone understand where we all stand.

All the stagehands avoided me as I returned to the edge of the stage. Kristin came over to me. "It's a mess. No one in the audience is leaving."

"Go tell the ticket sellers there's no second show tonight." I thought of Coffey. "And give refunds."

Kristin nodded, but she didn't move. She had a lost expression in her eyes. "What are we going to do?"

Her real question was, what am I going to do? And not only about tonight, but tomorrow, and the day after. Twenty-four, out on her own, her first job since coming to Vegas to be a showgirl. I had no sympathy. When I was her age, I'd been on my own for eight years, dragging Stevie behind me, scared to death our father would find us.

I kept rubbing my wrist, wrapped with a bandage, not a bracelet. That bracelet could, in the wrong hands, cause a lot of problems. For me, and for other people. Mostly for me, though. I had no idea what Kristin was going to do, but I knew what item number one on my agenda was.

"I'm going to kill him," I said.

CHAPTER TWO

IT TOOK ME SIX WEEKS to find where Colin was hiding.

I still visited the Marrakesh on the sly, hoping to pick up information about Colin, avoiding Barry Coffey where possible. He yelled a lot, but he kept his distance. So instead, he set Vin Behar on me. Every day, the walrus parked outside the apartment I shared with Stevie. A couple of times, he sent one of his flunkies to sub for him, and they used the same car he did. But mostly it was Behar. He followed me to the Marrakesh Casino, and he followed me home. When I went running in the middle of the night, more than once he followed me by car.

But never any closer than that. He stayed in the car.

I grew to loathe that brown sedan. On the twentieth day in a row, I peered out the front window and muttered, "Goddammit."

Stevie's grunt from across the room reminded me to watch my language.

"Sorry. Zeus damn it? Zeus smite them all to Hades?"

My elf of a sister smiled up at me and went back to her computer.

My clever sister tried all the standard ways to find Colin. Stevie sat at her computer, curled up in her tight pretzel and nibbling on the bottom of her braid, and pulled his cell phone records. And then a lot of the phone records for different Marrakesh departments. Honestly, computer security at the world's largest firms still sucks, even after all these years of practice they should have had. A few hours spent social hacking via phone—a friendly chat here, a short pretense at being a field rep there—and it didn't take much for me to get Stevie the information she needed.

The phone records didn't find Colin, though. At least, not directly. One of the ways I earned money during those six weeks was doing "intuitive" readings for some of the people I knew at the Marrakesh. The ones who couldn't be convinced my act was a put-on. I put on a good show and they got their money's worth, okay? The Thai hookers had one segment of the job market sewn up and drug dealing had never appealed to me, so I became psychic and it paid our bills. My biggest fan was Barry Coffey's administrative assistant, Eliza, and I was her biggest fan, because she paid in cash. Eliza had dated Colin briefly, before I was even in Las Vegas, until Coffey told her her job depended on being available to him. Eliza was a friendly, helpful little gal.

And then one day she wouldn't look me in the eyes and her laugh was a little too fake.

I told Stevie to pull all the records on Eliza's office phone, her home phone, and her cell phone. Stevie found a call to the office from Los Angeles from a phone belonging to someone named Anne da Silva. A cell phone that had been registered after Colin's disappearance. Anne da Silva was a writer for *People* magazine who already had a cell phone number (same cellular provider), a landline at her house, and a work phone.

Usually that sort of person doesn't need yet another phone line.

Stevie checked the location of the number that had called Eliza. Cell providers keep records of phone locations—Stevie told me they do that in order to improve service, not to track people, although the ability to track people doesn't hurt. The GPS coordinates for the phone showed it mainly being in two locations over the past six weeks: near Anne da Silva's house, and in an area of Hollywood filled with apartment buildings. The GPS coordinates were specific enough we knew the spot on the block.

Modern technology rocks.

The next day I went straight to Coffey's office, where Eliza was doing some paperwork. Without saying a word to her, I picked up her phone and dialed the number we'd found.

A man said, "Liza?"

I slammed the phone down. "He asked you to get his final paycheck, I presume?"

Eliza looked as though I might hit her. Word of what I'd done to Coffey had gotten around.

"You don't say a word to him," I purred. "Nod if you understand."

Eliza nodded.

I called Stevie and told her to get ready.

At six thirty the next morning, I stopped by Vin Behar's car, parked as usual by the parking lot to my apartment building. As I had on at least six other occasions, I handed him a foam cup of coffee. This time, in addition to the cream and sugar I usually added, I'd put in enough Rohypnol to stop a rampaging herd of rhinoceroses. In Behar's case, that probably would only make him sleepy for an hour or two. He thanked me completely insincerely. I went back into the apartment, got Stevie downstairs to the car with the two small suitcases I'd packed, and then drove past Behar, completely knocked out.

When we were ten miles outside Los Angeles, Stevie logged on to the cell network's records again. Colin's phone was in Hollywood, so I headed that way.

The GPS did not steer us wrong: we found Colin's Camry in the stall marked "22" underneath a shoddily-built apartment building. Same car, only the Nevada plates had been removed. Before going to see my beloved life partner, I decided to poke around his car. A quick use of handy tools unlocked it for me. The interior was spotless. Nothing in the glove compartment.

In the trunk, I found a brochure for the Marrakesh, a spare tire, and nothing else.

Dammit. I checked under the mats; I checked the interior of that tire. No bracelet.

I bounded up the stairs and knocked on the door of twenty-two. Then I stopped knocking and started banging.

No one answered. That was frustrating. I'd come quite a ways to find him, and now here he and his car were, and yet my bracelet was nowhere to be found.

"I'm going to go in and take a look around," I said.

In my earpiece, Stevie said, "Are you certain that's a good idea?"

I pulled a pair of latex gloves on. "We're married. I get half of everything, remember?"

So I let myself in and looked around. Colin's new digs in Los

Angeles made the apartment Stevie and I had left in Las Vegas that very morning look like a palace. The construction was cobbled together out of plywood and glue, with terrible insulation and carpets that closely resembled secondhand samples and weren't cut to fit the floor space closely. There were no closets at all. The bathroom had a tiny stash of supplies stuck under the sink in a basket.

"Oh yes, this is the right place."

In my earpiece, Stevie said, "Then please do this as fast as possible."

My sister: always worrying.

The bedroom had a futon on the floor, a chest of drawers against the wall, and a clothing rack like you might see outside the dressing room in a department store. The bed was a mess. The clothes I could see on the rack were Colin's standard mix of fitted tees and form-fitting sweaters and pressed denims. The man definitely liked to show off his physique as often as possible.

The clothes on the floor looked like a mix of Colin's standard wardrobe and a few more feminine pieces heavy on the lace and paisley. Since I would bet money I didn't have that Colin wasn't a secret cross-dresser, he clearly had a lady friend.

Of course he did. Colin always had someone.

The only thing on the counters in the kitchen was a pile of mail, including a utilities bill for this apartment made out to the mysterious Anne da Silva. The only cabinets in the place were extremely low-end kitchen units that could easily have been swiped off the sidewalk after someone's remodel. I checked all of them: they contained three pots and pans, a few dishes, and Colin's extensive collection of hard liquor.

I recognized several of the bottles I had bought in Vegas. They were my favorite brands, not Colin's. Typical bastard: Steals my things, takes my drink.

My liquor. But not my bracelet.

I slammed the last kitchen cabinet door shut.

The door made a different sound than the other door I'd also shut a little too fast.

I reopened each kitchen cabinet door and then slammed each one closed again. One of them made a lower-pitch thud that didn't last as long as its compatriots.

I knelt down and checked the cabinet, which was the one with the liquor. I took some of the bottles out and then felt around the cabinet.

The back of the cabinet had been removed. How on earth he'd done it I had no idea, but Colin was a clever one with the hacksaw and the screwdriver, and that skill didn't stop at the edge of the stage. The back of the cabinet box was now a case he'd wedged in there, hard to reach and almost invisible in the dark behind liquor bottles. I removed the rest of the bottles out, and then wrenched the case out.

It was a large briefcase.

What. The. Hades?

The briefcase was locked. Something hidden that well had to have interesting things in it, right? I fiddled with the combination and it popped open on Colin's birthdate. My poor dear estranged husband, always sticking with the classics. Inside were a bunch of boring-looking papers, a novel, and some actress's headshots. Maybe she was on some show Stevie liked.

The briefcase also had what had to be one of the worst false bottoms I'd ever seen. It might fool most civilians who wouldn't notice something tiny out of place, but to someone like me, the fake edge around the bottom of that briefcase stood out like a Maserati in a Safeway parking lot.

Of course, given where he'd hidden this briefcase, he wasn't expecting snoops to get this far.

I poked one fingernail under one edge of the bottom and lifted it up.

"Holy mother of Poseidon," I said.

"What is it?" Stevie's voice asked.

The bottom of the briefcase contained five neatly arranged packs of hundreds. Each packet was worth ten thousand dollars. Colin had fifty thousand dollars casually stuck inside the wall of this stupid, crappy apartment.

"Found a little stash of mad money," I told her. I fitted the bottom back into the case and closed it back up. I returned all the liquor to the cabinet and swept up all the sawdust. The case came with me as I continued to search the apartment.

Why did Colin have an extra fifty thousand dollars lying around? And were twenty-five thousand of them legally mine? Because I could use the cash.

After finding the briefcase, I did two more thorough sweeps through the apartment to reconfirm that my bracelet was not there.

He had my bracelet. I had his briefcase. We were going to make a trade. And then I was going to be completely done with Colin Abbott.

I returned to the car. Stevie, small and curled up in the passenger seat, put down her book as I got in.

"It's not there." I opened the case and started pulling up the bottom. "This was."

Stevie's sudden gasp reminded me how long it's been since we were around so much money. While growing up, this would have been the Christmas bonus for the employee my mother *didn't* like. "How much did you take out of here?" she asked me.

"None!" I was shocked. Pocketing a few dollars hadn't even occurred to me. Dammit, I was getting sloppy.

"Well, don't," she said. "We don't know where it's from."

"As in, are the bills sequential, listed as stolen by the Treasury Department."

"Yes, precisely."

"This money could go to a very good cause, like buying us a hotel room tonight."

She shook her head. "No, Dru." She held her hand out, and when I figured out what she wanted I slapped a pair of vinyl gloves into her palm. She slipped them on before refitting the false bottom into the case.

"Fine." I had a thumping headache. I was so close to the son of a bitch I'd married and no closer to my possessions. In the plus column, yet another day when a SWAT team wasn't lying in wait for me, so our father hadn't found me.

The bottom of the suitcase fitted in snugly; Stevie started replacing all of the items that had been in the suitcase. She stared at one of the head shots in it.

"Who is that?" I asked.

"Penelope Gurevich," she said. "She's an actress. She's on a nighttime soap opera called *The Night Glen*. It's got vampires and werewolves and witches and kissing and stuff."

Kissing. Stevie is so cute. "Do you watch it?" I asked her.

She shook her head. Probably the *kissing* bothered her.

"What's that other stuff?" I asked her.

She waved the paperback. "This is a novel."

"Thanks for the update."

"You asked." She glanced at the back before flipping through it. "Techno-thriller. Not my thing."

"Not Colin's either."

She skimmed the papers. "Rental agreement for the apartment," she said, holding up one set.

"Let me guess. The renter of record is Anne da Silva."

"You are correct."

"I'm not here solely for my looks."

She made a face at me, and then returned to the papers. "Not much. Flyers from nightclubs."

Annoying. I wanted a piece of paper that said, "I left my wife's bracelet at the following location." I gripped the steering wheel hard a couple of times and let go, trying to work off some of my nervous energy. "Where should we head now?" I asked her.

"You said that if it wasn't here, he probably left it at Anne da Silva's house."

That scenario seemed most likely. But that might as well be a wild goose chase.

And I didn't have to go chasing all over this horrible city to find where he might have hidden it. Now I had something he'd probably want back. He was going to come to me.

"Where would you like to spend the night?" I asked her.

"Wherever you think is best. Somewhere safe."

We had entered the US at points far east—from Montréal down through Vermont to be exact—and kept heading west. Down to Charleston, up to Chicago, down to New Orleans, through Texas, up to Nevada. It's said that immigrants to America kept heading west in order to find the American dream. When you've gotten to California, you've gone as far as you can.

I looked at my sister. "What's the point farthest west from

here?"

"Do you mean directly west from here, or—"

Oh. My lovely, literal sister. "Driving. If we drive west."

"Oh," she said. She didn't need to look at a map; she knows her geography. "Santa Monica."

"Let's go make camp in Santa Monica," I said.

◦◦◦

Stevie directed us on to Santa Monica Boulevard and we drove ten miles to the town of Santa Monica. The landscape changed from the busy, trafficky intersections of Hollywood, with its tattoo parlors and gigantic billboards of upcoming movies, through Beverly Hills and its neatly manicured sidewalks no one was walking on and Westwood, UCLA's hometown, to Santa Monica. It seemed like an upscale seaside enclave, with the nicer houses on one side and the seedier ones on the other.

The ten-mile drive took an hour and thirty-five minutes. Traffic in Los Angeles was everything it has been advertised to be. I couldn't wait to conclude our business with Colin and be on our way, to wherever our next destination was.

We parked on a residential street a few blocks off Santa Monica Boulevard, right under the "No Parking Without Permit" sign. The sign made Stevie anxious. "Dru, we can't pay the parking ticket," she said.

"We won't have to pay any parking tickets we don't receive," I said. "Let's both visualize us not getting one and we won't."

Stevie stared at me. "That's not how reality works, Dru."

If she only knew how many times I used my stunning powers of visualization to envision us getting out of a jam without any damn idea about how that might actually happen. "It does work that way, love. It absolutely does. It has to. Trust me on this one."

We tucked the briefcase under the backseat before walking over to Santa Monica Boulevard. Stevie stuck to my side like glue, looking at all the people walking by with a mixture of concern and fascination. Our first stop was at a cell phone store, where I bought a prepaid phone with a 310 area code. The first person I called, of course, was Colin.

His voicemail answered, because he was a smart boy and didn't recognize my phone number, I assume. After his terse greeting and a beep, I said, "Don't hang up, lover. I have your briefcase. Yes, that one. If you want it back in one piece, call me immediately." I rattled off the phone's number and hung up. Then I glanced at Stevie.

Still stuck to my side, she was gazing at the Third Street Promenade. It looked like an outdoor pedestrian shopping area, hugely busy, with lots of scantily-clad Angelenos walking around and buskers and musicians and mimes looking for their spare change. Stevie was always fascinated by bustling areas like that, even though actually being in one made her nervous and practically immobile with fear.

We are unbearably attracted to what we fear the most.

I have never analyzed what that might say about me.

Stevie desperately wanted to be the sort of person who could hang out and giggle and not care about anything except maybe getting her nails done.

One of these days, when we lived in the same locale for long enough and her head seemed to be in a good place, I would encourage her to take the steps needed to break out of her shell. Or at least loosen the edges a little.

"You want to go over there?" I asked her.

She shrugged. Not the sort of thing she wanted to have to make the choice about, I guess.

"Come on," I said. "Let's go take a walk and see what's on the Promenade. Maybe they have a cupcake bakery."

"Do you think they do?" Stevie asked.

"Cupcakes are very trendy these days, and this area looks intensely trendy," I told her. "I suspect we'll be in luck."

We did find a cupcake bakery. Stevie asked me to buy her a Meyer lemon cupcake, and I asked her for guidance on what flavor I should get. She told me to get the chocolate fleur de sel. I had one small taste of it—it was very good, although the chocolate wasn't bittersweet enough for me—and then held on to it, waiting for Stevie to finish hers and ask for "a bite of" mine.

My sister generally eats very well, but she does like her sweets. Once, when she was five, I found her in the room-sized pantry of our father's house in Sussex, her face smeared with chocolate. She stood there, a tiny little elf, deeply worried that I was going to narc on her. I was eleven. Who was I going to tell who'd even care? I took her to wash up and then sat with her while she lay in bed with a tummy ache.

While we sat on the bench and waited for Stevie to finish off two good-sized cupcakes, we noticed a number of bags going by with a Union Jack on them. I finally asked one of the pedestrians going by where the bags were from, and she told us there was a British shop around the corner. Stevie turned to me, her upper lip smeared with frosting and her eyes wide. I cracked up as I used a napkin to wipe her mouth off. "Yes, darling, we can walk over there and check it out."

Stevie missed Old Blighty something awful, even if she hadn't been there in eleven years, if she hadn't seen much of it while she was there, and some of the things that had happened while she was there didn't bear remembering. Her nostalgia was greater than her common sense. I'm not afflicted with sentimentality about anything. The present moment is always better than the past. Always.

We walked over to Ye Olde King's Head Pub, Restaurant, and Shoppe, which was right near the Promenade but not on it. The Shoppe interested Stevie the most: lots of teacups made out of fine china cheek by jowl with tacky souvenirs and electric kettles, and shelves and shelves of British food items like every single Cadbury bar ever made and boxes of PG Tips tea, which one of our nannies always compared to the sweeping left on the floor after the good tea had been sold.

She was Indian. She also didn't last very long, because, as so many nannies had done, she slept with our father. I can't remember her name.

My sister had her nose practically through the plate-glass window, looking at all the treats that she wanted to remember but didn't really know. She looked up at me. "Can we..." she asked, pointing in.

"Of course." As I opened the door for her, my phone rang.

The new phone.

The phone only Colin would have the number for.

"I'll be with you in there in two shakes. Don't touch anything." I pulled the phone out and moved to an area under an awning, out of the mid-afternoon December sun and away from any casual passersby.

I felt ever-so-cheery. "Hello darling!"

"Jesus Christ, Drusilla," he said.

It amused me to no end that at this moment he was perhaps a

tenth as enraged as I had been since he left. "I've been simply fabulous, sweetheart. How have you been getting on?"

"What do you want?"

"A simple exchange of possessions. I have something you want, you have something I want. Let's make a deal."

"You have to give me that briefcase right now."

"I have to, do I? That's not how this is going to work, husband dearest."

"You have no idea what you've done—"

I definitely hate it when men talk over me when I'm in the middle of speaking, as though I'm not saying a word. This is how you deal with an annoyance like that: you simply keep talking. It then becomes their problem whether or not they hear a word you say.

"First, I need to make sure you still have my bracelet. If you still have it, you have a hope in hell of getting your briefcase back."

"For God's sake, Dru."

"What's got you rattled, Colin? You have been a bad boy. Bad boys get punished. And I am very, very angry at you. So now we're going to do this the way I want to. Honk once if you understand."

"It has to be tonight." The words were so rushed, one on top of each other. He was desperate, no doubt about it.

Desperate men don't get to set the time schedule. "You send me a picture that you have my belongings," I said, before rattling off a gmail.com address Stevie had set up for us, "and then I'll call you, all right? Not before. Not one goddamned minute before. That's how this is going to work. Awesome, as the kids say. Oh, and by the way, Colin?"

"What?" He spat the word out. He was hugely furious. I had to stop myself from giggling.

"Let's have ourselves a divorce, shall we?" I dropped the phone in my pocket.

CHAPTER THREE

WHEN I WENT BACK INTO the Shoppe, Stevie was in the corner looking at the candies. I put my hand on her back and she jumped. She had been in that apartment in Las Vegas for every day we'd lived there. Every single day. No wonder she was so nervous being out among all of these laughing, lightly clothed people.

I rubbed her back a bit. "Candy after two cupcakes?"

"I was only looking."

My sister cracks me up. I tugged on her thick black braid. "All right, we can buy a few but you have to wait until after our next meal to eat them, yes?"

She nodded and then a smile burst out. My sister is quite pretty when she smiles. She doesn't do it nearly often enough.

She picked out several candy bars and a box of tea biscuits. While I paid for them at the register, Stevie looked through the door into Ye Olde King's Head Pub. I heard a sharp intake of breath, which inevitably signals an approaching storm of anxiety and fear.

I had to push the paper bag into her hand before she grabbed it. She kept staring into the pub.

I followed her line of sight and ended up at two men setting up a darts match in the far corner. The younger man—tall, nicely built, lovely glossy brown hair—was testing out his throw from the toe line. The older man—shorter, with a middle-aged man's body and a fringe of white hair around the crown of his head—was laughing with a few spectators as he opened his box of darts. Took me a second to recognize them as actors. Well-known enough to have drawn a good mid-afternoon's crowd.

This was going to be an excellent place for me to start looking for a place to stay.

Until I heard from Colin, that was my top priority. We could use some of my hard-earned cash for a motel room cheap enough to afford yet safe enough that we would wake up in the morning without a meth deal going on around us. But that was our emergency fund and I'd prefer not to touch it if I didn't have to. Usually I didn't have to. I'd found all manner of benefactor during our travels: a girlfriend who'd found someone to gossip and exchange clothes with; the older woman looking to mother the poor homeless (but clean and well-behaved) waifs; and, mostly, the men. Who pretty much all wanted the same thing.

I never kidded myself that that subject wasn't on the table whenever I met someone. Of course, the subject is always on the table when men and women are involved. A lot of women don't seem to want to acknowledge it, at least not directly. I, on the other hand, am a realist—there is not enough time to be modest about whether or not I'm attractive and how I can use it. I trained my sights on a man who I could look forward to staying with for a few days and who wouldn't mind having me around. He would need to be kind and generous—not only with money, although that didn't hurt, but with attention, with conversation, with attitude, and with space, especially after I sprang the second guest on him.

And the gentleman had to be the sort who wouldn't give Stevie a second look. I made pointed mentions that she was very, very young. One hint that they wanted anything to do with my sister and we were gone.

That scenario had happened once. At two in the morning. On our first day in Italy, where I didn't speak the language yet. The man made a move on Stevie, I decked him, and Stevie and I were out the front door in a flash. At least the summer night was warm and sleeping in a park wasn't horrible. And the police officer who rousted us was nice enough to drive us to the nearest youth hostel after he realized we didn't speak Italian.

Oh, that *carabiniere*. I stopped by his station to thank him for being so kind to us; he asked me out to dinner. By the time Stevie and I moved on three weeks later, I spoke pretty good Italian and he'd asked me to move in permanently. Sometimes I really missed him.

My attraction to cops is not really good for my long-term health.

The local British hangout in a city was always a good place to start when searching for a friend, because groups of British people in strange warm climates tend to be very helpful, glad of finding a kindred soul. That was how I'd found the magic act in Vegas. I'd met Kristin at the Crown and Anchor, and she'd taken me to meet Colin, who'd been working out a new illusion by himself. He took one long look at me, up and down, and asked me to step into his latest box. I did, I fit, I had a job. In celebration, I splurged on a very cheap motel room for Stevie and me. And after she fell asleep, I went back to where Colin was still awake and working, and waiting for me.

Stevie watched that darts match with keen interest. The older actor I recognized immediately: Sir Gareth Macfadyen, he of the multiple Oscars and starring roles in the West End and such. When I was fifteen and Stevie ten, I'd taken her to see him in *Much Ado About Nothing* at the Old Vic. She'd loved it; I hadn't understood a word. The younger actor took me longer to name. Liam Something. He was a TV actor who had been in lots of the shows Stevie liked to watch about detective inspectors and wartime correspondents and such. Stevie had told me his name once (at least once) when I made the mistake of asking what she was watching. She proceeded to give me a rundown not only of the current show, but the entire series and then the life histories of several of the actors.

Never ask Stevie a question you do not want the complete encyclopædic answer to.

Damnation, what was that guy's name? At last it came to me: Liam Bishop. Liam Bishop was quite the ladies' man, flirting with every female within radius and not a few who weren't. I had the feeling that grin had done a lot of work for him over the years.

My sister was staring at Sir Gareth Macfadyen with something approaching awe.

"You want to meet him?" I whispered.

She looked up at me, her big blue eyes even rounder, and she shook her head rapidly.

"Oh, come on, it'll be fun," I said. "First day in Los Angeles and look! Movie stars."

The back of her jaw popped out and her lips pressed together. She was grinding her teeth. She was afraid. And maybe seconds from a panic attack.

I rubbed her shoulder blades again, trying to get the muscles to relax. "It's okay, Stevie. I was funning with you. But we can watch them play for a while."

She looked at me.

"You will sit and no one will talk to you."

"Promise?" she whispered.

"You doubt my ability to run interference?"

She looked up at me then, under her thick black lashes, and I saw a hint of a smile.

"Smart girl." I cuffed her cheek. Stevie needed some kind of real-world entertainment after being cooped up in Las Vegas for six months. And I needed to find us a place to stay for the night. Just one night. Then we were getting the hell out of Los Angeles, first thing in the morning, after dealing with Colin. I had no idea where we were going after this, but I already knew Los Angeles wasn't it for me.

We took a table near the game and watched. The waitress came by and I ordered a pint of lager for me and a milk for Stevie.

Macfadyen seemed to be a friendly sort, chatting with several of the people standing around in between taking his throws. He leaned over the backs of chairs to hear what people wanted to say to him, whispered in the waitress's ear and made her laugh as he dropped something on her tray, borrowed a pen from one person to sign an autograph for another. Whenever the pub's door opened, he'd glance at who would come in, sometimes wave and say hi. Just a regular bloke. Except for one thing. Macfadyen never gave one person a lot of attention. Anyone, that is, except the woman sitting near his table. She was maybe around my age, dark hair, maybe biracial. She had a fabulous classical profile—definitely a beauty. Macfadyen looked at her fairly often. Once he laid his hand on her shoulder to get her attention, ask if she wanted anything to drink. She touched his cheek lightly in response.

So he was spoken for. Bishop clearly wasn't. He was the place to start.

I have no especial adoration of someone whose only claim to fame has been reciting someone else's words on television. Once you've watched your father tell some of the leaders of the free world how he is and isn't willing to work with them, you're not impressed by someone who got lucky because they're good-looking. Also, actors of both genders tend to be a mite self-involved. That could work in my favor; Bishop wouldn't be interested in anything beyond himself, so he wouldn't pay any attention to little things. Like my little sister.

After all, I'd really hate to smash that lovely face of his in.

Pint glass in hand, I left the table and moved closer to the game. I watched Macfadyen and his lady friend and yes, she was hot. Probably used to having men compete for her attention. Something else I noticed from this angle that I couldn't see before: she stared at Liam. A lot. Whenever Macfadyen was otherwise occupied, which seemed to be damn near constantly, she was focused on Liam, her body even turned toward him.

This was going to be interesting. I love interesting.

Bishop picked his pint off the table, and as he took a quaff, he gave me a once-over. By the time he got back to my face, I was staring back and not shyly. He had nice eyes, blue, framed with a thick line of brown eyelashes. Very direct. The eyes made up for the slightly pockmarked skin and then some. He had a square face and a slight cleft in his chin. And that wonderful body.

"Who's winning?" I asked.

"I am," he said.

"Is there money on the match?" I asked.

He leaned against the other side of my column. "Isn't there always?"

If there's a Brit involved there is. There's nothing they won't wager on.

"What's your name?" Liam asked.

"Who's asking?"

His grin froze on his face. Perhaps he was a little put out by my ignorance of his glory. "I'm Liam. And you are?"

"Drusilla."

"Hello, Drusilla," he drawled.

In my peripheral vision, I could see Macfadyen bending down to whisper something in the woman's ear, but she was staring daggers at Liam. Or perhaps she was aiming them at me. We were standing fairly close together, after all.

Amateur.

Never let the bloke see it bothers you. And if does bother you? Walk away. Men are like buses: there's always another one.

Macfadyen took his turn throwing and a few of the assembled crowd whooped. Seventy-eight points.

"Shit," Liam said.

When Macfadyen finished collecting his darts, he turned around and looked at Liam and me. His eyes were as green as when I'd seen him all those years ago. Either that or he wore contacts. I hoped it wasn't contacts because that would be disappointing. Macfadyen pulled his darts out of the board. "And that's five-oh-one," he said.

Liam took a pint off the waitress's tray and winked at her. The bloke who'd been expecting that pint started to protest, but the waitress reassured him another one would be on its way. "We're playing nine-oh-one," he said with careful enunciation. "So it's my turn again."

Macfadyen stopped in the middle of putting his darts into their velvet case. "The hell we are."

"I said nine-oh-one." Liam picked up his score sheet. "Did you hear five-oh-one?"

Oh nice, I thought. Change the rules of the match and insinuate it's the other player's fault, that he has bad hearing or something. Because of his age, perhaps.

The woman crossed her long, toned legs. Liam couldn't help but follow the motion.

Macfadyen noticed Liam checking out his girlfriend for a moment, and then smoothed out his brow and shrugged. "You want to keep playing because you've lost, that's fine."

He didn't know. He had no idea his girlfriend was putting the move on Liam.

Tsk, tsk.

"Getting tired, Gary?" Liam asked.

Macfadyen shook his head. "We can keep playing." He opened his dart case again. "But let's play for real money. Factor of ten?"

Liam hesitated for a second. "Brilliant." He picked up his darts and his beer. He drank and winked at me, as if I was supposed to be impressed that he'd managed to keep things going.

Macfadyen moved to the column opposite mine, putting himself slightly between the woman and Liam. Things were going to get nasty now.

A young woman, her boyfriend hovering behind her, touched

Macfadyen on the sleeve and held up a camera. Macfadyen said, "Yes, of course, I'd be delighted." She handed the camera to her boyfriend. Who, if he took the picture from where he was standing, was going to get me in the background. That was not going to happen if I could help it. It wasn't likely anyone would recognize me from a photograph. I looked a hell of a lot different when I was a kid, when I'd had short blonde hair, a short body, and no chest whatsoever. But why take unnecessary chances?

I quickly intervened, holding up my hand for the camera. "Would you like me to do the honors?" He nodded, and I took snaps of the three of them together.

Macfadyen stared at me, and for a moment I wondered, is there any reason he might recognize me? The only thing my parents had ever agreed on was a pathological desire to stay out of the tabloids, so my face wouldn't have been well-known. And we hardly would have traveled in the same circles in London, but there was always a chance. I gave him a flirtatious grin. He said something to the young woman, who handed him the camera. Which he then raised toward me.

I did what I always do. I turned away. When I turned back, he was handing the camera back to the girl, but staring at me. "Here you go." He gave her a quick, shy smile, the one he used in a hundred movies. When he looked back at me, he didn't have the smile. I got a raised eyebrow and a very studied look, as though he were trying to figure something out.

The dark-haired beauty noted Macfadyen's attention to me. She stood up and leaned into him, her hand lightly curving around his wrist. Marking her ownership.

Liam pulled his darts out of the board before he returned to where I was standing. "Do you live in Los Angeles?" he asked.

He'd clearly seen the woman's attention returning to Macfadyen, so he concentrated on me, moving this flirtation along. I shook my head. "Arrived today on holiday."

"Here to see anyone in particular?"

I raised one eyebrow at him. "The sights are fantastic so far."

He grinned at that. "Perhaps you, me, and Rachelle could head back to my apartment for a while."

"Rachelle?"

He jutted his chin at the woman sitting with Macfadyen.

"Isn't she with Macfadyen?" I asked.

"She's keeping her options open."

"Does he know that?"

Liam shrugged. "Is your hotel room closer?"

"I don't have one."

There was an immediate tenseness in his spine that drew his torso away from me. Only a few millimeters, but it was enough to signal that he didn't like that answer. "Well, you see…"

I could have helped him out of his awkward pause. I didn't. I let the empty space widen. I'm good at that.

He cleared his throat. "I have an early call time."

I shook my head, as though I couldn't for the life of me understand what he was attempting to imply.

"You can't stay at my place tonight." He grinned. "But we can have fun anyhow."

Oh, could we now? I'd already started feeling iffy about Liam —changing the rules of the darts match mid-stream set off warning bells enough—but this confirmed for me that he was not my idyllic prospect for the evening. Time to have fun. "That sounds lovely," I said.

Liam's attention went back to Rachelle. Who glowed. But she

was careful not to be too obvious about it, so that Macfadyen wouldn't notice.

I wondered if Liam was interested in Rachelle for her sake, or simply to annoy Macfadyen. Who cared? It didn't change what I was about to do. Liam wasn't an option anymore. I glanced over at Macfadyen. Older, true, but probably had much nicer accommodations than Liam anyhow. And he wasn't that much older.

So the task at hand was to separate Macfadyen from Rachelle.

I sent a hand signal to Stevie, telling her to stay put, because I was going to be busy for a little while.

"You said you have a 'call time.' What's that?" I asked Liam.

That annoyed him. "It's when you have to be on a movie set."

"Oh, you're an actor, too? I mean, I recognized Sir Gareth over there. Of course." The "of course" had the intended effect.

"And what do you do?" Liam asked, his voice icy.

"I'm a psychic," I said.

His eyes widened and he backed up, just a step. Actors are such a superstitious lot.

I nodded toward Rachelle. "She's not going to leave him. I mean, she might get together with you behind his back—"

The way his gaze jerked slightly to the left told me that had already happened.

"—but he can do so much more for her than you can."

From the way Liam's mouth tightened, I'd scored a direct hit with that one.

I smiled at Macfadyen, who was pulling out his darts. He narrowed his eyes at me, wondering what was going on. I gave a quick tilt of my head toward Rachelle and Macfadyen looked over at her. Then I grabbed Liam and kissed him, hard. He didn't take long to respond in kind. He was a good kisser.

I couldn't see Rachelle's reaction clearly, but she definitely had one. And Macfadyen had to have seen it.

When I pushed Liam away, I looked over at the older actor. He was gazing at Rachelle, completely neutral. I suppressed my urge to grin.

"Your turn to throw," I said.

Liam went to the throw line and I wandered over to where Macfadyen had taken up residence against the wall.

"What was that for?" he asked quietly.

"I was wondering if you knew."

"Damn." He shook his head.

"Also, he's an asshole, and she deserves him."

That made him chuckle. "That he is."

"They have plans tonight."

"How do you know that?"

"He tried to include me in them."

Rachelle smiled over at Macfadyen brightly. And in the middle of gazing at him, she took a quick peek at Liam, who threw his last dart.

"How did I not see this?" Macfadyen asked.

"She's been working damn hard to make sure you didn't. You could make things easier on yourself, though. And on her. And not get into a nasty and pointless discussion about what the two of you are going to do tonight."

He raised his eyebrows at me.

"Ignore her, and take me home with you instead," I suggested.

Macfadyen seemed surprised by my proposition. Perhaps it was just the straightforward way I put it.

"What?" he said.

"You tell her off, you make the grand exit, with me; she does whatever she's going to do anyhow."

He raised his eyebrows and appeared to think about this. "When?"

"Now is good. Unless you're not interested in my companionship."

"No," he said slowly, "I'm beginning to think it's a wonderful idea." He gave me the lopsided grin as he took my hand in his and our fingers interlaced. He looked over at Liam. "You can pay me tomorrow, Bishop."

"What the fuck are you talking about?" Liam asked.

Macfadyen cocked his head at the board. "Do the math. I've got to leave. *Ciao.*"

Rachelle stood, furious. "Gary!"

"You appear to have other plans, darling, and now so do I. Have fun, you two." He waved goodbye to her with his other hand. I did likewise.

Once outside, on the sidewalk, Macfadyen planted a big kiss on my lips. More in the way of a thank-you than foreplay. No need to rush that part, after all.

"This should make tomorrow's scenes all that much more fun," Sir Gareth said.

"Scenes?"

"We're doing a movie. Liam and I are the villains." He glanced at me through narrowed eyes. "Easier to spot the bad guys if they have English accents. Anyhow. This is his first big movie and he's acting the total prick."

"He'll learn, I take it?"

Sir Gareth shook his head. "No matter how big you get, it ends. It always ends. It's not a pretty process, but it's a predictable one."

"You don't seem gleeful about it."

"Oh, I'm not. I am gleeful about getting out of there, however."

"My pleasure."

A block from the King's Head, he pulled out a ring of keys and pressed a button, which unlocked the doors on the blood-red Mercedes two-seater roadster, low and curvy and gorgeous, that I was standing next to. His car. Oh, yes, this was definitely the right man to have left with.

Sir Gareth had stopped a few feet from the car, keys in hand, and he was staring off into space. I walked over to him, and he appeared not to notice I was there.

"Are you all right?" I asked.

"I'm a complete fool, aren't I?" he said quietly. "I didn't notice what was going on."

"Are you in love with her?"

"No." He shook his head. "I simply wonder if I've become the old man I used to make fun of."

Time to snap him out of this. I needed him here and now and ready to do anything I asked. "I have a story that can top yours. My husband left me during a Las Vegas magic act. And we weren't in the audience, we were on-stage."

That startled him enough out of his reverie to look at me for a few seconds. Then he burst into laughter. A deep, true laugh, not one for the stage. "I apologize," he said after he managed to calm himself down. "That's not funny."

"You're right. It's not funny. It's completely hilarious."

He laughed again. "Yes, I'd have to say it is."

I grabbed his hand and led him over to the car. He opened the passenger door for me.

"A gentleman."

"Not really." He winked at me.

It was my turn to laugh as I got into the car. It was clean and nice and smelled like new leather and a lot of money. I wanted to sink into the passenger seat and never, ever come up for air. It was more comfortable than the futon I'd ditched in Las Vegas. Hell, it was more comfortable than any bed I'd been on a very long time.

I gripped the armrests. "I think I need to marry this car."

He got behind the wheel. "This car is a total slut and will break your heart every chance it gets."

"Where are we going, Sir Gareth?"

"Gary," he said immediately as he slammed his door shut. "It's Gary."

"You don't like Gareth."

"I don't like how everyone insists on calling me Sir. And they do it here more than anywhere."

Gary—seemed very odd calling a man like him Gary—said he lived in Pacific Palisades, which was north of Santa Monica and likewise bordered on the Pacific Ocean. "Very ritzy," he drawled. "I don't have one of those compounds, like everyone else seems to. It's a regular house."

Regular house, my arse. The regular houses in Pacific Palisades were large and professionally landscaped. The amazing estates were up the hill. And he lived up the hill.

We drove up to a giant wrought-iron gate, complete with intricate curlicues and evenly-spaced pikes. Gary pressed a button on his sun visor and the gates swung open, allowing us to continue up a long, windy private drive, which ended in a courtyard paved with bricks in concentric circles. A giant fountain stood in the center of it, splashing away over spotlights installed in the base. He drove around the fountain to park in the four-car garage, which he opened with another button on the visor.

Beyond the courtyard stood a gigantic two-story house that seemed to go on forever. The outside was layered with pink stone and the roof topped with Spanish tiles. The style referred to as Mediterranean. And sometimes as Tuscan. Tuscany is a wonderful region of Italy, very beautiful, filled with romantic farmhouses and delectable Italian men. Stevie and I lived in the attic of one of those farmhouses for two years, ten miles outside Florence. I did housework and chores for the little old lady, and every so often I took Stevie into Florence so she could look at the art while I looked at the men. Tuscan architecture has as much to do with the surrounding land and hills as it does with the terra cotta or the red tiles. It looks wrong plopped down in the middle of another culture.

The house, the gardens, the fountains, and surrounding garden were arranged so perfectly, giving a surreal quality to the estate. Or, if not surreal, theatrical. Like living life on a stage set. So maybe Tuscan was the exact right style for it.

The door to the garage opened, but we didn't drive in. I turned to look at Gary, whose hand was still on the button built into his visor, and he was staring straight ahead. His breathing had sped up and his face was flushed. I hoped he wasn't having a heart attack. That could wait until after.

"This is a bad idea," he said.

"Excuse me?"

"I shouldn't have—I'm sorry. I can't do this. I can't have you here." His voice had gotten very tight, enunciating each syllable.

I put my hand on his arm and he yanked it away. "Gary,

what's going on?"

He glared at me and then roared, "I made a mistake." This was a man who had a voice designed to be heard clearly on the last balcony. My ears rang and he blinked, as though he needed to get a handle on himself. "A mistake," he said in an almost whisper, a kind of apology. "Listen, I'll drive you back to Santa Monica. I'm sorry. I don't know what I was thinking—"

I leaned over and turned off the car. He glared at me. "Shhh," I said quietly.

He shook his head. "I don't want—"

"Shhh," I said, as I stroked his arm rhythmically. Eventually, I switched to a mantra of, "Calm and easy."

We sat like that for a long time, in the car outside his garage. I made reassuring noises and continued to rub his arm. His breathing started as rapid and shallow but slowed down, matching the pace set by my hand. It was a trick that had worked wonders with Stevie many times. I'm good with panic attacks.

It took well over half an hour. I thought the skin on the palm of my hand might rub off before he'd get back to normal.

I stopped when he lifted his arm out of my touch and covered his face with his hands. Then he dropped his hands in his lap and cleared his throat, but he wouldn't look at me. "I don't know what came over me." His voice was just a shade higher than it had been. He was lying. That was okay. Whatever had happened—the panic attack or whatever—embarrassed him that much.

"This isn't about you...You're a very lovely woman..." Gary was having trouble finding the words. It's so much easier when people give them to you, I guess.

"Are you going to be all right?" I asked.

He nodded, still looking at the garage instead of at me.

"Would you like me to stay tonight anyhow?" I asked. "So you don't have to be alone?"

He shook his head and finally glanced at me. "No, I don't think that's a very good idea." He chuckled, as though that were the understatement of the year. "I'm not going to be very good company for the rest of the night." He turned the car back on. "Where are you staying?"

"I still need to take care of that," I said as morosely as I could without laying it on too thick.

He looked at me as he moved the car out of park. Instead of turning around to head back to the front gates, however, he drove around the far side of the estate, on the gravel access road.

"What are you doing?" I asked.

We came to a small two-story pink house, a tiny replica of the main house. Small in comparison to the main house, of course. Large by most mortals' experience.

"That's my guesthouse," he said.

I looked at the house. Then at him.

"You could stay there," he said. "No one's using it at the moment."

We'd gone from a possible one-night stand to some kind of panic episode to this. Who was this man?

"Are you serious?" I asked.

"The least I could do," he said.

I turned away from him to look at the house again. And then smiled. I wiped the smile off my face before I looked back at him again.

"Oh, thank you," I said.

CHAPTER FOUR

GARY DROVE ME BACK TO Santa Monica. I told him I had to run a few errands, like getting some groceries for that big empty fridge in the guesthouse before I came back. I also had to get my sister, of course, but I didn't mention that part.

When I got back to the King's Head, Liam and Rachelle were gone and Stevie was still at the table where I'd left her. Her glass of milk was finished and my beer was still sitting on the other side of the table. The bag with the candies on it was still clutched in her hand.

"Need to use the loo?" I asked.

She nodded rapidly.

"Come on." I put money on the table for a tip and then took my sister by the hand. "I have a place for us to stay tonight. I'll tell you about it when you're done."

Stevie's eyebrows knitted a few times as she tried to phrase her next question. Something like, *And how did you arrange that?* But Stevie, for all her high IQ, chooses to live in a world of an eight-year-old. An extremely sheltered eight-year-old. And much of that is my fault.

I held my hands up in surrender. "He simply offered the house. That's all there is. Honestly. Can we go?"

"Sir Gareth Macfadyen?"

"The one and only."

The movie lover in her came out, intrigued and nervous. Her mouth made an O, and then she popped up to follow me to the car.

I crumpled up the parking ticket I found under the windshield and threw it in the backseat of the car.

While we bought dinner, Stevie told me what she'd found out about Penelope Gurevich while waiting for me. Penelope had been a child star from age four to age twelve, and then spent her adolescence getting awkwardness out of the way to become a stunning twenty-five year old, on her first series (a nighttime soap) as an adult, and starting to get a lot of press. She was featured in articles in *People*, *Us*, *In Style*, and *Elle*, and that was this month alone. She had a dog named Buddy and a cat named Pookums. She had lived in Sherman Oaks but had moved "over the hill" to be closer to the water. She was estranged from her mother, with whom she used to live. She wanted to do movies.

"The same story, over and over," she told me.

Celebrity journalism at its finest. I wondered about this Anne da Silva character Colin had hooked up with.

As we drove to Gary's house, Stevie stared out the window at the wide panorama view of the California coast. "Wow," she said. "It's so very beautiful."

Gary had given me a remote control for the gate and the keys to the guesthouse. The access road around the estate allowed us to bypass the main house altogether. Which was fine by me, since I had neglected to mention Stevie's existence to our host.

Stevie waited at the back of the house while I walked around inside, closing the drapes that faced the main house. Once inside, she floated through the house. First she studied the kitchen, of course. It was larger than the usual postage stamp, with a full array of appliances and a breakfast nook. We had a living room that didn't double as a bedroom. The living room had a sofa and love seat set in blue-and-white stripes—boring, but as far as I could tell, never used. The whole place had the distinct smell of dust and stale air. It hadn't been opened in quite a while.

Stevie opened the window in the dining area. "An entire house sitting here unused?"

She must not remember the estate in Berkshire, I thought. Stevie's memory is excellent, but she can block things out if she wants. I opened one of the front windows to get some cross-ventilation before dropping the drapes over it again. Then I headed to the stairs. "Come on, let's see up here."

The upstairs: two bedrooms, two bathrooms. Stevie's wide eyes told me she was thinking along the same lines I was. We'd lucked into unbelievable luxury.

Ah, how one's standards change over time.

"Which room do you want?" I asked her.

Stevie stood in the hallway between the two rooms, looking from the pale yellow of one to the green and silver stripes of the other. "I want to stay with you."

"But that's it, Stevie! You don't have to! Isn't that marvelous?"

Her small oval face tilted up toward me. "Please?"

It was too much to ask her to adjust so soon to being able to spread our wings. That was my special talent, not hers. We wouldn't be here long and it might be crueler for her to get used to sleeping in her own room before we had to cram into a closet again. "Okay," I said.

She smiled so wide I thought her cheeks might split.

I went out to the car to get our bag. By the time I came back, she'd set up her computer. "Colin has it."

On the computer screen was a picture of my bracelet on a messy countertop. Where had he taken that photo? I wondered. I didn't remember a countertop like that in his apartment. "Anything else?"

"He says he'll be ready for you at about eleven tonight." Before I could ask, she added: "It's six now."

We ate dinner and I passed out on the sofa in the living room for two hours. Stevie shook me awake. "Let's go over the map and familiarize you with the general layout of the city."

"Show me," I said. Despite my eyesight, I'm not very good at reading street signs. Or anything else, but street signs in particular. I have to memorize maps the hard way to learn a place.

She pulled out the *Thomas Guide*. We began with a little lesson on Los Angeles geography and the layout of the main streets on the Westside. The curve of the Basin, which made roads that had been more or less laid in a southwest-northeast line (Wilshire, Santa Monica) turn due east-west. The main streets that ran through to the ocean. The boulevards and freeways. Where Beverly Hills was in relation to West Hollywood or Brentwood or Pacific Palisades, where Gary's house was.

I could go back to Colin's apartment the exact way I'd driven to Santa Monica. But I had other choices.

Hell, if I could memorize how to navigate Paris, Los Angeles should be a snap. I nodded.

Just as I kissed the top of her head, the phone rang. Stevie glanced at it. "It's Colin."

"He's going to try to weasel out of meeting." I grabbed the phone. "I'm on my way, keep your trousers on. For once."

There was a long pause. "Oh God, Dru. Things have turned to shite here. I've definitely fucked up this time. I need your help." He sounded like hell. Something terrible must have happened since we first talked.

I was not only incredulous at his request, I went ahead and let him hear it. "You want me to help you? I want one thing from you. My bracelet for your briefcase. Then we're done."

He kept talking. "I've walked right into a massive shitstorm with Penelope. Jesus. She's just left here. I don't know what to do."

I was so busy remembering Penelope was the actress in those photos I almost missed him adding: "And you're in it, too. I was trying to help her. It's all a bloody mess."

"I'm in *what*, Colin?" I said.

"Jesus, Dru. Blackmail. Get over here, would you? She's accusing me of blackmailing her. *Us* of blackmailing her. I don't even know how your name came up."

My name? *For what?* "How the bloody hell am I involved with this?"

The startled look on Stevie's face was my first clue that I'd started shouting.

"I'll explain everything. Hurry. I need your help."

"You need my help?"

"You're the best at fixing problems."

Oh, that was me, all right. Ms. Fixer. "I'll be there. Don't expect me to be nice about it."

I considered throwing the phone at the wall. Why in the hell had I ever gotten involved with this man? Oh yes, that's right, he paid me to. When Stevie and I arrived in Las Vegas, we were dead broke and I thought Stevie was going to need some kind of massive therapeutic intervention, because she was repeating herself, losing her train of thought, having nightmares. When Colin offered me ten thousand for a simple marriage ceremony, of course I said yes. As it turned out, hibernating for six months in a dinky, featureless Las Vegas box worked some kind of magic. I never did find her that therapist.

Depending on what Colin had gotten me involved with, I might be the one in desperate need of a professional head-straightener.

My sister was looking at me over the edge of her knees, her hair draping the sides of her face. She started rocking back and forth, holding herself in a tiny ball. "What happened?" she whispered.

I told her.

She closed her eyes and rocked a little harder. "What do you think he did?"

I went straight from fear into fury. I had no idea what the hell Colin had been doing, but I was supposed to figure a way out of it for him, just as I'd figured out how to revamp his show and I'd figured out a way to turn the middle of the act from the draggy bit it had been into one of the highlights by doing my mind-reading act. "Hell if I know. Again."

Sometimes I get so damned tired of figuring things out for everyone else.

Stevie saw something on my face she didn't like. "Dru, don't."

"Don't what?" I snapped.

She tucked her chin back into her knees. "Don't do whatever you're thinking about doing."

I knew what she was saying, of course. How could I not? She knew better than anyone what could happen when my temper gets the best of me.

I tried to smile. It probably came out as a fixed, evil stare. "I'm not thinking about doing anything."

She reached out one thin, bone-white hand and put it over mine. Her hand was so much smaller than mine. And cooler. "Everything's going to be okay, Dru. You didn't have anything to do with what he's talking about, so there's not a problem, right?"

I pushed back the black bangs off her face. "Here's what I want you to do while I'm gone. Sit tight, and watch the telly. I'll give you a call when I'm done with Colin and reassure you that he's still alive and in one piece, okay?"

She nodded. I kissed her forehead and grabbed my purse.

I was glad Stevie had faith that I was going to deal with Colin in a rational, careful, adult manner. Because at the moment, I was so furious I had no such faith in myself.

CHAPTER FIVE

IT WAS MIDNIGHT BEFORE I arrived at Colin's apartment. I found a space a block away and considered myself lucky, because I hadn't seen much parking. The streetlights cast little skirts of light here and there, leaving enough dark patches to make me hug the street-side of the sidewalk. I can take care of myself and I don't seek out trouble. It finds me often enough anyway.

As I neared Colin's apartment, I saw a light brown sedan at the end of the block, near one streetlight. A common enough car, but a light brown sedan sat outside my Las Vegas apartment every day for six weeks, Vin Behar sitting in it, watching my comings and goings morning, noon, and night. What a coincidence that a similar light brown car, down to the dent on the front bumper, was right here, by Colin's apartment.

In my universe, there's no such thing as a coincidence.

I walked right past Colin's building. In the front seat of the car was the glow of a cigarette held in a beefy hand.

Vin Behar was here.

How in the hell was Vin Behar here?

As I got nearer, the passenger side window slid down. The odor of sweat and cigarettes and sour cheese wafted out of his car. "So you found him after all," he said to me. "Congratulations."

Vin Behar, as large and ugly as ever, was right in front of me. This was a long way from the Marrakesh Casino. Vin looked like the cop he used to be, except older and meaner and with extra gut. He gave me the creeps the first time I'd met him and my feelings hadn't changed since then. I wanted away from him and his ragged cuticles and short-sleeved shirt that I knew had the armpit stains burned in, even if I couldn't see them in the dark car.

"Why are you here?" I said.

"Maybe I followed you." He grinned.

Maybe he'd planted something on my car. A GPS tracker was a couple of hundred dollars. A lot of money for a tightwad like Coffey. The boss must have been desperate to find Colin.

"Did you get a good morning's sleep?" I asked.

He spat out the window. Lovely man. "You're going to pay for that."

I appeared to consider the idea. "No, don't think so."

Behar smiled at me, those ugly tobacco-stained teeth dark in his mouth, and he started his car. "Go see loverboy."

I walked back to Colin's, wondering why Behar was here. If he was supposed to bring Colin back, shouldn't he be in Colin's apartment, wrestling my husband into a gunny sack or something? Why was he outside Colin's apartment, so calm?

Screw them. Screw them all, *hard*. I would go in to that

stupid, tiny apartment, deal with Colin, and then leave him to his own problems. It couldn't be much harder to get divorced than it had been to get married, could it? Hell, my mother had managed three divorces by the time I was fifteen.

At the stairs, I hesitated again. Move it, I told myself; let's get this over with.

The thumps of my footfalls should have alerted Colin to my presence, prompted him to open the door. But the door remained closed.

I peeked in through the bars over the side window. No lights on, no one moving around.

"Colin?" I said.

After waiting a few seconds, I rapped my knuckles on the door. That apartment was so tiny he had to have heard it. But he didn't show.

I had arrived late, but damn it, I'd told him I was coming. Colin should have been on pins and needles, ready to talk, ready to get me to help him out of whatever he'd been babbling about on the phone.

Colin did not come to the door.

When something smells wrong, do not be around. And if you need to stay and not run far, far away, at least make it seem as though you are not around. I reached in the pocket of my jacket and took out a pair of latex gloves.

After I had the gloves on, I tested the door handle. If I'd needed to, I could have jimmied open the door—hell, breathing hard probably would have done it. But the doorknob turned.

My breath caught and I stopped pushing the door. Alarms went off in my head. Of course, there were lots of possible reasons for the door being open and Colin not answering. Maybe he'd walked to the nearest Starbucks for a midnight cappuccino. Or perhaps he'd gone out for a pack of cigs for himself, taken a walk around the block, gone to do some food shopping while waiting for me.

I pushed the door open.

The smell of copper hit me first. On top of the copper lay a faint acrid odor, like the wind near a portable toilet. Urine.

Turning on the light showed me Colin on his side by the kitchenette, his back toward the door. The back of his head was a pulpy red mass, mixed with plaits of his golden hair. Red flecks decorated his white shirt; a large red stain soaked the carpet under his head. I walked in a wide circle around him until I could see his face, with his eyes wide open in surprise. He'd left a puddle of vomit on that dusty carpet. His jeans were wet, which explained the smell of urine.

Colin looked like a part, a gruesome part, of our Grand Guignol stage act, with much better visual effects and an awful, horrible smell. It seemed unreal. It had to be unreal. I had to be hallucinating. There was no way he could be dead.

I leaned down and touched the side of his throat, my gloves smooth against his skin. His body was warm, but nothing pulsed under my fingertips. It had been two hours since I talked to him. How in the hell could he be dead?

Oh my God. Colin was dead. Dead.

I've seen dead bodies before. Even ones whose heads have been cracked open. And the smell is horrible and the sight is horrible and neither of those is the worst part. Someone who had been alive not too long ago was silent forever. Their soul, their spirit, whatever you call it, that animates the human body and gets it through the day is gone and there is no going back.

I wasn't even aware I was crying until a tear dripped onto Colin's sleeve.

Come on, Col, get up and wipe yourself off. Fun and games are over.

A glint from his hand got my attention: his hand was over my bracelet. He'd been holding it. Blood had smeared on the faint etching, highlighting the words there: IN C SE F EM G NCY LL and the phone number. That phone number. The number I couldn't call ever again. Had Colin called it? More important, had anyone answered?

I thought about taking the bracelet. I even reached for it. But it was there, under his hand, and it was going to be obvious someone had disturbed the body taking it.

Near the other hand was his cell phone.

When I stood up, I did notice the bottle of gin that had been tossed aside, its glass smeared with blood and hair and flesh. Bombay gin. My brand. I was willing to bet folding money that was the bottle I'd left at Colin's place in Vegas. Zeus in a sidecar, my fingerprints were on that bottle.

My bracelet. My fingerprints. I had to get out of here.

Colin, what did you do? Why would someone do this?

Behar had been sitting there in his car. Waiting for me? Waiting for me to come in here and see this? Waiting for me to get caught in here? He'd driven away as soon as I'd gone up the steps.

I ran out onto the top of the steps and promised myself I would find a pay phone and I would call 911, but until then I was getting the hell out of here. And maybe I wouldn't use the first phone I found. I could put a little space between me and this.

As it turned out, I didn't need to find a phone at all.

The first patrol car, lights and sirens blaring, rounded the corner.

Someone had called the cops. Behar, most likely. Or, if Behar hadn't killed Colin, whoever did kill him. And Behar had to know who that was.

I stripped off the latex gloves, shoved them in my pocket, and pulled out my cell phone to call Stevie as I walked down the steps. No use waiting until the last second to get her working on this problem.

And there was no question that I had quite the problem staring me in the face.

She answered after one ring. "Is everything okay?"

"Find me a defense lawyer."

She stuttered a number of noises, like she wanted to ask something but couldn't find the words. Then she managed: "We have no money."

"The money in the briefcase, Stevie. Use it."

"We don't know where it came from—"

"Stop arguing, and start dialing."

The patrol car slowed to a stop in front of Colin's apartment. The officer got out and shined a flashlight right at me.

"You're at Colin's?"

"I'm at Colin's. Hurry it up."

I popped my phone in my pocket and settled down to wait.

CHAPTER SIX

WAITING AROUND AT A CRIME scene is not only not glamorous, it's distinctly awful. For one thing, there's no comfortable seating.

The first uniformed cop out of the car bounded up the steps to Colin's apartment while the second one, a red-haired guy named Ulriki, took my statement, which was as close to the truth as I would get: he was my estranged husband, we were getting together tonight to talk, I showed up, and he was dead. I did not volunteer the words "Penelope Gurevich," "blackmail," or "Vin Behar." One thing at a time, and right now the necessary thing was shutting the hell up.

The presence of cops attracted the attention of neighbors. The street went from lifeless to full of people in about ten minutes.

I realized we were in LA when I overheard one woman asking the man next to her, "Where are the cameras?" and the man replied, "Nah, I think this is for real."

The second pair of cops blocked off the scene with yellow police tape. Then one of them, the only woman of the four, asked me for my statement again. I asked her if we could talk under the stairs, away from the growing crowd of people. She thought I wanted to get away from the noise. In reality, I needed away from the cameras that were coming out and focusing on me.

After I talked to the second cop, I stood in the shadows under the stairs and waited for the next time I had to tell the same damn story again. Stevie hadn't called me back, which meant she didn't have good news for me yet.

When the Ford drove up and double-parked behind the second patrol car, I knew two things: the homicide detectives had arrived, and I would be leaving soon. Either with police escort, or without.

The driver got out—thin, wiry, shorter than my one hundred and seventy-five centimeters. Under the street lights, his skin color looked Hispanic and he had the flattish nose of a Central American Indio. He had an empty expression that must have taken years to develop.

The second detective got out and I wondered whether he was free for dinner, and then whether I would be free to join him. Or at least out on bail. Forget dinner; I wanted to talk about breakfast. Great gods above, people really were better looking in Los Angeles. He was maybe a decade younger than his partner, taller, and muscular. I admit to being deeply shallow and preferring men who are in damn good shape, which he was. He seemed congenitally unable to smile. I was willing to work very, very hard on that problem. He glanced around the scene and stopped when he came to me. I saw the barest twitch in the side of his lips. A good sign. A very good sign.

Was being sexually attracted to one of the homicide detectives investigating your husband's death a normal reaction? I'd ask Stevie, but at a question like that she'd blush and hide in a corner for a while. Until such time as she'd researched the answer in a couple hundred books, half of them in German, and had a prepared a treatise on the topic.

Then one of the uniforms pointed me out. My current object of serious lust glanced at me, and then said something to his partner, shielding whatever he was saying from view. From my view. But not before I saw that twitch flatten right out and the shoulders stiffen enough to indicate the shields were going up. Clearly, I should make other breakfast plans. And I needed to watch what I said to him. The most likely suspect in someone's death is immediate family. A marriage like ours, doubly so.

I hoped Stevie was having luck finding me a lawyer. Any lawyer. Who was willing to accept a down payment of cash from an unknown source.

Once in my life, I needed to find out if there was an easier way to do something. There had to be. For once, I needed to try that option first.

The detectives walked toward me. My pulse raced and my solar plexus seized up, which meant my nervous system was in working order. My father used to say the only people who weren't tense around the police were other cops and criminals.

My father: a man never nervous around cops.

After all, he had half of Scotland Yard on his payroll.

My affect when I'm nervous is to get languid. Relaxed. Some have used the word "cool" and others "patronizing," but in my own defense I was raised to be patronizing—people were either of our class or they were below it. Just because my station in the world has fallen precipitously doesn't mean all that early training went to naught.

When the detectives got to me, the badges came out with introductions. The tall one with the nice body and the not-so-nice scowl was Detective Samuel Gruen. The twitch in his lips developed into a hard stare. All right then—he would be playing the bad cop. His partner was Detective John Vilar. Vilar had a softer, less confrontational stance, and a sadder air. I wondered how long each man had been doing this job.

Vilar's eyes were soft and brown. "Mrs. Abbott." His voice as polite and sad as his demeanor suggested. "We'd like to ask you a few questions about your husband."

Very nice. The power plays were starting. Excellent. I put on one of my tight half-smiles and looked at Vilar. "It's Thorne. Drusilla Thorne. I don't use Abbott." I gave his partner a swift glance. Gruen didn't change expression; he shifted his weight, and I could tell he'd wrapped up this case in his mind.

Vilar nodded sympathetically and made a note in his book. Along the lines of how I was obviously the murderer, perhaps. He wrote another line in gorgeous handwriting I couldn't make heads or tails out of. As I've said, reading isn't my strong suit. He looked up. "Ms. Thorne." What a soothing, musical voice he had. "Can you tell us what happened?"

Gruen stepped backward and started walking around the area under the stairs, which was a not very subtle way of circling me. I felt intimidated, which I was sure I was supposed to. Now that he was not a Possible Prom Date, I was not in danger of being overly helpful. Not that I ever am, to be honest.

My father's number-one rule echoed in my mind: *Never*

volunteer information. Despite the fact that it came from my father, it was still good advice that has come in handy a number of times. "I don't know what happened." I spoke quietly, which made Detective Vilar lean in closer to me and Gruen stop pacing. "I think my husband's been murdered."

Gruen looked me up and down in a way that made me think maybe breakfast was back on. He stopped when he got back to my eyes. "That's a nice outfit. You have something planned for today?"

I shook my head. "I like to dress well, Detective."

He nodded, his gaze still on me. He had beautiful hazel eyes. "Do you often carry latex gloves in the pocket of your nice outfits?"

I believe the only reaction to have to that was: *Fuck.*

The gloves were showing.

"Don't answer that."

The voice startled both me and the good detective, and we turned to see who'd joined our little tête-à-tête.

The man standing there wore the most expensive suit I'd seen in quite a while. He wasn't handsome—plain, with thinning blonde hair on top—but what he lacked in conventional attractiveness, he more than made up for with the most direct stare I'd seen in a while. He carried a dark leather briefcase and he looked as comfortable telling us what to do as, well, only a successful lawyer could be.

A lawyer.

My lawyer.

Stevie's supernatural powers could make a religious convert out of me.

"Nathaniel Ross. Good to see you again, Detective Gruen."

Gruen gave him a malevolent look that made me damn glad he didn't have me in an interrogation room.

Ross took me by the elbow. "I need to talk to my client."

He started to pull me toward the street, where the lights and the cameras were, but I shook my head and pulled him toward the darker alley on the side of the house. I didn't want to be seen.

What can I say? Acting guilty is a habit with me, formed at a tender young age. When I was, after all, guilty at least eighty-five percent of the time.

"You're quite well-known, aren't you?" I asked, smiling enough to seem flirtatious.

He shrugged, as if to say *Of course I am.* "My being your lawyer is going to make the cops look that much harder at you."

I nodded. "So you're expensive." As if the shoes hadn't told me that. "What on earth sort of payment did my sister offer you?"

Ross raised an eyebrow at me. "Sister?"

"My sister didn't call you?"

"I don't think he's your sister, no."

"He?" Fire of Hades, had Stevie managed to overcome her fear of leaving the house and of meeting strangers in order to ask Gary to help us? And he had said yes? "Does he have a name?"

"I'll just say I was surprised he doesn't have a stronger Spanish accent."

And the answer became clear: "he" was Roberto. Roberto Montesinos, that is. A very wealthy man. Also, my stepfather, and most probably the man who had told my mother not to save me that night eleven years ago when I was covered with blood. *Now* he saw fit to get me a lawyer.

Roberto could not have known where I was for the last eleven years. So the question became: How had Roberto known I was in trouble so fast? And if he knew where I was, did my father?

I glanced up at the window of Colin's apartment.

No. I was not going to go there. I smiled and nodded. "Ah. Of course."

Ross held up a business card. Nice linen stock and raised printing. On both the front and the back were phone numbers in blue ink. He tapped the number on the back of the card. "You need to call him in the morning," my lawyer said. "And then tomorrow you and I need to have a talk."

"I'd prefer to talk to you first."

"That's what I said. But strangely, that point was non-negotiable."

It wouldn't be, not with Roberto. "And you're not going to argue anything you're not paid to."

The lawyer's eyes narrowed. "Something like that. Call after you've talked to him."

I assumed the number on the front was his cell. I looked at him with a sideways glance. "I look forward to it, Counselor." Though if I were being truthful, I wasn't. At all. Of course, as a rule I'm not truthful, either.

<hr />

Nathaniel Ross got the police to release me. Powers of persuasion beyond mortal ken perhaps. When they released me, it was 4:30 Tuesday morning. I took Sunset Boulevard for the long drive back to the guesthouse in Pacific Palisades. Sunset was empty, or nearly so. I didn't think about that during my drive back. Nor did I think about how someone I knew, someone I'd been married to, had been brutally murdered tonight. I didn't even think about how the detective who inspired such unclean thoughts had pegged me as the murderer.

No, I mulled over how to tell Stevie that Roberto was back in our lives in a big way. If the thought of dealing with him made me want to jump in my car and head for the Mexican border, it might blow one of Stevie's circuits. She'd freak out or pass out. Or become a complete and utter mess, unable to take care of herself in the simplest ways.

Deep down, I suspected she had those little meltdowns to give me something to focus on when things got very, very rough. Which was very thoughtful of her, but I didn't want her doing it when, for the first time in years, I wanted to have the damn meltdown instead.

The house was dark and Stevie was sitting in the living room, facing the kitchen. The phone was still clutched in her hand, resting on her knee. It wouldn't surprise me to find out she'd been frozen in that exact position since I called. I flicked on the overhead lights and tried to smile. It was a complete and total failure as a facial expression.

"You're back." Her voice was full of fear, as though she were expecting me to hit her for not being able to do the impossible. Whereas I had gotten over that urge a decade ago. "I never found —"

"Everything's going to be okay, sweetheart."

"What happened?" she said.

"Colin's dead."

She gasped.

I told her Colin had been murdered, with none of the gruesome details. Not to spare her, surprisingly, but because I didn't want to relive it again. Even so, I couldn't wipe the mental image of his open eyes over a large and spreading red pool on the carpet any time soon.

I mentioned Behar's appearance outside the apartment, what

the cops asked me about, and, lastly, gently, the attorney who showed up.

"Courtesy of Roberto Montesinos."

Stevie sucked in her breath and stared at me. I nodded.

I gave her the business card Nathaniel had given me. She glanced at both sides. "I have the feeling we're going to need these phone numbers. Program them into my phone."

She nodded as she put the card down on the coffee table. She'd memorized them with a glance. My poor little sister, who remembered every single thing she'd ever read. It was a wonder her brain didn't explode.

Focus, Dru. "I need to call Roberto in the morning."

"If he comes to Los Angeles, you'll need to meet him in person."

If he comes to Los Angeles. My sister, ever the optimist. Like there was a chance he *wasn't* coming. "Yes, I will."

The guesthouse was quiet after that. Not much to say. After eleven years and twice as many identities and untold amounts of covering our tracks, it was over. Our journey was over. We had reached the Pacific Ocean, and there was nowhere else to go. It was time to see Roberto.

"What time do you want me to wake you?" Stevie asked.

The sky was already lightening for sunrise. My hands were shaking from an overdose of adrenaline. On a bright new day when I needed to be fresh and alert, I wasn't going to sleep. "I'm much too wound up. I'll go for a run."

She looked at me. Then she shrugged and nodded.

Running was the best way of starting my day off with a bang. While I changed into running clothes, Stevie went into the kitchen, hunched over her laptop. I opened the back door. "Be back in half an hour."

She lifted her hand and waved without taking her gaze off the screen.

The road from Gary's palace down to the lowlands of Pacific Palisades was narrow and winding, and I had a mild worry a Ferrari might tear around one of those bends. Mostly the chance of anyone being up at this hour in this area was small. Their maids and assistants might be out, but those people have to worry about speeding tickets and take it a little slower.

Sunset Boulevard was crowded with cars headed out of Pacific Palisades. The commute to Los Angeles had started, poor bastards. I followed the road—Chautauqua, Stevie had said; praise Hermes, I would never have to spell it—down to the start of the beachfront park. I pounded out a quick roundtrip of five miles on the sand, racing against the sun as it rose in the sky. My skin isn't quite as sensitive as Stevie's, but it still can't handle too much direct sun. "Death frozen over" is a good look for me. It keeps my skin smooth and soft, and in a world of tanned or over-freckled women, I stand out.

In Las Vegas, when I ran, I ran in the middle of the night. In the open air when I could, in the casino's gym otherwise. I hated being indoors. Flying outside was the way to go.

If I'd been familiar with the Pacific Palisades and Santa Monica areas, I would have had my usual faster pace of six minutes a mile flat. The beach made me wish Stevie and I were going to stay in Los Angeles permanently, because it was runner heaven. Runners headed all different ways, with different routes. Plus, there was varied terrain—rough and smooth, hilly and flat—to run on. I was ecstatic. Or, as ecstatic as I ever get when sex isn't involved.

The final push up the hill to Gary's house was fabulous,

draining any excess nervous energy. Once the static was removed, I could focus on what I needed to do. And what I needed Stevie to do.

At the estate, I found our host yelling bloody murder at the top of his lungs.

He was standing behind the guesthouse—Stevie must have had a massive heart attack—yelling, "Jesus fucking Christ, what is this piece of shit doing on my property? Can you fucking hear me in there?" He was facing the guesthouse, his back to me as I came up the service lane. When he finished yelling and didn't get a response, he kicked what must have been the source of his frustration: my car. Nice.

"They can fucking hear you in Encino," I said. I wasn't quite sure where Encino was, but I was sure of that.

He whirled around, glaring at me. He slammed his fist onto the hood of my car, which had to have hurt, but he didn't so much as wince. "What the hell is this dogshite doing on my property!" Spittle was flying out of his mouth.

"It's my car." I took a step closer, but not too close. No need to escalate this. "What's the problem?"

His rigid body radiated fury. Both hands flexed in and out of making fists. "Get the fucking hell off my property!"

Gee, that was fast. I hadn't even asked to borrow money yet. "What?"

"You come here, you dirty the place up. Get out. Today. Now."

My car was not attractive, but it wasn't that bad. Something else was going on. Maybe he'd forgotten I existed. Gods, that would explain a lot. Like what he was doing picking up women in bars and giving them places to live.

"Do you remember me?" I asked, making my voice a lot softer.

"Of course I do," he snapped. "Get off my property by noon or I will have the police here." He pointed a finger at me. "Do you understand?"

His offer of the house the previous night was clearly open-ended. So either Gary didn't remember that conversation, or he hadn't meant what he said, or something more bizarre was going on. Had the police come by, asked him about Colin's murder, and he'd decided he wanted no part of it? "Yes, I understand," I said.

"And nothing had better be missing from in there."

He stalked away then, leaving me on the gravel driveway. He rounded the corner of the guesthouse, heading toward the main house. I waited for a minute to see if he was going to come back and say anything else. I was hoping for "Didn't mean it" or "April Fools."

He didn't come back.

Fabulous.

I went into the guesthouse to find Stevie and get her to pack things up. She was sitting on the bed in the room we'd slept in last night, still and quiet, her hands on her lap as her legs dangled over the edge. "What happened?" she whispered, as though Gary might be right behind me.

"Your guess is as good as mine. Possibly somewhat better."

The way she tilted her head to the side told me she didn't believe me.

"I swear to you, last night he was kind and generous and… sweet. Now this."

"What should we do?"

"If he's going to call the police on us—well, on me—that's one more complication we don't need. I have my appointment to get to this morning." Neither of us dared say the name *Roberto* out loud.

"Choice number one. You come with me and wait."

That was a non-starter. Not only would Stevie not be allowed to grace Roberto's august presence, it would terrify her to be that close. She shook her head.

"Choice number two. You stay here and pack everything up, and I will do my damnedest to be back by noon."

"What if he comes in?" she whispered.

"Lock every door. Deadbolt everything. And if he does get in…cry. A lot." I held up the Vegas phone. "You call the cops."

She studied the way her feet were bouncing against the side of the bed.

I sat down and put my arm around her. "Everything's going to be okay."

That got her to look at me. "No, it's not."

She had a point there, but I wasn't going to concede it. "Everything's going to be fine. I will be back by noon." I kissed her forehead and headed into the bathroom to shower.

Chapter Seven

THE LOBBY OF THE PENINSULA Hotel is not the fanciest hotel lobby I've ever been in. I'm not sure which hotel should get that distinction, because they all sort of blur after a while. Also, I haven't been in very many fancy hotels in the past eleven years and undoubtedly they've all upgraded in the interim. But when I did stay in them—and I did, quite frequently, up until I was about sixteen and a half years old—I stayed in the hotels where the staff knew they were better than the vast majority of the patrons and were not shy about advertising this knowledge.

Many of these hotels were in France, which will probably not come as a surprise.

The Peninsula Hotel in Beverly Hills is snooty and lavish and exclusive, and yet no one working there would dare say they were better than the people who came in. They might think it. But they won't say it, and that already puts them several thousand notches above hotels like the Georges V in Paris in my book.

Not that anybody's been asking me for my opinion of these places during the last eleven years, mind you.

There were lots of people at the Peninsula, early in the morning. Businessmen in suits, Japanese tourists preparing to go shopping, film producers in Hawaiian shirts and grimy yet pressed linen Bermuda shorts. Most of the people there seemed to be heading for the restaurant to get breakfast.

I didn't fit in. I was dressed too well. The less money you have, the more you need to avoid looking desperate. So I had dressed in one of my best serious outfits. If the funeral you're going to is your own, it's polite to save the undertaker some time.

My execution was scheduled for eight a.m. and I arrived only half an hour late—which for me, arriving at a place I don't want to be, doing something I don't want to do, at anywhere near the appointed time, counts as punctual. The concierge's name was Genevieve and she looked like a movie star. Genevieve the Magnificent smiled and said, "Hello. May I help you?"

"I'm here to meet someone."

"What is the guest's name?"

I smiled. It probably didn't reach my eyes. "I'd really prefer not to say out loud."

Her smile suddenly didn't get any further than her mouth either. She'd been waiting for me, I guess. "Your name?" she asked.

"Drusilla Thorne."

Genevieve nodded and typed something on the screen in front of her that I couldn't see. "I'll have Clark escort you."

Clark was a tall, good-looking young man who in Genevieve's movie would be the movie star's gay best friend. He had a smooth face and amazing skin and he introduced himself as though I were his valued customer. "This way," he said, and he led me through the marble hallways and out into a fabulously lush garden, one you wouldn't expect to find in the middle of the grounds of a hotel in Beverly Hills. But everything's a movie set, when you get right down to it, and this place was no different.

The villa was a separate building on the hotel grounds, a large house operated by the hotel. Clark led me through the hotel's security. Ten meters from the villa's front door was a highly muscular guy in his thirties with close-cropped black hair and a casual outfit that would allow him to fend off attackers without much effort on his part. His fraternal twin waited ten meters to the far side of the villa. These would be the guards we could spot easily, the ones attackers would go for first. There were probably at least two others, but I'd have to work on spotting them and I wasn't that interested. The guard closest to us gave Clark and me thorough once-overs, although I'm sure to the hotel clerk it looked like perhaps the guard was checking him out.

He wasn't checking Clark out any more than he was sizing me up. Don't get me wrong. Ex-Mossad agents can be as gay as anyone else. However, they don't check out possible prom dates while they're on the job. They're sort of like asexual killing machines until it's time to call it a night. Then they party way harder than almost any other highly trained servicemen, possibly exceeded only by German paratroopers.

Clark held out his badge. "She's expected," he told the bodyguard, who nodded and took over Clark's duties. The bodyguard escorted me to the door of the villa and indicated I should open it.

He stayed directly behind me. Harder for me to use peripheral vision on him.

I walked into the villa, which was luxurious and overwhelming; for all that, it was also a fancy hotel room. I didn't pay attention to the quality of the wood floor or the design of the immaculate modern kitchen that would have been a jewel in any high-end home. I stared into the living room.

The sole occupant of the living room sat on the silk and chenille sofa, the table in front of him piled high with papers and notepads. The fireplace was fully ablaze. Three phones littered the area near his teacup. His shoes were off and his stockinged feet were rubbing rhythmically against the Tibetan carpet. His reading glasses sat perched on the end of his nose and he seemed deeply engrossed in whatever he was reading—the financials of a company he was thinking of buying, a report from his tech division on a new product they were developing, or maybe *Entertainment Weekly*. Whatever Roberto Montesinos Degollado paid attention to, he gave it his full attention.

Eleven years ago he had told my mother to hang up on me. That was his way of paying attention then.

Roberto had gotten older. Of course he had; a decade had passed. I had last seen him eleven years and six months ago, at my sixteenth birthday party. Tensions were riding high between me and my mother at that point and I wasn't too concerned about what Roberto was doing. Since then, his hairline had receded some and he'd gotten streaks of gray through the thick black hair still left. His face had sagged a bit and he'd put on some weight around his middle. He looked like the older brother of the man I remembered.

When the guard and I entered the foyer, Roberto looked up from whatever he was reading. He stared at me for a good thirty seconds, probably as startled by the changes eleven years had wrought in me as I was by his.

After those seconds went by, he nodded. The guard moved from behind me and slipped out the front door of the villa. I guess he'd been waiting to get confirmation that it was really me. Maybe if Roberto hadn't been sure, he had orders to snap my neck.

It had taken him the full half a minute because I looked a great deal more different than the girl I had been, that was for sure.

Roberto folded his glasses and tucked them into the pocket of his shirt before he stood up. "Trudy," he said.

"It's Drusilla."

He stopped moving, as though he were surprised I were arguing the matter. Identity is always a power game. Always.

He was the first person to teach me that explicitly.

Roberto nodded. "Drusilla." He walked over to where I stood, unable to move. He spread his arms. "May I?" he asked. I guess when I didn't fight over the issue, he gave me a big hug, the kind he used to give me all the time when I was younger. I decided to stop fighting and let myself enjoy it for a second. I did not hug him back. He still smelled like cinnamon and coffee and whatever weird aftershave he now used.

"It is good to see you again. Jane will be amazed. You are all grown up now."

"I always was."

He thought about that. "Yes, I guess you're right about that. You look so different now, *bella*."

"Amazing what changing one's hair color will do."

He leaned back and studied me. He could have mentioned my height, or my body, or any of the thousand things that were different. "Your eyes are so old now."

I shrugged. "We have all changed in the past decade."

"Why do you have that accent?" he asked.

"This year's voice. Suits my purposes." I stepped away from him and looked around the villa. "It must suck being really rich. You have homework all the time."

"I love what I do." He grinned. Of course he did. He always did. So long as everything worked out neatly. So long as no one caused any trouble.

Mistake number one: being the person who always caused trouble.

"Please, come, sit down," he told me. He lightly grasped my arm and led me over to the sofa. I took one of the armchairs. I wasn't getting any cozier than I needed to. "Can I get you anything? Espresso? An aperitif?"

"Is this how today's going to be?" I slouched on the chair. "Do you think I don't remember how you feel about people who drink alcohol this early in the morning? Or at all, ever, even on their own time? Is this how today's going to be?"

He laughed. "I have had men working for me for fifteen years who can't seem to remember that rule. You're still sharper than any of them."

"Doesn't say much about your executives."

"Says more about you, *cara*." He settled on the sofa. "Perhaps you'd like something to eat then."

His question reminded me I hadn't eaten since sometime the previous afternoon. "I'm fine," I said.

He nodded and tapped a button on one of his phones. "*Tomás, dos cafezinhos, por favor. Y pasteles.*" He leaned back on the sofa and draped his arm over the back. "You're in some deeply serious shit, you know this, right?"

Oh, the time-honored technique of sweetness and lightness, viciously interspersed with direct tough talk. I laughed. "You're the one who hired the lawyer, you tell me."

"You are not this cold, this dispassionate about what happened."

"Cold? Roberto, someone murdered my husband. They bashed in the back of his head. They went out of their way to make certain it looked like I did it. I don't have time to be emotional about this. I have bigger problems to deal with. There will be plenty of time to be all torn up about it later."

"I see some irony in our reconnecting over such a circumstance."

"I don't think you mean irony." Then I slapped my leg with an exaggerated motion. "Oh, you mean because I used a cricket bat to —"

He held up a hand. "I don't need or want the details."

"Why am I here, Roberto? Why are we doing this?"

He leaned forward. "Because it is time you came home."

I shook my head. "Stevie and I are doing fine, Roberto, thanks."

He launched out of his seat and looked down at me. "You aren't doing fine!" he yelled at me, and I flinched. Roberto had a disturbing voice when he yelled, intentionally designed to make recipients afraid. "You're under suspicion of murder. You are living like a pauper, relying on other people's handouts. You're still the caretaker for your younger sister. You're not doing well at all, Trudy."

A series of knocks on the door interrupted his tirade. He muttered something and then yelled, "Come in."

The door to the villa opened and a young man with curly black hair and wearing a blinding white chef's coat entered. He held a silver tray that had two coffees, two glasses of water, a pitcher of water, and a tray of pastries on it.

Roberto leaned forward and cleared a space on the glass table in front of him. "*Muchas gracias, Tomás*," he said. Then he waved his hand.

I tried to make eye contact with Tomás as he went about his business, and not only because he was very handsome indeed (although too smooth-faced for me). I wanted to see how well-trained he was. He never once so much as glanced in my direction. Tomás put the tray down, he bowed, and then he retreated, leaving as silently as he had come. I might as well have been a ratty throw on the armrest of the chair for all I existed. Tomás would not have heard whatever Roberto had been yelling. Wild horses would not get him to discuss anything said in his presence.

Roberto always had the best staff.

When the front door closed again, Roberto stood by the fireplace, leaning his head against the antique white wall and trying to collect himself. "Please. Enjoy."

The pastries Tomás had brought in smelled heavenly. And I knew they would taste better than they smelled, because Roberto is a man who has always enjoyed the finer things in life for themselves. Even when he was a struggling young stockbroker in Barcelona, he decided he would rather eat once a day than eat inferior food. He was a lot thinner as a young man.

"Don't mind if I do," I said. My nonchalance would have been fabulously executed, had my stomach not taken that moment to grumble loudly. I picked up the coffee, which was thick and smelled heavenly and tasted twice as good. Then I tried one of the small spinach and walnut pastries and thought maybe going home to New York City might not be all that bad.

Except for one minor detail. Well, I suppose technically she wasn't a minor; she was twenty-two years old.

After my second pastry (sweet potato and spices) I decided to give in and not pretend that I wasn't hungry and this wasn't heaven. I must have eaten five before I finally came up for air. The entire time, Roberto circled around the room, sipping his own coffee, watching me. He was not only nervous and upset about my presence, but he was a good host. He wanted me to enjoy myself.

When I finally came up for air, I said, "Why isn't Mama here?"

"I didn't want to get her hopes up."

"So...you haven't told her you've found me."

"I had no idea what I was going to find. I cannot let you break her heart again."

"Break her heart?" I screamed. "Do you know what she did? I begged her for help and she hung up on me."

"She didn't know what you had done."

"She knew I needed help. What else did she need to know?"

Eleven years ago, my mother had rejected me when I needed her most. She had been a difficult mother in some impossible situations, and I had been a terrible child. I had hurt her in some dreadful ways. But when I called her, blood spattered all over my clothing, she hung up.

Roberto sat across from me again. In his hands he had a photo album, the old-fashioned kind with printed out photos affixed to page after physical page. Such a casual maneuver. Not a casual man.

I opened the photo album, and my breath stopped.

It was a picture of my mother, Jane. She still looked marvelous, with her blonde hair and big blue eyes that I always wanted. I desperately wanted to look like her. I began asking to get my hair colored when I was ten so I could be blonde like her. She was eighteen when I was born, which meant she was only forty-five now. In this picture, she could have easily passed for early thirties, with almost no crow's feet or wrinkles. All natural. I knew she wouldn't have had plastic surgery.

She looked the same. What was different was that the picture showed her with her arms around two children: a girl and a younger boy who looked so much alike they were clearly siblings. They were darker than my mother and resembled Roberto quite a lot.

"Consuelo is six and Alejandro is four. Connie and Alex. I am very proud of them."

Stevie had kept up with gossip about my family. I knew they existed. But much like she had with me and my brother, Mama kept her new kids out of the tabloids.

Roberto didn't have any other children. His first marriage, to a woman named Zarita, had lasted for twenty years. She died a few years before he met me. After she died, he moved into the expansive co-op apartment directly beneath our three-floor penthouse monstrosity on the Upper East Side. I was nine and my mother was already married to stepfather number one, Jimmy. Roberto talked to me as though I were an adult—well, maybe not an adult, but he didn't talk to me like I was a baby, the way Jimmy did. Roberto treated a whiny nine-year-old with kindness and respect. And Jimmy was a son of a bitch who liked to pinch me to make me cry or hit me where the bruises wouldn't show.

Roberto gave me espresso. He thought ten years old was a perfectly fine age to drink coffee. It turned out I liked hot chocolate better. He took me to Washington Square Park and let me play chess. I was terrible but I had a great time. When I was twelve, he started letting me hang around his office downtown, running errands for the workers there, like buying sandwiches or photocopying articles.

One day, my mother stopped Roberto in the lobby of our co-op and asked him, viciously, why on earth a forty-three-year-old man was showing so much interest in a twelve-year-old girl. He said, "Madame, why don't you ask your daughter why she prefers to spend time working for me instead of home with you?"

My mother had immediately marched into my room and said, "Tell me what Mr. Montesinos meant," and I showed her the left side of my rib cage. Jimmy was gone less than an hour later, screaming about lawyers and million-dollar settlements. My mother, who had been insanely wealthy all her life and knew better than he did how to play this game, shook her head. He didn't get a penny.

However, a year later she married Patrick. The less said about him, the better. Jane always had to be with a man, which is how she ended up with so many terrible ones. I sincerely hoped Roberto had been a better husband than the first three had been. The best that can be said about them is that they taught me to be self-reliant.

I counted backwards from a thousand to get a grip on myself. "Family reunion time is over. What is it you want, Roberto?"

"As always, you are very efficient. All right then. You have quite a mess here in Los Angeles. We need the police to find whoever did this."

"And find the actual culprit?"

"Exactly. Then, you need to come home to New York City. You have been a very busy girl for the last eleven years."

I wondered if he knew how busy.

"My investigators have managed to trace you backward to Lucrezia Forni. Care to give me the names you had before that?"

Lucrezia was my name when we lived in Firenze. That had

been about five years ago.

He knew how busy I'd been.

"How did you find me?" I asked.

He raised an eyebrow. "That doesn't matter."

"Oh, it matters quite a lot. I vanished off the face of the earth eleven years ago and suddenly you know where I am."

"Perhaps it wasn't suddenly."

"Given some of the situations I've been in over the past few years, you would have shown up a long time ago if that were true. For example, Lucrezia got into a scrape or two."

"Yes, she did. You know, if you needed money, you could have asked us for it. Instead of robbing our villa."

"Yes, but robbing the villa in Venice was more satisfying. Not to mention fun." Actually, it hadn't been either satisfying or fun. I'd done it as a way out of a bad situation I'd been in. But he didn't need to know that.

Roberto clapped his hands. "All right. Here's what we're going to do. You're going to move here, to the Peninsula, so we can keep an eye on you—"

"No," I said.

"What?"

"We have a place to stay," I lied. "I'd rather stay there."

"That is not acceptable."

My turn to shrug.

He smiled tightly. "After this murder investigation is dealt with, you will come home to New York. Yes, things will be a madhouse for a while."

"Madhouse? Roberto, are you aware that my father wants me dead?"

He narrowed his eyebrows, as though he hadn't the slightest

idea what I might be referring to. Then he shook his head. "Stop being dramatic."

"I destroyed a billion-dollar deal. The man can hold a grudge. He sent one killer after us already."

"When?"

I snorted. "Eleven years ago?"

"What happened?"

"I didn't kill him, if that's what you're asking."

I did, however, let the man die. All I'm going to say is, it was him or me, and I'm extremely fond of me.

"Just the one?"

"Thank Hades I had proper training in how to hide. We've stayed hidden for eleven years to avoid him."

"You will be safe. We can protect you."

I nodded, as though everything he were saying made sense. I had a somewhat different take on it. "So where would Stevie and I go when we're in New York?"

And Roberto did the worst thing a negotiator can do: he hesitated.

How on earth could he not have had an answer for that question ready? I was reminded immediately of some of the best advice I'd ever heard on the subject of discussing difficult subjects, and what do you know? It came from none other than Roberto Montesinos. Always tell the truth if you can, he told me. If you can't tell the whole truth, tell as much of it as you can. If you can't tell the truth at all, say what you'd like to do. And if you can't say that much, keep your mouth closed.

Roberto had his mouth firmly closed.

"Oh my God," I said, trying not to laugh. "Mama still calls her 'the bastard,' doesn't she?"

"*Bella*, I don't pretend to understand your mother's attitude toward Stevie—"

"I understand it. It's looney tunes. She still blames a baby for breaking up her first marriage. Stevie had nothing to do with being born. She wasn't responsible for my father fucking around with a ski instructor. Or with half of the women on the Eastern seaboard. Or every seaboard."

"Everything that happened as a result of your father's—"

"Let's go with 'evil'," I said.

"His more unfortunate influences on your family…Jane regrets it."

"Well, if she hadn't met him, she certainly wouldn't have ever met me, would she? How many problems would that have solved right there?"

He slammed his hand on the armrest of the sofa and stood up. "Your mother loves you. Why can't you believe that?"

Did he want an actual list of reasons? "Look on the bright side." I picked up my glass of water and leaned over the back of my armchair. "If Stevie had never been born, you might not be married to my mother right now. Ever thought about that?"

"Every day," he said. That surprised me. "Every day I wonder what my life would be like if I didn't have Jane and Connie and Alex."

Nothing like that had ever come out of the mouths of Husbands One through Three. I would bet money on that, and I'm not the betting kind. Son of a bitch. Well, good for Mama. "I'm not going home to New York unless Stevie comes with me."

"Your sister will be taken care of, Trudy. Sorry, *Drusilla*. For God's sake, she needs help, not to continue living as you have been. You know this."

"So. She needs a better living situation…just not with me."

This time he didn't hesitate. "No, not with you."

"And I don't get to know where she is until…"

"You show you can act like a responsible adult."

"And in a few years I won't need your say-so, will I?"

On my thirtieth birthday, I would become one of the richest people in the world. And I wouldn't need Roberto or anyone to run interference for me. Visions of my thirtieth birthday had gotten me through a lot of sleepless nights.

He smiled, much more sadly this time. "There is no money unless your mother and I say there is money."

It took me a few seconds to understand what he was saying. He was telling me that the trusts I'd been waiting on no longer existed. One of his hands tapped on the armrest of the sofa and the other one picked at the lint on his trousers, and I knew I was screwed.

Years ago, I figured out Roberto Montesino's tell. I probably could have made several more fortunes than I already had telling competitors about it, but at the time I was ecstatic that I could use it to beat him at the penny poker games we played. He was such an expressive man that if his hands were moving, he was telling the truth, and when he could sit quietly without so much as doing finger flexes, he was lying.

His hands were still in motion. There was no money. He'd done something to screw me and my inheritance over.

"You stole my money."

"Everything is right where it should be. We have no idea if you even have the ability to act in anyone's best interest, including your own. You will need our help. You aren't prepared. Your dyslexia was and mostly likely still is catastrophic. And if, as you say, your father still wants revenge, you need protection. Until you are ready, until you are prepared, there is no money waiting for you."

The shock of what he was telling me started washing over me, in hot, acidic waves. I felt like I was going to throw up, fall over, burst into a mad rage. I clenched my hands shut instead. "I'm not going to abandon my sister."

In that moment, I wasn't entirely sure I believed what I was saying. Roberto could be forgiven for thinking he'd won.

He stabbed his finger in the air toward me. "You don't have much choice in the matter. We're going to get you squared away here in Los Angeles, and then you come home to New York."

"Whether I want to or not."

"Yes, even if you don't want to."

After eleven years of hiding away and making sure Stevie was safe, it was all over. And no one was going to look out for my little sister the way I had. Which meant if I were physically separated from her and her location could be found, it was going to be open season on her, as a way to take revenge on me.

I probably shouldn't have murdered that guy when I was sixteen, but trust me, I had a very good reason at the time.

CHAPTER EIGHT

I WAS SO LOST IN my own thoughts that I don't even remember the walk to the valet stand. The first thing I was aware of was the handsome man standing there. No, handsome was an insult to this man. He was the sort of gorgeous that made you want to say, "Knock me down and fuck me right now." I was sure I knew him from some movie, some TV show. If Stevie were with me, she'd be able to spout his entire career, including visits to chat shows and charity work. Thick black hair, tan skin, big brown eyes framed by long eyelashes any woman would kill for. And a body with a flat stomach and tight arse. He smiled at me and I thought, He asks me back to his room, I'm going. After the day I'd had, a quick one with someone who looked like a Greek god was exactly what I needed.

"Your ticket, ma'am?" he asked with a slight Mexican accent.

At which point I realized he was the valet.

Are all LA valets better-looking than most movie stars? I

wondered. I handed him my parking voucher. Holy Zeus, at this rate I was never going to leave LA, because there were a whole lot of men here I needed to meet, and in a hurry.

If I'd taken Roberto up on his offer of a villa, I'd have had a room handy I could use with my new friend here for fifteen minutes or so, but oh well. This wasn't my lucky day. Yet, at any rate.

The valet took my parking tag from me. A nasally voice said from somewhere behind me, "She don't need the car yet." And I knew it definitely wasn't my lucky day.

Hermes Trismegistus, Vin Behar was an ugly man. He grabbed the parking tag from the valet's hand. He crushed it in his fist and had it in his pocket in seconds, and I wasn't getting it back because there was no chance in hell I was putting my hands anywhere near his trousers. He gripped me on the upper arm, his fingers digging into my bicep. "The lady's staying for a drink."

"Take your hand off me or lose it."

He knew I could back that up and took his hand away. But in a quiet voice to match my own, he said, "We talk, or I tell the cops about your trip to visit this guy here."

I wanted to get far, far away from him. But for the moment it was more important to find out what he knew. There were a lot of people staying at the Peninsula. "Who?"

Behar pulled out a tape recorder, and then glanced at the valet. "You wanna do this here?"

The valet took the hint and moved away.

"I don't want to do anything with you anywhere."

"Your husband dies, and you come here to see Roberto Montesinos. Think the cops might be interested?"

Dammit. Behar knew Roberto's name. That was bad. "The

cops are already interested in what you were doing outside Colin's apartment last night."

Behar grinned, an ugly sight even on the best of days. "I was in Vegas last night. With lots of witnesses."

Of course he was.

His meaty thumb with peeling cuticles pushed the Play button, and my voice said, "Yes, Roberto, nine sharp." The thumb lifted, and the player clicked off.

I looked at the player, rather than at Behar. "Where did you get that?"

"Cellular ain't secure. And here you are, at Montesinos' hotel, right after your husband got shut up. Come on. We're going to have us a talk."

"This should be amusing. Or some definition of amusing. Not the one I generally use, of course."

We ended up at an outside table, shielded from the afternoon sun by a giant white canvas canopy. A miniature fountain with dancing waters played nearby to the soft strains of Mozart. I tried to figure out which piece it was. All of that music history crammed into me, and so little of it stuck. Stevie, on the other hand…

Stevie. What on earth was I going to do about Roberto's demand I return to New York and abandon Stevie? Behar might be threatening me, but I had real problems on my hands.

"Buy me a drink," Behar said.

I spread my hands out. "No money."

"You gotta pay for parking."

"Or talk my way out of it." I'd been betting that the hotel had been instructed to take care of my parking. Otherwise, my car would sit here a very long time. Which would be an unfortunate handicap in a driving town like Los Angeles.

"You spend an hour with Montesinos and you got no money?"

Hm. Good point. I was off my game. And he hadn't even offered me some, the stingy bastard. "I'd offer to let you search me, but you're disgusting and you're not getting an inch closer to me. Say whatever it is you have to say. I've a long and unpleasant morning that's getting worse by the second."

"I want a hundred thousand not to mention Montesinos to anybody."

That got to the point.

"While I'm spinning miracles, would you like me to arrange for you to somehow become attractive?"

He spread his hands on the table. "That's in addition to the money your dead husband already owes me."

Colin owed Behar money? I laughed. "I don't do drugs, Behar, but if I did them, your supplier would definitely be on speed dial."

He grinned. His teeth were discolored and yellow. "You think I'm lying about this?"

"Yes. Sorry, was that too direct for you?"

He tapped a button on his recorder and I heard Colin say, "Of course it's fifty-fifty, you twat." Then Behar saying, "Then where's mine, you jackoff?" And Colin saying, "She's been on location for the past month. I haven't gotten the goddamned money. Can't give you what I fucking don't have."

That was definitely Colin. I had no reason to believe that Behar had fantastical sound-editing skills, so that was most likely an actual conversation between the two of them. Zeus in a side cart. Colin had been working with Behar.

"I want my money," Behar said.

I wasn't going to let him know his recording had served its purpose and rattled the hell out of me. "Let's think back to the part where I'm not certain I can afford to get my car out of parking, shall we?"

"Your boyfriend has it."

Boyfriend? If I'd had a boyfriend anytime in the past few months, I'd be a great deal more relaxed than I had been.

Then it dawned on me he meant Roberto.

I stifled a giggle as I stood up. "You think you're so clever because for whatever reason I talked to someone who might or might not be Ricardo Montalban—"

"Roberto Montesinos."

"Right. Whoever. And you're going to blackmail him for a million trillion dollars because of…me? Here's a tip. Someone who wants to be a blackmailer has done other bad stuff. Comes with the territory."

"Speaking from experience?"

I shrugged. "If this guy Renaldo has that kind of money lying around, he's probably not a stupid man. And he'll shut you up pretty fucking fast."

That was a safe bet. When I was thirteen, I watched Roberto shred a would-be blackmailer to smithereens using only a few of the things Roberto had dug up about him. By the end of it, the man had been begging for Roberto to spare his family. Nobody's life is perfect, some people's less than others, and Roberto was born knowing how to find weak spots.

"Let's go." Vin stood up. "Time's a wastin'."

The single saving grace of being marched through the lobby by this cretin was that it was not the worst thing that had happened to me all day…although it ranked in the top five. We headed straight for the walkway that led to the villas, which took us past Genevieve the Magnificent. She leapt to her feet and intercepted us. "May I help you?"

"We know where we're going," Behar said, and he tried to keep walking.

The concierge at the Peninsula was no wilting violet. She got right in front of him and said, "Our guests value their privacy. Please tell me who it is you're here to see. You can wait in the lobby while I contact them."

"Montesinos, lady."

"Sir, if you're going to be belligerent, you're going to have to leave the hotel."

"You let her in to see him."

Genevieve appraised me, her attitude several degrees below zero, as though she'd never seen me before. Beautiful move. Then she flicked her attention back to Behar. "Please ask whoever you want to meet with to make an appointment to see you elsewhere. These gentlemen will escort you to your cars."

Behind us stood two linebackers in matching suits and quiet shoes. Neither one had a pretty face, but with bodies like those I was willing to overlook that problem. Their bodies weren't so much attractive as solid and willing to pummel.

It would be nice to have that kind of power again. And I would. As long as I left Stevie by herself.

"Call him," Behar growled.

"Unless you have a tape of Colin saying, 'Help, Drusilla's murdering me,' I don't give a flying fuck what you do with it."

Behar gave me a cracked one-sided smile. His teeth were yellow. "Yeah, you do. 'Cause you haven't walked out of here yet."

He did have a point there. I took that as my cue to begin walking toward the front door.

Behar caught up with me, tailed by his linebacker. "You got

twenty-four hours. And the price just went up."

"Keep dreaming of big paydays, see where it gets you. And we've both seen what happens to people like that in Vegas, haven't we?"

My car was already waiting, out at the curb, engine running. The valet opened the door for me and I handed him my last five as I got in. Why, I don't know. He must have been used to much larger tips at a hotel like this, and at the moment I needed to keep any money I could lay my hands on. The valet winked at me as he closed the door. I didn't have enough energy to wink back.

Behar's tape didn't worry me. Or, to be more truthful, several larger problems had gotten in line ahead of the tape and it had to wait its turn. I was also certain Behar would not take that tape to the police unless he had to. Or unless he'd already gotten the payoff money. He seemed like the type who wouldn't stay bought.

Errand number one for the day was done: face Roberto Montesinos and survive. That got a big check mark in my mind. Surviving Behar was just a bonus on top of that. Errand number two: discuss my situation with my lawyer. I took out my phone. Stevie had put Nathaniel as speed dial two. She, of course, was speed dial one. Speed dial two picked up on the first ring. A perky female voice asked who was calling and, when I identified myself, told me how to get to the lawyer's offices. No mention of a meeting time, so they were waiting on me.

Wow, it had been years since anyone had waited for whenever I could bother myself to get there.

It's good to be the king. Unfortunately for me, the king in this situation was Roberto, not me. But I'd make do.

The second I put my phone back in my pocket the mobile rang again.

"Who was that?" Roberto asked.

I told him who Behar was and what he wanted.

"Your husband was working with this man?"

"It comes as shocking news to me as well, Roberto, in the possible case that you care."

"Do not mention this to the police," he said.

"Have you always thought I'm this much of an idiot?" I hung up on him. And then I turned the phone off before I started the car up again.

CHAPTER NINE

AT SOME POINT, CENTURY CITY must have been zoned for lots of tall office buildings with mirrored outsides tinted copper. And nothing had numbers on it, making it hard to double-check that this was the right building before I drove into the correct valet-only car park. The other cars within easy reach of the valet were Mercedes or Lexuses, with one Ferrari and one Porsche (a Carrera, not a Boxster) mixed in.

I had the feeling my poor Chevy would be hidden away somewhere deep in the bowels of the garage, safe from contaminating the others.

Two men, in their mid-thirties and power suits, were waiting by the elevator when I walked up beside them. A blonde and a brunet, two of my favorite kinds. Their conversation trailed off as I made eye contact with one, and then the other. When I smiled, the taller one said, "Hi," and the second bloke adjusted his tie.

Sometimes your day is working out such that you need to give yourself a little ego boost here and there.

The doors opened to a futuristic control center staffed by one woman, who looked like an efficient dominatrix with perfect makeup and hair tied up in a smooth bun. The red headset matched her red outfit, which led me to suspect she had several headsets to choose from. On either side of the desk was a pair of giant, and locked, doors. The rest of the office was closed off. If an angry client came through here, she was the only one they'd see, and she looked like she'd be comfortable with the pump-action shotgun she probably kept under that desk.

She told me to have a seat before pushing a button and saying something softly into the microphone.

I flipped through the magazine at hand. It was all ads, and I couldn't for the life of me figure out what some of them were selling. In one, the woman in the picture was completely naked, so it couldn't be clothes or shoes or diamonds. Then one pair of the doors to the inner sanctum opened and a young brown woman walked through them. "Drusilla?" she said, unsmiling. Hers was the voice from the phone. Probably Nathaniel's secretary or assistant or whatever they're calling them these days. "Follow me, please." She ushered me through the gates.

Once through, she said, "I'm Carmela Tanner. I'll be handling any scheduling with Mr. Ross." She led me through a web of corridors marked by the polish of the wooden inlays and lack of decoration of any kind. I was ninety percent certain I could find my way back to the start unaided, if I needed to, and no one with weapons was chasing me. Most of the doors were closed, and any glass walls had thick white curtains in front of them. Carmela and I could have been strolling through an abandoned building, for all the signs of life I saw there.

I rubbed my fingers across my palms, which were faintly warm and moist. My husband had been murdered and I had to see a criminal defense attorney and that situation was making me nervous.

We stopped at one door and Carmela opened it for us, quietly and efficiently. The office was large but felt small due to the number of bookshelves, packed full of those matching sets of books every law student must receive upon passing the bar exam. Stacks of file folders sat on every available surface. The man behind the desk was busy scribbling away on (what else?) a yellow legal pad and did not look up as we walked in. His hair was a darker blonde than it had appeared last night under the harsh street lamps, and he was also younger than I'd supposed last night. Those wrinkles came from hard-grinding work, not years. He had well-maintained hands, though, which would be important if he ever made his way in front of a jury. I hoped I did not need a lawyer for a jury.

My main introduction to criminal lawyers came via the portly, sweaty guy in Baton Rouge who wore a shiny suit. He asked my boyfriend of the moment, "Who arrested you?" followed by, "How much you got?" My boyfriend borrowed money from me to pay off the cop, and never paid it back. And then he had the gall to ask me for rent money. I had the gall to ask, "Who are you again?" It wasn't an amicable parting, but it so rarely is.

"Mr. Ross," Carmela said, her voice wavering with a touch of uncertainty.

He finished what he was writing with a stab at the paper and then he looked up. I smiled. He didn't return the favor. Instead, he dropped his pen and indicated the leather chairs facing his desk. "Carmela, a couple of waters."

I had to decide which chair to sit in. Physical position is so damned important in so many endeavors—for one thing, it determines who has the power. I chose the chair farther away from the desk. When he looked at me, he'd see me sitting there, relaxed and comfortable, instead of right up against his desk. Also, I had the sun behind me, which would put him at a disadvantage.

Before I sat, I reached out my hand over the desk. "I don't think we've had a proper introduction." He had a firm but not crushing shake, which I appreciated, but he also didn't lengthen it by as much as a fraction of a second, which I didn't appreciate as much. Had I lost whatever charm I'd worked on the guys in the elevator, or was he immune to it? I usually get some reaction from males, even the gay ones. He wasn't pinging my gaydar, either. Nathaniel was going to bear watching.

As I sank onto one of the giant leather armchairs, I crossed my legs. *That* he noticed. My inner sense of comfort rose quite a bit. He wasn't oblivious of me. I relaxed a little and flexed my foot a tiny bit, which enhances the curve of the calf muscle. But almost as quickly as he'd glanced at my legs, he picked up another legal pad and skimmed it, as though he hadn't observed anything. "Let me tell you what I already have here, and you can fill me in on anything I'm missing. Your husband, Colin Abbott, was murdered late last night at an apartment in Hollywood." He glanced at me. He had brown eyes, with lots of gold highlights. "A case like that doesn't warrant as much attention as this one is starting to get."

"What's different this time?"

"He had some kind of relationship with Penelope Gurevich. You know who she is?"

I nodded. "A television star?"

He grinned. He had a nice mouth. "Yeah. Cops get nervous

when celebrities get involved in murder. You don't seem upset or surprised that your husband was, uh, seeing someone."

"I didn't care. We didn't have that kind of relationship."

"How could you not care? You'd only been married six months."

"It was a green-card marriage. Which might be a problem in and of itself."

"Trust me. Marriage of convenience sounds a lot better than wanting revenge for getting dumped by the love of your life for a TV star. You have any friends back in Las Vegas who will swear about the state of your marital bliss?"

Oooo. Mr. Sarcastic. I liked him more and more. I gave him a couple of names and phone numbers. A few girls Colin had dated, and one or two of the guys I went out with. Nathaniel shook his head, while he wrote them down. "Weird setup just to get a green card," he said.

"Colin's work permit was running out and he couldn't get it renewed. Seemed like the easiest way."

Nathaniel glanced up from his legal pad. "I thought the green card was for you."

I shook my head.

"Are you sure?"

I smiled. "I'm American. Raised in England." That was true, but that was also the story I'd dreamed up for Drusilla, since her passport was American. "Colin was Australian. His family emigrated to Canada when he was about ten, but he was Australian."

He wrote something down. "Did he pay you?"

"Yes. Ten thousand dollars."

"For a green card."

"Is that too little or too much? I know it's illegal."

"Least of your problems. Still have it? No, probably not." When I didn't respond, he looked at the paper again. "When you got to LA, where did you see him?"

"I didn't. I found his apartment. He wasn't there."

"So you knew where he was staying?"

"Yes."

"But you weren't staying there with him."

"No. I didn't have much to say to him. We needed to work a few things out and then we were done."

"Were you going to give him back the money?" He raised his eyebrows at me. "The money he paid you to marry him?" Before I could respond, Nathaniel wrote something else down. "Did Colin gamble? Maybe owe someone money?"

I shook my head. "No. That's not the kind of risks he liked to take. He thought gambling was for idiots."

"Do you gamble?"

"Never had the money to lose."

He tossed his legal pad aside and clasped his hands together. And he looked at me. He was not making up for lost time checking out my figure. This was the assessing stare of, well, a lawyer.

And if this was the guy on my side, I was in deep trouble.

The door behind me opened and Carmela walked in, carrying a tray holding two bottles of water. The lawyer stared at me the entire time Carmela was in the room. As she left, he picked up a bottle and took a drink. Then he put it down and looked back at me again.

"I need you to help yourself on this. You're not helping yourself much. Or at all. Colin left Vegas—" He glanced at the legal pad. "Six weeks ago? And, when did you get to Los Angeles?"

"Monday."

"Monday. That's yesterday. Did you happen to notice he had left you before that?"

Neat. My lawyer was baiting me. Unfortunately for him, I'm very good at keeping my emotions in check. "Why yes, I did. I had no idea where he was. Until I found him, I had a few things to take care of."

"Why didn't you know where he was?"

"No one knew where he was! He'd disappeared right in front of me."

"Even the casino knew your husband was in Los Angeles."

I speak six languages and can make myself understand or be understood in a handful of others. I completely lost the ability to fathom what Nathaniel had just told me. "Sorry, what?"

He rifled through a couple of papers on his desk. "This morning, before you got here, I talked to the general manager of the Marrakesh Properties, Barry Coffey. Do you know him?"

"We're acquainted."

"The magic show was scheduled to go on hiatus six weeks ago. Colin had some outside—"

"That's bullshit," I said.

Nathaniel glanced at me.

"I don't know why Coffey would say that, but it's a simple lie."

"He was clear. He's having the casino's lawyers send me the contracts today. But he mentioned he knew Colin lived in Hollywood."

This was insane. Coffey had spent much of the past six weeks yelling at me about Colin's disappearance, even though I clearly hadn't gone with him.

He had to be covering for Behar. Somehow. I couldn't see the con in that one, but it had to be Behar.

"You need to look into Vincent Behar. He's the main security guy for the Marrakesh—"

"I've run across him already."

"And he wasn't in Las Vegas last night; I don't care what he tells anybody. He was sitting outside Colin's apartment, as if he were waiting for me to arrive. He either killed Colin or he knows who did."

Nathaniel made a couple of notes on his legal pad, and then he stood up and walked around the desk toward me. He was looking at me the whole time he moved, so I steeled myself to look at his face, using only my peripheral vision to get a reading on the rest of him. He wasn't especially tall, about my height, but he moved like he owned the room. I couldn't take my eyes off him.

"So, Colin ditches you in Vegas, leaving you broke and alone. You track him here in Los Angeles and find him banging Penelope Gurevich. Who gives him a lot of money."

"As far as I can tell, his girlfriend is named Anne da Silva."

"Oh, even better. You find him with multiple girlfriends. Suddenly, Colin's dead and a shitload of money has disappeared." He sat on the edge of his desk and looked down at me. "In case you're wondering? Looks bad."

"I'm not sure what you're getting at."

Nathaniel snorted. "We've been talking for what, fifteen minutes, and already I am absolutely sure you're not that stupid. Neither am I. You're in trouble. Tell me everything you know, because the more reasons the police have to look elsewhere, the better."

"I take it you've had clients who killed over money."

He reached over and picked up the legal pad. "The first person

I ever defended was a twenty-year-old who murdered his brother over twenty-five bucks."

"What happened with that case?"

"Plea agreement."

"Then?"

Nathaniel flipped through the pad, put his finger on a series of numbers. "He got ten years."

"And?" When he didn't respond to my prompting, I added, "What happened to him then?"

He looked up at me with those dark brown-and-gold eyes. "Knifed to death after three."

He was very good at pretending that outcome didn't bother him. He was probably dynamite in court. "If it comes to that, I'm not going to plead."

"So I've heard."

"What's that supposed to mean?"

He walked back around his desk. When he was turned away, I went ahead and did a much more complete body scan than I had before. "We've come to the trickiest part of this little scenario. The part we're not supposed to talk about but we are anyhow. You know who's footing the bill for your defense."

"Yes. So?"

Nathaniel leaned back in his chair as he stared at me. "Hm. Let's see. You're married to a man who, according to you, disappeared on you, left you in debt, left you holding the bag for the act. Suddenly you have an incredibly wealthy man who's footing the bill for you on certain things. A husband might be kind of a liability in a situation like that."

I smiled. It may have come out more like a baring of teeth. "Between you and me, I'm the sort of girl who takes the money and runs with nary a thought to her own marital status." I leaned back in my chair and tilted my head to one side. "Here's one of my rules for this relationship. We're not going to mention you-know-who's name. Ever. He has nothing to do with this case."

"Don't be surprised if the prosecutor brings him up."

"So your job is to keep me very far away from the prosecutor."

My lawyer tapped the end of his pen against the legal pad before turning the pad to a new page. "Where are you staying?"

"With Sir Gareth Macfadyen." Why bother mentioning the guesthouse? Nathaniel wasn't going to believe me about Roberto, he wasn't going to believe me about anyone else, so I might as well let him think the worst.

Which he did. He looked down at the paper, but not soon enough.

"Not making this easy for you, am I?" I said.

"You're going out of your way to make this hard. How long have you known him?"

Didn't take long to come up with the answer. "Since yesterday."

He wrote that down. "Yesterday? The same day you came to Los Angeles?"

"Yes."

"You met him and went to live with him the same day?"

I shrugged. "Don't tell me. That's also a reason for me to knock off my husband?"

"In this town? Women will dump their husbands for one date with a Golden Globe nominee."

"You've been hanging around the wrong type of women, Counselor." I flicked an invisible piece of lint off the end of my skirt.

He glanced at me, and then returned for a longer, direct look. Then he put down the pen and gave me his full attention. Not the case. Me. "Let's get a few things clear. I have only three rules for how I do my job." He held up one finger. "Never decide whether or not the client's guilty. That's not my problem." He held up another finger. "The job is always about the government's case, not the client's merits, so I pick my battles carefully." He held up a third finger. "And lastly, never fuck a client. No matter what. So you can stop, now. We don't have time and it's not going to happen."

I didn't say anything.

"Did I offend your delicate sensibilities?" he asked.

I shook my head. "I'm sure you would have, if I had any." Then I leaned toward him. "Did you say 'fuck a client' or 'fuck over a client'?"

He laughed. "Fucking someone over is just part of the job description. So I guess we're in agreement."

"We are? About what?"

"You let me do what I do best, which means you stop making my job that much harder for me."

He stood up. We were done.

Nathaniel opened the door to the reception area. "You have any more ideas about who might have killed your husband, give them to me. Don't be stupid and decide to find out for yourself. The cops are already looking for a good reason to arrest you. Don't make it easier for them."

I passed him, and then stopped short in the middle of the doorway and turned around. He nearly walked into me and our sudden closeness disconcerted him, exactly the way I'd wanted it to. "Tell me, Counselor. Those three rules of yours? How many have you broken so far?"

He backed up to put a little more space between us. He didn't seem in the slightest bit surprised I'd asked that question. Maybe he'd been waiting for it. "All three."

"All at once or individually?"

He shook his head and smiled, sadly. "It was a long time ago. Which is why I take them very seriously."

"Oh. Pity. I'd like to meet her."

"Why, so you can compare notes?"

"So I can give her hell for ruining you for the rest of us."

He stared at me for a few seconds before he looked away. "Keep your cell phone on. The police are going to want to talk to you."

I started to walk away and then looked back over my shoulder. "Do keep me abreast of what's going on, Counselor."

He went back into his office.

Chapter Ten

IT WAS THE MIDDLE OF the afternoon by the time I was ready to return to Stevie. I felt as though I'd been working in the brickyard all day. I drove up to the house, drumming my thumbs on the steering wheel and running through what I was going to tell her about my visit with Roberto.

Stevie was not stupid. She could guess my family wasn't going to welcome her with open arms. I like to avoid hysterics whenever possible, and that goes double with my little sister. So I would go with my usual approach and say nothing. If she asked, then I'd tell her. But not until.

Knowing my lawyer probably thought I was guilty wasn't even the worst thing that had happened so far that day. Roberto's decree was all I could think about. On the upside, I'd have no worries. I'd have the family's protection. I could use my real name again. And Stevie could get all the medical care, physical and mental, she could use.

The downside is I could never see if it was working for her.

Damn it, my mother could hold a mean grudge. It wasn't Stevie she didn't like—she didn't even know Stevie. My mother was still furious that her first husband, the one she'd married against her parents' objections, had knocked up a ski instructor, which humiliated her and led to a horrible divorce. I think I first loved Stevie so much because she made my mother so crazy.

Ah, Stevie. What in the hell was I going to do?

Since I hadn't called within the past four hours, she must have become somewhat concerned.

When I walked in, my sister was nowhere in sight and the inside of the house was darker than the outside. "Stevie!" I called and I dropped my keys on the counter.

No response. The TV wasn't on. No noises from upstairs of her running down to greet me. Which was strange, because where else could she be? She wouldn't have left. She had to be somewhere in this house. "Stevie?" I yelled in my loudest, angriest voice. "Sweetie, where are you?"

Stevie does sleep like a stone from time to time, but she always responds to that tone. Always.

No answer.

The combination of Colin's murder and my having to see Roberto had frightened her but come on, I'd been in worse predicaments. True, I couldn't think of one at the moment, but that was only because I was worried, not because I didn't have a raft of possibilities to choose from.

She wasn't in the living room or the downstairs bathroom or the laundry area. Or the coat closet. I ran upstairs, two steps at a time. She wasn't in either neatly-made bed. She wasn't in either bedroom closet, her usual place to find solace when she was alone: dark, cramped, easy to hide in. There weren't even any clothes on the floor for her to hide under. She'd spent some of the day tidying up.

Hide under. Of course. We hadn't had beds that were set off the floor in donkey's years.

I picked up the bed skirt of the bed in the larger room. Nothing. I went to the other bedroom and picked up its yellow bed skirt.

Empty. And dust-free. Good housekeeping.

Could she have left the house by herself, agitated and afraid because I might be in trouble? Had she run into Gary or some other stranger? Had she feared that I might not return from seeing Roberto?

Not a chance. Not even that level of fear could get her to leave this house voluntarily.

I went into the bathroom to see if there were any clues there. Her bath towel was damp, so she'd showered. The shower stall was empty. The linen closet: shelves full of towels and bed sheets and not a bit of my sister.

The only place left in the house I hadn't checked was the attic, and I wasn't even sure there was an attic, or how you'd get into it. If Stevie were panicked, the attic wouldn't have been an option anyhow.

Think, I told myself. Check every possible space she could wedge herself into.

Across from me was the built-in sink and vanity. Two sinks, each with a cupboard underneath and three columns of drawers flanking them.

I pulled open the doors under the sink: tile cleanser and toilet bowl bleach.

But there was another sink, a bigger sink.

I raced downstairs to the kitchen. There, under the kitchen sink, curled up in a tight ball, was Stevie, fast asleep.

Looking at her, my first thought was that the wrong one of us had learned to squeeze ourselves into the narrow spaces of a magician's coffin.

Relief washed over me, together with an urge to slap her silly for scaring me so badly. There was my sister, curled up around the sink pipe, her head tucked into her shoulder, her other arm at an unnatural angle to make herself fit into the cramped space, and she was asleep.

One doctor—in Vienna, naturally, because why not go to the source—tried to explain away Stevie's behavior as post-traumatic stress disorder. I had argued with him, saying that she'd always been a little strange, even when she was a toddler, sucking her thumb and doodling in Latin. At least, I think it was Latin; I know I couldn't make heads or tails of the writing and it wasn't Greek, because that uses a different alphabet. The doctor had asked, "Was her home life unusual?" and that shut me right up. He then asked if there was any particular event she might have found especially stressful. We left his office.

I put my hand between her head and the wall of the cabinet, leaned in close, and then screamed, "Stevie!" right in her ear.

Her head banged backwards, against my fingers, and her eyes flew open. Her feet kicked against the wall of the cabinet and one knee slammed into the drainpipe.

She was awake now.

She looked at me with eyes wide with terror, until she processed what she was seeing and realized it was me. She squirmed, trying to get herself out of the contortions she had gotten her body into. I grabbed her under the knees and behind the back and pulled her out. Not the easiest stunt in the world—my sister, though slight, still weighed eighty-five or ninety pounds—but one I'd had enough practice with. She served as my main weight set, as I'd found it tough to work out at a gym on a regular basis.

I plopped her onto the limestone counter. "Mind telling me what that was all about?"

She gave me a wide-mouth smile and then threw her arms around my neck. "You're here! You're all right!"

I gave into the hug for a moment before pulling away as much as I could, given that her fingers were digging into my upper arms. "I'm more concerned about you at the moment. This is a new one, even for you."

"You're here." Tears were streaming down her cheeks.

She had been expecting me not to come home. She'd been afraid that once Roberto had me in his sights, I was going to disappear and she would be alone.

Which was the general idea, yes. But one thing at a time.

I moved her curling bangs out of her eyes. "Everything's going to be okay." So much for telling her the truth. I'm a terrible sister. "But you've got to tell me why you were under there."

She hopped off the counter and immediately sank to one knee. "Ow, my foot."

"Sit. Your circulation's probably iffy." I filled the kettle for her and put it on the stove. Stevie and her cup of tea. Even made properly—and it so rarely is, especially in America, where people tend to make tea with water not quite hot enough poured over stale leaves and left steeping for much too long—I thought tea was a waste of good water.

I checked some cupboards. "Didn't we buy some wine?"

She opened the drawer with the kitchen towels in it. I took a towel and the bottle of Cabernet Sauvignon she'd hidden there. Then she opened another drawer and without even looking into it reached in and pulled out a corkscrew. "You said you would call after…"

I used the towel to wipe off the neck of the wine bottle. "After I saw Roberto. Right. My bad. Sorry, I've been distracted today."

"I started to get scared. Like maybe you wouldn't return. And then…" She seemed as though she were searching for the right words to say it. "And Sir Gareth came to the door. Rang the bell."

Oh Lord. That would have frightened her to death. Especially after this morning. I wondered what Gary wanted.

She pulled down a teapot from its spot in the glass-fronted cabinet. "He was calling your name."

"Like this morning?"

She shook her head. "No, completely different. He sounded contrite. He said, 'I'm sorry, please come out.' It was…" She shook her head. "He heard me moving around in here. So I hid. I picked somewhere no one would look."

"And you fell asleep."

She ran hot water into the teapot and shook it around.

"I called your name several times."

Her mouth made a small *o*. "I must have been quite tired."

"Must have been." We didn't say anything for a few moments. The only noise was the water in the kettle revving up. Stevie had to be thinking about the same thing I was. Was she on the verge of another catatonic attack? Or was she catching up on twenty-two years of getting little to no sleep? And did she have to do this right now, when we might need to vacate the premises at a moment's notice?

Okay, there was little chance she was thinking that last one. But I certainly was.

While I opened the bottle, she went to the glass cabinet, pulled out a delicate wine goblet (perfect for an aromatic red), washed it, dried it, and handed it off in time for me to pour. For all of her faults, Stevie makes an excellent companion: cook, washerwoman, and sommelier rolled into one.

The kettle whistled and Stevie took it off the burner to let it cool down to the proper temperature for the best cup of tea. "Tell me what happened today."

I gave her the short version of my visit to Roberto, surgically removing both his offer of money for Stevie no longer being in my life and how relieved I had been to see him after all these years. I mentioned how surprised I felt to see pictures of my new little brother and sister. Then I told her about Vin Behar's showing up at the Peninsula and his blackmail attempt.

"He followed us from Las Vegas."

That reminded me. I needed to check the car for a sensor. Then I filled her in on what Nathaniel Ross, criminal defense attorney extraordinaire, was like. I took a large swig of the excellent Cabernet. It was fantastic. Stevie loathed anything stronger than 2% milk, but boy, had she read up on her wines.

She poured the tea from the pot into her cup, letting it pass through a strainer. "So what is your plan?"

"I think I need to talk to Anne da Silva. Find out what Colin was doing that he somehow dragged me into."

Stevie added the proper amount of milk—not cream, never cream, cream was for cretins—to her cup of tea. I sometimes mused we should move to Japan, so Stevie could study their tea ceremony in depth.

"How are you going to talk to her? Introduce yourself as Colin's wife?"

"That is an excellent question." And I didn't have one damned idea.

Sometimes exercise helps clear the cobwebs, so I went outside and searched the car for an hour, looking for some kind of device Vin Behar could have used to track us to Los Angeles. Nothing. Dammit.

I showered and then lay on the living room sofa, listening to Stevie knit and wishing I could nap like a normal human being.

"What you could do," Stevie said, needles clicking in perfect rhythm, "is use one of the posters from the show."

I saw where she was going with that. "We'll need to go to an art store."

"You agree this will work?" she asked.

"It's a brilliant plan, Stevie."

She gave me another wide-mouth smile. "Thank you. I know," she said with perfect sincerity.

CHAPTER ELEVEN

ANNE DA SILVA, *PEOPLE* MAGAZINE celebrity journalist extraordinaire, was the renter of record on Colin's apartment, though clearly he—or someone else—had been giving her the money every month to cover the rent. However, she lived somewhere else, a house in Beachwood Canyon. Which was nowhere near the beach, of course. Beachwood Canyon was the Hollywood Hills, not far from the Hollywood sign, and a few miles from Colin's place.

Stevie said, "The real estate listings call Beachwood 'funky' which apparently means run-down, yet expensive."

"Funky hill people," I told myself as I drove to Anne's house in the morning. Because of traffic I arrived at half-past nine, which seemed to be about perfect. No writer I'd ever met got started before ten, and then only with a firm deadline and a check in hand.

I followed Stevie's detailed instructions through the narrow and curving canyon roads. There were lots of bungalows, which must have been the realtor's term for these small, one-story wooden houses, many of them covered with sun-warped wooden shingles. More than one looked like a thatched-roof wonder spirited in from the Emerald Isle. The streets were narrow and shady, lined with old trees that formed a canopy over the road, keeping the area cool. Or relatively cool, given how baking hot LA was supposed to get during the summer. Beachwood Canyon was an area that appealed to me much more than most of LA had so far. Not that the city appealed to me at all. I wanted to get my bracelet and be elsewhere.

To New York? Or elsewhere? Alone or with Stevie?

I couldn't think about that. One problem at a time.

Anne's house was two-story and modern—a square white block with wide windows and red doors—in a shady stretch of a dead-end street. A Land Rover was parked outside, and, according to Stevie, Anne owned a Land Rover.

I parked on the street and pulled the now-framed poster from *A Night of Grand Guignol Magic* out of the backseat. Colin was prominently featured; Kristin and I were the interchangeable blonde and brunette in the back. I wouldn't have agreed to be on the poster if I had been recognizable in it. Colin had zero problem with showcasing himself, so that worked out well.

It took Anne several minutes to answer my two rings of the doorbell. As soon as I came to the conclusion perhaps she'd spent the night at a friend's house for comfort, she opened the door. Her eyes were red and puffy, she was wrapped in a blue robe much too thick to wear on such a warm day, and she had one arm wrapped around her waist. Protecting herself from the outside world. She looked like the photos Stevie had found of her. A cute, round-faced woman, with her glossy brown hair cut in a pageboy. She was wearing glasses and she had no makeup on, but this was her.

I took a deep breath. "Ms. da Silva?"

She cocked her head to one side. "Who are you?"

"I'm here about Colin."

She blinked and her mouth opened and closed a few times.

"I'm Drusilla. Did he ever mention me?"

She shook her head.

Why would he, I asked myself. "Ah. Then this is fairly awkward. May I come in?"

"Say whatever it is you came here for."

Okay, so she wasn't a wimp. She was going to leave me out here on the stoop. "I worked with Colin in the magic act in Las Vegas. Did he tell you about that?" Anne nodded and I turned the poster around. It had the desired effect: She couldn't stop staring at it. "Colin talked about you. And I thought you'd like this."

She pressed one fist against her mouth. Her jaw started trembling. "Oh, my God."

"May I put this down?" I jutted my chin toward the foyer, and she stepped aside to let me bring the picture in. I rubbed the palms of my hands together to wipe away the sweat. "This brings me to the other reason I'm here. This is awkward. But I hope you can help me." Anne folded her arms across her chest—more self-protection. "I swear to you it was only a green-card marriage, but I am Colin's wife."

Her immediate reaction was crystal clear: she'd had no idea he was married. "Oh my God." She shook her head. "Whatever. Just get out."

"I need your help."

It was a minute before she could allow herself to speak. "What? What can I help you with?"

"The first reason I came was to see if you'd been told about what happened. To him." I gave a weak smile. "I see you have. And you don't have to believe this, but I understand how you must feel."

She stared at me for a few seconds before she shut her eyes and shook her head. "You have no idea."

I almost said something like, *Hey, lady, I was married to him, remember?* But I am nothing if not polite in the service of getting what I want. "The other reason is something he said to me the night he died."

Her face softened, going from hostile to curious (and still hostile). She wiped her nose with the balled-up tissue. "You talked to him?"

"Yes, a little. We needed to discuss a few things. Divorce was at the top of my list." I held up a hand. "You don't need to believe me, okay? I came to Los Angeles looking for him, and when I found him, he said he and I had big trouble because of someone named Penelope. "

At the name "Penelope," I got Anne's full attention.

"He told me she had just left—"

"He said what?" she shrieked.

Interesting. I waited a few seconds to see if she had anything to add to that. She didn't.

"There was some kind of bad situation he was in because of her. He called it a 'bloody mess.'" The irony of his using that phrase right before he died hit me as soon as the words left my mouth. "I'm hoping you can tell me who Penelope is."

Anne paled before my eyes. "He didn't know her. How could he...They'd never met." She sank to the ground, wrapping herself in a tight ball.

Oh, Colin. Colin, you bastard. Seeing two women, who

happened to be friends, and neither was aware of the other? It's one thing to play around, it's another not to tell everyone what the game is and who's scoring.

"Who is Penelope?" I repeated, softer this time.

"She's my…a woman I know. An actress. Penelope Gurevich. You've probably heard of her."

I pretended to think about it for a second. "No."

"She's on TV." She looked up at me. "You're sure he said that?"

"I'm guessing you don't know why he might have been in trouble because of her."

She pursed her lips for a second, considering something. Then she said: "You were the mentalist. You did the mind-reading act."

Wonderful. He had mentioned my existence, except not by name and not the part where we were married. Not that it made a difference. "Yes. Among other things. But—"

"Colin wouldn't tell me how you did it."

No good magician gives away his secrets. Also, he didn't know. "It's magic."

"So read my mind. He said you were so good."

I was baffled by her request—didn't she want me out of there? —until it dawned on me she wanted proof. Proof that I was the one from the act. Fine. I sat down on the ground across from her, close enough to gauge her reactions.

"Your name is Anne. You're a writer." She was trying not to react, but her temple twitched. That was my baseline for a hit. "This is the first murder you've ever experienced of someone close." Hit. "You told Colin to get out of that apartment, maybe even to come stay here, but he wouldn't." Hit. I could have told her why. Colin had a pathological need to have his own private space.

I rattled off other things as fast as I could, some hits, some misses. Standard stuff, not hard to guess with what I knew about her from Stevie's research. And as a finale I said, "And you really, really want to start drinking, even though you know you absolutely shouldn't."

Which I thought would be safe to say about anyone on a morning after their lover had been murdered.

When Anne's eyes widened, and her mouth opened, I knew I'd hit the bull's eye without even meaning to.

"How did you know?" she said. "Colin didn't know."

She seemed so bewildered by my guess I wanted to comfort her with something like, "I saw your 60-day pin." But there was no sign on her or around us of any kind of AA involvement. I kept looking at her. "You don't tell anybody?" I asked.

"Not a lot, no." She leaned against the wall. "How did you do that?"

I shrugged.

"Maybe you really are psychic." She smiled weakly. "A lot of people would like to talk to you."

She didn't know the half of it. "There's only one person I need to talk to at this moment. I'm sorry I upset you. I hope your day gets better."

She looked up at me, pleading, wanting reassurance. "He said he was in trouble with Penelope?"

"The bad kind of trouble. Not romantic trouble, no. He sounded as if he could barely stand her."

"Could barely stand who?"

The sudden intrusion of a male voice startled me. Instead of flinching, I glanced up. There, in the doorway, was Detective Samuel Gruen. All six foot something of him, staring at me.

"Good morning, Detective," I said.

Anne clutched at her robe, as though he could see right through it. "Who—"

He held his badge out and introduced himself. "I have some questions about Colin Abbott."

She ran a hand through her hair, messing up those perfect bangs. "I think—just a minute." She scurried off through her living room toward the back of the house.

I reached my hand up to him. "Mind giving me a hand, Detective?"

He crooked his head as he regarded me sitting on the floor. Then he gripped my hand—his skin was cool and, damn, did he have a firm hold—and I rose to my feet. Of course, when I stood up I fell against him, as though I were trying to get my balance. My hand pushed against his chest for a second. Which was long enough to answer one of my questions, which was that his physique was not only for appearances.

"Thank you for the assist, Detective." I looked down at my hand, which he was still holding. He dropped it.

It's not nice, but men are so much fun to flirt with. Particularly the ones who don't want you to.

"What are you doing here?" he asked.

"Don't worry, I was leaving."

"How do you know Anne da Silva?"

I picked up my purse off the ground, stretching down in as slow and sinuous a movement as I could without being pronounced about it. He watched. I pointed to the framed poster. "I came here to give her that."

"You woke up this morning and decided first thing you'd stop by and have a talk with your husband's girlfriend?"

"I'm almost certain you're not supposed to talk to me without my lawyer present."

From his slight nod, he was well aware of that. Perhaps he was hoping I wasn't. "You don't seem bothered your husband was sleeping with her."

"I'll have my lawyer fax you a list of the girlfriends Colin had in Las Vegas. No, it didn't bother me."

"You were going to tell me who Colin could barely stand."

"I'll be happy to tell you at the proper time."

"This have anything to do with Penelope Gurevich?"

I shrugged. "So many things are possible, Detective." He was fast. I wondered what else the police had managed to find. It was time to stop talking to him. That was a good idea anyhow, nicely muscled body or no.

Anne popped around the corner, having thrown on a polo shirt and Bermuda shorts. Her hair was still a mess but she'd washed her face.

"It was my pleasure meeting you, Anne." I took her hand in mine for a light shake. "May I leave you my number?"

She nodded and found a pad of paper and a pen on a table in the living room. Writers are so good with that sort of thing. I scribbled my new phone number in my carefully-practiced handwriting. I ripped it off the pad and handed it to her.

"You're leaving?" Gruen asked.

"Alas, yes, I must be going."

He looked back at Anne. "I need to ask you a few questions."

"Do you want to come in?"

It hadn't dawned on me why he'd stayed in the doorway this whole time. I laughed. "Oh yes, that's right, it's sort of like with vampires, isn't it? They have to be invited in."

At the same time as he started to enter the house, I squeezed past him in the doorway. He froze. I said in a low voice, "See you around, I hope."

"You will," he said, his voice a notch or two huskier than it had been.

I was out on the front steps, feeling certain I'd gotten the better of him, when he added, "And yeah, I'll take that list of names."

I got into my car without checking to see if the detective was still looking at me. If you check, the effect is spoiled.

My hands were trembling a little as I put them on the wheel. Which left me wondering who'd gotten the better of whom.

I got home and gave Stevie the run-down about Anne. She had no idea her friend Penelope knew Colin, she had no idea what Colin might have been doing with Penelope that made him so scared, and, most worrisome, she was a hell of a lot more devastated by Colin's death than I was, which looked bad in front of the detective.

"But usually you're good at acting," Stevie said, which was both true and not what I wanted to hear right then.

One of the phones rang. Since it was the one in my purse, it was the new Los Angeles number, which narrowed down the possibilities for who could be calling: Colin, Gary, the police, Roberto, Anne, or Nathaniel Ross. And I was almost entirely certain it wasn't Colin.

"I bet it's Ross," I said.

Stevie put down her needles. "I'll answer it for you." She looked at it. "The number's blocked. Hello? Who is calling, please?" Her eyes widened with surprise. "Just…just a second."

She held out the phone to me. *Penelope*, she mouthed.

Penelope? I sat up and grabbed it from her. "Hello?"

"Hi there!" said a bubbly, unfamiliar voice. "Hi! It's me!"

When in doubt, act stupid. "I'm sorry, you have the wrong—"

"Drusilla! It's me, Penelope! You're in town, and I'd love to get together!"

I nodded at Stevie, and she sat back on the sofa, her knitting forgotten.

"We *really* need to talk, Dru!" she continued.

"I'd love to," I said slowly.

Penelope told me we could meet at her *favoritest* place in the universe, a juice place on Venice Boardwalk. Because, as she put it in one giant unstoppable rush, "I hate vegetables but my nutritionist says I have to have them and I'd rather drink them than eat them any day. Come soon!" It didn't sound so much like an invitation as an order.

After I hung up, I waited for Stevie to tell me what the hell that was all about.

"It's the boardwalk in Venice. She wants to meet you in public."

"Why does she want to talk to me?" I grabbed my purse. "Let's go mad and guess this has something to do with Colin. Come on."

Stevie didn't move. Her shoes remained by their spot at the coat closet and not on her feet.

Yesterday I left Stevie alone for hours, with disastrous results. What would happen if she were alone even longer? "You should come with. It'll be fun. You can meet a TV star."

She shook her head. "I will if you need me to, but...I don't want to."

She didn't want to?

She should be anxious to spend a little time with me. Where was the girl who could stick like Velcro? Suddenly she could take me or leave me?

I stared at her. "There's something on the telly, isn't there?"

She gave me the lip press of annoyance. "Yes, there is," she said, not looking at me. "But you don't understand."

"Oh for Chri—Zeus's sake, they rerun those detective series twenty times a day."

"Chelsea versus Arsenal."

Well, if that wasn't Stevie in a nutshell. My husband's been murdered, I'm going to have a chat with the person he mentioned before he died as having threatened him, and Stevie has to let her obsession with football get in the way of helping me out. Football. She'd never watched a match while she lived in England, either at a stadium or on the telly. (Stevie at a stadium with tens of thousands of rabid football fans? Please. She wouldn't have made it past the first gate.) She'd never kicked a ball, let alone played. Her fanatic devotion to Arsenal—*Arsenal*, for Christ's sake, as if that weren't proof of her complete and total detachment from the real world— was wholly a manifestation of her desire to go home. A home that never existed, of course, but Stevie was never one to let reality get in the way of a good fantasy. Whereas in the here and now, I got to deal with the reality.

I glared at her. "You want to stay here and watch a football match?"

She rocked back and forth, ball-heel, ball-heel, several times, not looking at me, before she nodded. She tilted her head toward the floor and said, "The telly has all the pay sports channels."

My first thought was, might as well enjoy them, because they probably won't have all those neat channels at the group home. But

I clenched my jaw and stopped thinking about Roberto and New York and my inheritance.

"Fine," I said, not caring much whether or not she heard my teeth grinding. "Let's go over the map and you can show me where I'm headed."

Chapter Twelve

PENELOPE WAS IN THE JUICE Heaven hut when I arrived at Venice Beach. She wore a fuchsia cropped top with matching short-shorts, the kind that require a Brazilian bikini wax. Compared to some of the other girls in the juice store, though, Penelope was wearing a burka. Who needed clothes when the weather keeps you warm? She signed a few autographs and, from where I sat, I could hear her squeal of appreciation every time someone recognized her.

I sat on a stone bench across the pedestrian walkway, camouflaged by the constant foot traffic. Venice Boardwalk was crawling with people. And why not? It seemed to be California personified. The March day was warm and sunny and the beach stretched out for miles, with the Pacific glistening beyond—the water was freezing cold, which explained why no one was swimming in it. Walkers, rollerbladers, and bicyclists covered the boardwalk, passing the shops on one side and the line of street sellers on the other. At my bench, I had a street artist to my left, ready to do a caricature of any tourist in oil crayons. On my right was a giant display dedicated to the legalization of marijuana, manned by a chap with blonde dreadlocks and an untrimmed beard. I was downwind from him and he smelled like samples were available. Also, like he hadn't bathed in a while.

Penelope stepped out of the juice place, holding a gigantic foam cup but not drinking from it. She looked up and down the block, perhaps wondering where I was.

I stood up and waved. "Penelope!"

She waved at me and flashed her too-white smile. "Hi!" She dashed across the pedestrian path, dodging a few rollerbladers, and came over to me. "Hey! You're here!" She looked at my dress. "Wow. Vera Wang?"

"How are you today, Penelope?"

We started walking down the beachfront.

She swung her honey-brown ponytail over her shoulder. "I'm so glad I'm off the set today. Doing a series is a grind, you know? It looks easy, but it's so much work. Hey, you want some juice?" She offered me her cup.

I shook my head. "I have a dinner engagement tonight." The same one I always did, with my sister.

She shrugged, and then took a sip. "This is like all I'm going to eat today. Seriously. I have got to drop five pounds before this photo shoot next Monday, and I retain water like anything." She snapped her fingers.

I knew I was supposed to ask, "Lose five pounds from where?" I don't like to play other people's games. So instead I said, "Where would you like to chat?"

She raised one index finger off the cup and pointed to a building a few blocks up the beach. "I live right here. Bought it like two months ago. It's so fabulous having my own place. But there's not much furniture. It's not decorated yet, okay? I've been away at a location shoot for forever and just got back two days ago."

As we walked, Penelope babbled on about interior designers.

"I think I want a Tuscan kind of feel to it," she said.

I stifled my first reaction and went for a neutral response. "Many people do seem to like that, it's true."

"Oh! I just love the way English people talk! I wish I'd been born there and had an accent. Instead I'm from Merced. You ever been to Merced?"

I shook my head.

"Don't. It's completely the ass of the universe."

"I'll wager you've never been to any of the Baltic states," I said.

"I've been to Baltimore, does that count?" Then she laughed.

As we walked, we discussed fashion, as though we'd talked about it before. She told me about the gossip on her co-stars, none of whom I knew. She said hello to everyone who said hello to her. It was surreal, walking along the pathway, chattering away with the woman who had threatened Colin in some way, shortly before he got himself murdered. I found it tough to believe she could have killed him, if for no other reason than she was five or six inches shorter than Colin and she weighed about three hundred tons less. She was bony. Penelope had a body built to reassure male viewers, not threaten them.

Her building was a large, shallow sandstone arc that faced the Pacific Ocean. "Every condo in there has an ocean view."

"Every condo goes from one side of the building to the other?"

She nodded.

"So the ones on the end must have wrap-around views."

Another nod. "And I have one of the end ones!" she burbled.

In the lobby, Penelope tried to wave me past the guard's desk with a smile and giggle, but he insisted I had to sign in anyhow. I signed the book with my beautiful copperplate signature, all carefully placed angles and perfectly-sized loops. Whenever I get a new name, Stevie has me work on the signature until I can do it without hesitating, and every name has a different writing style. I can't read any of them, of course, but they're very pretty.

I can even do it with either hand. That particular skill hasn't come in handy yet, but I'm sure it will one day.

We went up in the elevator, which required a card key to operate, to the nineteenth floor. The top was the twentieth, so Penelope hadn't scaled all the heights of fame yet. The décor down the hallway to her condo had nice touches: The hallway carpeting was black with gold paisleys, and the walls were painted with various sizes of stripes in pale pink and yellow.

It wasn't fabulous. But it looked nicer than anywhere I'd lived in the past few years. Up until Gary's estate, of course.

"Ta da!" Penelope said as she opened the door—into an empty apartment. When she had said it was empty, I hadn't expected actual emptiness. The entire contents of the place were one red Barcalounger in the middle of the living room, one half-full ashtray on the white Berber carpeting beside the lounger, and a wine glass on its side nearby. The only decoration was in the hallway, where a poster for *The Night Glen* was tacked onto the wall. There was nothing else I could see in the place.

Even more overwhelming was the smell. Penelope smoked like a fiend, because every pore of that place was filled with cigarette smoke, a scent that appalls me as much as it beckons me to return to its loving embrace. I prayed the overpowering smell of the cigarettes in the condo wasn't going to stink up my clothes.

The living room did have an impressive view. To be specific, the balcony off the living room did. Venice Beach was right below, on the other side of the street, and beyond that stretched the Pacific.

We were at the end of the continent. I couldn't run any farther west. Nowhere left to go.

Penelope bopped into the kitchen and I followed. "I need a drink," she said, throwing her foam juice cup into the sink, which was already filled with plenty of dishes and other juice cups. "Want some wine?" She pulled the bottle out of the refrigerator. "I'm not much up on wine, but this is a really great brand." She held out the label toward me. I didn't need to. I recognized the label. Queen's Lace Pinot Grigio.

Colin's favorite wine.

Interesting.

My stomach threatened to go on strike and look for another body to live in if I had anything to drink before I'd had my first decent-sized meal. And I didn't quite trust what might be in that bottle. Nathaniel hadn't mentioned a thing about toxicology reports, so I didn't know if Colin had been drugged or not. This tiny woman would have had to have had some kind of help in overpowering him—such as using chloroform or elephant tranquilizer—if she wanted to kill him.

Vin Behar had been sitting outside Colin's apartment.

"Oh, are you AA or anything?" She didn't wait for my answer. She put the bottle on the kitchen counter and picked a wine glass out of the sink. A quick wash and wipe and she was good to go. "I'm thinking about doing AA." She filled her glass. "It's a great place to meet people in this town. AA is like the best place to network." She giggled over the top of her goblet, embarrassed. "A lot of people do. If my show doesn't work out…something to think about, right?" She took a gulp of wine, swished it around in her mouth like mouthwash before swallowing, and then topped off the glass with another slug. As she stuffed the cork back in the bottle, her eyes started to fill with tears. "This was Colin's favorite wine."

"Yes, I know," I said. "Did you spend a lot of time with him and Anne?"

She put the bottle back into the refrigerator and looked back at me with a half-grin. "No. We spent time alone. Hope you didn't mind."

I rolled my eyes. Hope she didn't think she was special. She wasn't special; she was obvious and heavy-handed. What could she have done to make Colin so damn frightened right before his murder?

She led me back into the living room and started to pull open the door to the balcony, where there were two chaise-longues facing the ocean, with an overflowing ashtray between them. A strong cold breeze came in and Penelope shut the door.

"Fog's coming in." She giggled and drank about a third of her wine. "Come on."

She led me down the hall, past the poster, to the bedrooms. We passed the first two, which contained opened, rifled moving boxes or racks of clothes. Then we entered the master suite, which was larger than the living room and had a bigger balcony that looked out over Venice toward Santa Monica. The room had a king-sized bed with the black-and-white checkerboard satin duvet, a flat-screen TV on the wall, and a bedside table with the ashtray, the pack of Marlboro Lights, and a lighter on it. The telephone was on the floor. Clothes had been scattered wherever she'd been standing when she removed them. A highboy stood in the corner, forgotten.

Penelope propped up the pillows on the bed against the ornately carved headboard. "This is kind of weird, but it's so comfortable." She reached for the cigarettes and lit up. She blew the smoke into the air and I waved it away. "Oh, sorry! I'll crack open the door." She pulled open the balcony door and then hopped back on the bed. And sat there for a moment, as though she'd forgotten why in the hell she'd asked me there to begin with.

"So." She looked over at me. I raised my eyebrows at her. "Um…how do we start?"

Start having a discussion or having sex? I thought. "Let's discuss what happened last night, Penny."

"Penelope. Just Penelope." She laughed without a genuine drop of humor. "Never Penny." She smoked her cigarette and stared off into space for a moment. Then she turned her head to look at me, head tilted forward so she was looking up at me through her lashes. It's a powerfully seductive position. I've used it often enough myself.

"This whole thing with Colin—it's totally weirded me out. I mean, I was talking to him at his place last night." Her hand slid over mine and she interlaced our fingers. "The whole conversation we had, then he was murdered…"

She squeezed my hand so lightly, I almost mistook it for a nervous twitch.

Almost.

Except Penelope was gazing at me at the same time, in a way that was supposed to make me think "longing" but instead made me think "deliberate." The squeeze was a maneuver to make it clear she was flirting with me. Getting us in bed together was a move calculated to put me off-balance. She wanted me wondering what was going on, which would leave her in control.

Her first mistake? Thinking she could put me off-balance by sitting on a bed with me. Please.

"You know I'm Colin's wife, right?"

"Oh, uh huh." She took another puff. "I feel I'm really close to you, in a funny way, you know?" She put the cigarette in the ashtray and then leaned against the pillow, light golden brown eyes turned toward me.

Fantastic. Had he given her the idea he'd married a lesbian? "You were at his apartment last night? Have you told the police that?"

"I really don't want them to know," she said.

Right. Let me put that on my Not To Mention list. "How did you meet Colin, anyhow?"

"God, stop being stupid. Look, I'm upset about what happened last night, okay?"

A quick flash of what I'd seen last night interrupted my intention to remain cool. "You're upset? Colin got murdered. I found him. His head was bashed in and he's dead. What is this game you're playing?"

She chewed her lip in an adorably vulnerable sort of way. Most women who wear makeup would never do that to their lips, and since she was on TV she should be used to wearing makeup. But American women tend on the whole to be far more casual about their appearance than European women.

Also, Penelope was playing a role. And the character she was playing would chew her lip to indicate vulnerability.

Helios's sidecar. Fine, I'd give her an opening. "Last night

Colin called me, said something terrible had happened between the two of you."

"I shouldn't have said what I did, okay? I was just so…" She waved her cigarette around for emphasis. "So scared. You can understand that, right?"

"Honestly?" I said.

She nodded.

"No!" I screamed in her face, which blew her back on the bed a few feet. I got off the bed and started walking around. "No, I have no goddamn idea what you're talking about. What in the hell were you and Colin up to?"

Her facial expression went from soft and giddy to focused and not at all giddy, which suited me fine. She sat up against the pillows and crossed her arms. "Listen. How much more damn money do you need?"

"Believe me when I tell you, I am the wrong person to ask that question."

"Come on. Stop jerking me around. I shouldn't have said it, okay? I'm not really going to the cops. Just give them to me."

I thought about what Colin had said last night. "He told me he already did."

"He didn't. Lying son of a bitch."

I pinched the bridge of my nose. "Let me see if I can follow along here. You paid him some money, he gave you something, and once you had it in your hot little hands you said you were going to sic the cops on him for…what was it? Blackmail? But it turned out you didn't get it, he's dead, and you've got me here."

"Come on. This is me. I just want them back, okay? They're mine. He got them for me. I've already paid for them."

"What did he get for you?"

She rolled her eyes. "Why are you being such an idiot?"

"Why Colin? How did he get involved with you?"

She gave me a look. "He said he could help me. I thought he did. He didn't."

How like Colin. A pretty woman bats her eyelashes at him, and he falls all over himself to help her out. Not that I could complain too hard about that—I'd made use of that character flaw of his myself.

How could Colin help her, though? Why on earth would she ask him instead of the studio publicist or someone like that?

Oh. She had told me, hadn't she? *He got them for me.* He had stolen something for her. He gave it to her, she said she was going to accuse him of blackmail, and then he told her he'd given her the wrong thing. She wanted the right one.

I stared right back and let the silence go on for a while before I said, "I don't have it. Must still be in his apartment." I knitted my eyebrows together. "Unless…"

"What?" she screamed.

"The cops found it?"

Penelope relaxed and she smiled. "Believe me, if the police had found anything like this there, I'd have heard about it already. Give them back."

I nodded. "I have one more question, Penelope."

She stared at me for a second, and then dramatically rolled her eyes.

"How did you get my phone number? It's less than a day old."

She took a long drag on her cigarette. "You're unbelievable, you know that? Get out."

"It's a simple question."

"Get out!" she screamed. She didn't have a trained voice: the pitch went sharp in the upper registers. "Stop calling me, get out, and give me my goddamn pictures, all right?"

Pictures. Photos. Blackmail. I thought back to the head shots of Penelope in that briefcase. Not those. Something bad enough to be worthy of stealing. And maybe of murder.

The other thing she said came to me. "Love, I need to point out *you* called *me*."

She shook her head and her mouth opened and closed a number of times. She clearly kept thinking of things she wanted to say to me and then kept thinking better of it. "Fifty thousand more. But that's it. Not a goddamn penny more."

Fuck me. What in the hell had Colin picked up for this woman? It was making her a lot more than fifty thousand crazy. Whatever Colin had gotten was worth much, much more than that. Intriguing.

"Done. I'll look into it first thing tomorrow."

"Why tomorrow?" she snapped.

I gestured toward the window. Night had fallen as much as it could in such a lit-up city during our little sojourn here in her bedroom. "I think a flashlight moving around his apartment might be noticed. And the cops might be watching it."

She gave me a half-grin. "I knew you were going to be reasonable. Nobody needs to call the police about anything."

"For fifty thousand? I can be extraordinarily reasonable. I also need to go."

Penelope got off the bed and swayed over to me. She looked me up and down. When she got close to me, she lifted her arms around my neck and raised herself up on her tiptoes to give me a light kiss. "Let's talk tomorrow," she whispered.

I rolled my eyes and pushed her away. She fell back on the

bed. "Does that act work on many people?" I asked.

She grinned. "Colin sure liked it," she said.

I laughed. "I'm sure he did." I picked up a tissue and made a show of blotting her kiss off my lips. "But he had lots of women he liked, Penelope. Some of them better than you."

That was how I left her in her bedroom, letting myself out her front door. I signed out with the security guard, winking at him as I handed back the pen.

As I walked back to my car, I was certain of one thing: whatever Colin had gotten for Penelope, he hadn't given it to her and that had pissed her off something fierce.

And I knew exactly where it would be. Luckily for me, it was nowhere near his apartment.

CHAPTER THIRTEEN

THE GUESTHOUSE WAS WARM AND smelled of citrus and sounded like a sports announcer with a horrible Geordie twang. A plate of fresh orange cinnamon scones was on the counter, the kettle was on, the coffee pot was full, and somewhere in the living room, the giant TV showed a close-up of several athletic men with tight, perfect bodies running around the pitch in shorts and sweaty shirts.

For a second, I found myself wondering if Stevie enjoyed watching football for the same reason I would, but I shook my head. I doubted Stevie had even discovered boys yet.

Stevie came bouncing in. "Arsenal, one-nil. What's up?"

"Let's hope they keep the penalty kicks to a minimum, because we have work to do. I need the briefcase."

She came back with the briefcase and a plastic supermarket bag filled with the cash. I put down the scone I'd taken a bite of—

heavenly, as always—and shook my head. "Put the money away. I need the case." I poured myself a cup of coffee. No need to rush. The briefcase was going to be fine for the next hour or so, whereas these scones had a marked shelf life.

When I was done indulging, Stevie swept off the counter and we put on gloves. She opened the case and angled it toward the nearest light, but the light wasn't enough to show the inside. I needed a flashlight.

"Should I get the torch?" she asked.

"Please."

She found our trusty Maglite wherever she'd hidden it and held it over the briefcase, shining the beam all around the edges and over the interior satin.

Stevie shook her head. "I don't see anything in here. Are you sure—"

"Where's the best place to hide something?" I asked her. "Hide it in a place that's already got something hidden. If you opened this and found the money, would you keep looking? Hell no."

"I'm not certain your experience is enough data to cover everyone's reactions," Stevie said.

I ignored her. "And it's small, whatever it is." I lightly drew my fingers over the bottom of the case, then in and around the pockets on the top.

Stevie poked and prodded at the lining of the bottom of the case. "Wait!" Her face fell. "No, sorry, that's a bump from the false bottom."

At the same time as she said that, my fingers trailed over a bump on the top edge of the case.

There should be slight irregularities with the bottom, since Colin had installed a fake layer to hide the money. There shouldn't be anything wrong with the top. I grabbed the flashlight and shined it around the edge of the top. "Move over. I need to see this better."

"There?" she said, pointing to a flaw in the lining.

I peered closer. "No, that's a tear in the cloth. Over here." I tapped the side where I'd felt the bump and then dragged my fingertips over the spot again. A closer look made me wonder how I could have ever missed it in the first place.

The false bottom in the briefcase was a lovely piece of work. On the top of the briefcase, the black satin liner had been cut and reattached. As a result, it was pulled to one side. Extremely sloppy work for someone of Colin's talents.

I slipped my fingernail under the edge of the satin lining. The edge came up, but then I hit the thick strip of glue holding the lining in place. "Get the nail polish remover."

She came back with a bottle of remover and a box of cotton swabs. "Couldn't find the tweezers."

"This'll do." And I set to work.

One of the reasons I was being so careful and neat about it was that the police had to see this briefcase. At some point. I'm not oblivious of the facts of jurisprudence. I wanted to make my snooping seem less obvious. I would snoop, and then I would re-glue. And that was it.

To remove the glue, I had to swab the underside of the lining and then tug, ever so gently, to separate it. Stevie wandered between the kitchen and the living room, alternately watching me and the match. It took me an hour to unseal the top edge of the lining from the leather case.

Which is right when we heard a series of sharp knocks on the front door.

Gary stood in the doorway, peering into the guesthouse. Stevie was looking over her shoulder at the door, paralyzed, yet in position to bolt at any moment.

I muttered a number of maledictions in various languages, mostly at myself for not having considered that he might be around. I wiped my hands on a towel as he rapped on the door again. I swung it open and stood in the middle of the doorway to prevent his coming in. "What?"

"Hm?" He looked at me, and then shoved his hands into his jacket pockets and looked down at his feet. "I came by to apologize." When I didn't respond, he grinned with embarrassment. "For my outburst yesterday." His eyebrows knitted for a second. "It was yesterday, right?"

"It was. Apology accepted." As to how sincere his apology was? Who the hell knew. The man had two or three Oscars. No one should trust a damn thing he said, ever. That was good advice about anyone, to be honest, and I should know. I started to close the door.

He put his hand on it to keep it open. "Is that Chelsea?" he asked, glancing at the television. Stevie, who was still staring at him, nodded. "Hullo, I'm Gary Macfadyen." After a quick comparison of the two of us, he nodded. "Is she your sister?"

"My what?"

"Your sister. You couldn't have a daughter that age. You look a great deal alike." He moved his hand by the side of his face. "Your hair. The eyes."

He needed to get out of here. "Gary, darling, we're in the middle of something, so if you'll excuse us—"

"Can I come in?" he asked, in a small voice. "Look, I am sorry about the way I behaved. I...I get that way, sometimes. I didn't mean anything by it."

"Oh. You get that way sometimes. Then that's all right then. Please, feel free to come by and scream at me once in a while."

He winced at my sarcasm. "Do people not give you an apology very often, or, are you simply incapable of accepting one?"

He was right. I needed to be nicer. At least until such time as we could leave. And the best way to be nicer is to have an excuse for one's bitchiness. "Today is difficult. My husband was murdered yesterday."

"Oh my God. I'm so sorry."

"So you'll excuse us." I started to close the door

He held up his hand to stop the door. "Do you think I could watch the match? My house is somewhat...quiet."

Even famous actors can get isolated and lonely in their hilltop palaces. It wasn't that surprising. Lots of millionaires didn't have one person to call friend. But his loneliness didn't change anything as far as I cared. My focus wasn't even on myself at that moment, difficult as it might be to believe. I needed to find out what Penelope was so concerned about.

"Honestly, it's not a good idea," I said.

His look of dejection was heartbreaking as he nodded and turned around.

I closed the door. "You okay?"

Stevie nodded.

"I think I have the case open. Let's have a look."

Stevie followed me into the kitchen. I put on my gloves and tested the edge of the satin lining: it was completely detached. I reached into the space beyond with my index finger, which poked into something flat and plastic, with a hard edge. It hurt. I held the lining open and turned the briefcase upside down.

Strips of film negatives shot out onto the kitchen table. I

shook the case again. Nothing.

Hard, sepia-colored film negatives. How low tech.

"Actual celluloid?" Stevie said. "How low tech."

"Someone didn't want them found easily, that's for certain."

She picked up one of the negative strips and held it up to the light as I stripped the latex gloves off my hands. They had the nail polish remover on them, and I didn't want to chance hitting the negatives. She turned the strip this way and that, before she dropped her hand and put the strip back on the table with its fellows.

I picked it up. Took me a few turns of the view as well to figure out that the picture showed a blowjob.

Unfortunately, that was all I could tell about it, because it was a tiny image with lights and darks reversed.

"Well, well, well," I said.

Stevie's face was pale and she stared at the floor, unable to speak.

"Stevie. Breathe. Inhale. Exhale." I squinted at the strip of images, trying to see if I could make out the faces clearly enough to identify.

"You think it's Penelope?" Stevie whispered.

My poor sister. She had her reasons, I reminded myself.

I held the negative strip up again. "We need to get these developed before we should draw any conclusions about them."

"Do you think he was blackmailing her?" Stevie asked.

"Blackmail would explain the money." I lowered the first photo strip and picked up the next one. More of the same, at least from what I could see. "And Penelope is rather agitated about this situation, which is understandable."

"But…" Stevie said.

I glanced over at her. "But what?"

"That's what I'm waiting for you to finish. There's some contrafactual you want to add."

The only language my sister doesn't know: the one the rest of us mortals speak. "A contra what?"

She sighed. "You want to add something like, 'If such and such had occurred,' where such and such could not under any circumstances occur. You want to say that this whole thing with Penelope could have happened if...?" She waved her hand in the air.

The kitchen was quiet except for the quiet thumping of the dishwasher.

"Oh, all right. I was going to say, 'If Colin were capable of blackmailing someone.' Which he couldn't be. Except maybe he was." I slammed my hand on the counter, frustrated.

"Blackmailing who?" came a third voice, definitely male.

Stevie and I stared at each other for a second before we turned around to the actor leaning in the kitchen doorway, watching us. My sister took a step back toward me, and I put my hand on her shoulder to reassure her.

"I locked the door!"

"You didn't. It was open. I returned to give you this," he said, holding up a bottle of what looked to be an excellent syrah, and from Stevie's intake of breath I surmised it wasn't cheap, either. "By way of apology and because of your husband. But I can see your grief takes different forms than many people's. Blackmail?"

"You need to leave now, Gary."

"What's going on?" he asked.

Stevie looked at me, her eyes wide with panic. "What do we say?"

Of course, she said it in Hungarian.

"Have any ideas?" I replied. "Like how long he's been standing there?"

The actor nodded. "You won't answer questions and you're looking at photographic negatives and there's a pile of money over there and you say your husband's been murdered and now the two of you have suddenly lapsed into another language. By the way, this isn't at all suspicious. Or intriguing."

"Are you okay?" I asked my sister, in English.

She glanced at Gary, and then turned back toward me. "I'm okay."

Great. I considered Stevie's needs taken care of. I turned toward Gary. "You want to know what's going on? My husband was murdered yesterday. I think he was murdered over these photographs. Was it blackmail? I have no fucking idea. I was married to him for six months and I have no idea what he was doing or why I hadn't clued into any of it. And now I'm the center of the inquiry and I'd like to know why. There. That clear things up for you?"

"Are you okay?" Stevie asked me.

I gave her the hand signal that meant I was getting a migraine. She pulled out our med kit and rummaged around until she produced the bottle of migraine aspirin. She shook two out, put them on the counter, and went to fetch a glass for water. It gave her something to do.

When I was busy trying to swallow those god-awful pills, Gary said, "What's your name?"

"Stevie," she said quietly.

I snapped my fingers. "Eyes over here, your worship." I needed him gone, but more importantly I needed Stevie to get working on a problem. Thinking reduced her anxiety immensely. "What's the connection, Stevie?"

"Why does Colin have these pictures? How did Colin even know Penelope?"

"And how am I somehow involved?"

"We need to give those pictures to the police," Stevie said.

"We will. We will give these pictures to the exceptionally attractive Detective Gruen. Right after we find out for ourselves what's on them."

Gary leaned his chair back on two legs and held onto the doorframe for support. "This is the best thing that has ever happened to me."

"I wonder where we can get them developed that won't get us arrested," I said.

"In LA?" he said. "Thousands of places. But you don't—"

Stevie shrugged. "We can buy the chemicals we need and do it here."

"How much is that going to cost?" I asked.

"Girls," Gary said.

She shook her head. "It's not terrible. I'll make a list of what we need and tell you where to go to get them."

"You want me to buy a bunch of chemicals where I have to read the fucking labels? Sorry. Next plan."

She thought about that for a second, and then nodded. "Good point. Perhaps we can find a lab that rents space by the hour."

Gary dropped his chair to the floor. "Girls!" he yelled. That man had amazing vocal presence. Of course he's known for that, but it's thrilling up close and personal.

We both looked at him.

"Photography happens to be a hobby of mine."

It took me a couple of seconds. "You have a darkroom here."

"Why, yes, I do."

Stevie and I looked at each other.

"Lead on, Macduff," I told him.

He glared at me, and that was not an experience I wanted to repeat. Ever. That man had a scary, well-practiced glare. "Christ, don't say that," he muttered.

As he led us over to the main house, I remembered about fifteen years ago he'd starred in *Macbeth* for the BBC, a weird techno-modern version with updated clothes and robots and cross-dressing. Even Stevie hadn't liked it, which meant it was unsalvageable dreck.

Stevie looked at me. "It's 'Lay on, Macduff'. Not 'Lead on.'"

"Thanks ever so much for the update," I said.

We went in the French doors at the back of the house and up the staircase made out of slabs of travertine marble. The house was dark and hollow. Every sound we made echoed off the walls. I wondered how he could stand living here alone.

Upstairs, he led us down a long green carpet past several heavy Brazilian cherry doorways, to the one at the end of the hall. "Here it is. Let me know if you need anything. Like a proofer."

"Thanks, we'll be fine," I told him. I blocked off the entrance to the dark room with my arm to keep him from following us in.

Stevie put her arm across the doorway to block me from coming in. "You can't be in here," she said.

"I need to see what you're doing."

"Darkrooms tend to be small, and you take up too much space."

Stevie was the only person on earth who thought I was too large. Given how small and thin she was, this attitude troubled me sometimes. And I would worry over whether she had a body image issue when I had the time.

"Stevie. These pictures." I didn't need to say the obvious.

"I'll be okay. I don't need to look at them to develop them."

She slammed the door in my face.

❧

The room at the center of the upstairs was a fabulous media room I coveted deeply and sincerely. One entire wall was the screen, set to that Chelsea v. Arsenal game—wasn't that over and done with yet?—with life-size players. Large, soft armchairs in blue and gray ultrasuede were parked at various spots around the room, each with its own side table and small snake light attached on the edge.

Gary was at the other side of the room, a script in his hand while he kept an eye on the match. He grinned at me and pointed to the refrigerator at the side of the room before going back to his reading. I pulled out a beer to sip while I waited.

"Are you interested in this?" I asked, cocking my head at the screen.

He shrugged and held up a black remote control. I nodded and he tossed it to me. I channel-surfed until I got to an Errol Flynn movie—oh, wasn't he beautiful—and lounged back in a chair.

The next thing I knew, Stevie was pinching my cheek.

I slapped her hand away. "Could you try something simple, like saying my name first?" I asked.

Gary was still sitting in the lounger at the far side of the room. "She did. She also tried yelling it. Then she tried shaking you. I suggested using open flame next."

Stevie's disappointment bloomed all over her. "You've been

drinking today."

"That happens every day. Get over it already. You've found something?"

She nodded. Her lips pinched and she kept fiddling with the strands of hair that had escaped her braid.

I put a hand on her arm, which was trembling as though she were freezing, so I pulled her into a tight embrace for several seconds. She struggled a bit and I let go. "You should see this," she said quietly.

I started to follow her. So did Gary. I asked him, "Don't suppose I could tell you to fuck off for a bit?"

He shook his head. "Don't suppose you could."

The three of us went back to the darkroom. Stevie had not lied. It was cramped. The two of us wouldn't have lasted two minutes in there together while she worked, especially when the only light was dim and red. The cramped confines were much easier to deal with when the room was bathed in normal white light. A number of wet sheets hung from a plastic line. What had been so difficult to see in the negative strip now showed clearly in black and white: A blonde girl, wearing heavy makeup but with the baby cheeks of a young girl giving a blowjob to an older man in a tux.

The man's face was half cut off by the angle of the shot. I didn't recognize him. The young teenager was Penelope Gurevich.

"Seems very definitely blackmail," Stevie said.

I massaged the back of her neck with my fingers. How many of these photos were bringing up waking nightmares for her? I didn't give her enough credit for working through things that made most people want to cry. "I'm sorry," I whispered into her hair, over and over. If only I had killed the bastard earlier. Before I realized how stupid I'd been. How stupid my father had encouraged me to be.

"It wasn't your fault," Stevie said.

I widened my eyes and took a deep breath. "Are the rest of the pictures like this?" I asked her.

She pointed to the last sheet on the drying line without looking at it. "More or less."

The contact sheet showed all the photos on the strips. Penelope had things done to her on film that I would never have suspected she had even heard of, let alone participated in. Hell, some of them would have given me pause. And she was so young. I chuckled to myself as soon as I thought that. When I was thirteen, I'd been having sex regularly with an older man, too. But however old she was here, it was young. Much too young.

"Poor Penelope." Then I remembered what a manipulator she was and added, "Perhaps."

Gary leaned in close to the second picture on the line, and then he stepped back, his eyes a tiny bit wider than they had been. He glanced at the first photo, and then joined me at the contact sheet.

"Holy shit," he said.

"What is it?" I asked. "You want a larger version for your personal collection or something?"

He shook his head and turned away, as though he could unsee the pictures. "Give the negatives to the police and pretend you never saw them."

"I'm going to give them to the police. Why does no one believe I'm going to do that?"

He flicked the corner of one of the pictures without looking at it. "You don't recognize who's in these pictures, do you?"

"Yes, it's Penelope—"

"Not her, you idiot, who gives a damn who she is. Him." He pointed to another picture. "And him. And him."

I looked at the pictures again. Nope, a couple of older white guys getting their jollies. I shook my head.

"He's a producer by the name of Aaron Ueberfeld." Stevie's sudden intake of breath told me her knowledge of movies was paying off. Gary seemed pleased that somebody present had a clue about what he was talking about. "This one is Ian Jack Reynolds, and he's currently president of Lang Studios. And this chap, I don't remember his name, he's got a development deal at Warners, but at the time this picture was taken he was most likely the guy in charge of the PAN television network."

I berated myself for being so witless. My father certainly would have axed me off his strategic council for missing something so obvious. "These pictures aren't about Penelope. There were much bigger fish in the sea."

"Your husband had a monstrous problem on his hands." Gary reached up and fingered the edge of one of the pictures, the one with the Lang Studio president in it. "Jesus Christ."

Stevie cleared her throat. "So where did Colin get these?"

Good question.

Gary laughed to himself. "What's so fucking hilarious about this is how sanctimonious these sons of bitches are. Take this one." He pointed to Ian Jack Reynolds. "His wife is the Grande Dame of Los Angeles charities. The perfect holier-than-thou couple. Utterly hilarious, given what she was like when she was an actress. In these 70s movies, playing the hippie chick. And it was typecasting, if you know what I mean. Amanda da Silva was no virgin—"

"Who?" I said slowly.

"Amanda da Silva. Well, Amanda Reynolds, but she was

Amanda da Silva then."

Funny. I'd met another player in this game who had the last name da Silva. Coincidence? I don't believe in coincidences. Stevie must have been thinking the same thing I was. I nodded at her. "Find out if they're related."

She was already heading out the door and back to her computer.

Gary stood in my path. "What did I say?"

I picked up all the photos. "Thanks for the darkroom. It's been a real help."

He lightly grabbed me by my upper arm. Touching without permission is not advisable under the best of conditions. With substantial effort, I checked my initial impulse to flip him over backward.

I stopped and picked his hand off of me. "Don't."

He didn't seem to pay any attention to my reaction. He leaned in toward me, crowding my space. Gary Macfadyen wasn't a big man but he always felt imposing simply through his presence. "Listen to me. You have to get rid of those."

I held up the pictures. "These?"

"Get rid of them and pretend you never saw them."

"What happened to the man who thought that this was the mostest and bestest fun ever?"

He didn't smile. "This isn't a game. You are dealing with heavy-duty shit here. Get rid of them. Walk away."

"Where is this sudden concern coming from?"

"You're involved with murder and blackmail and who knows what else." His hands curled into claws. "And you've brought it into my house."

Half an hour before it had all been a giant lark. Before that, contrite. Before that, raging.

"You're bipolar, aren't you? You're supposed to be taking medications and you're not."

The startled blink was all the response I needed.

"This up-and-down behavior—you're rapid cycling."

He gritted his teeth. "Get the hell out of my house."

"Oh, I will. Not right now. But very soon. I need something else from you first."

"For the love of Jesus," he yelled. "What is it now?"

"First off, I want you to start taking your meds. You have them for a reason. Take them. For another thing...I need to find a good psychologist immediately. Go ask your friends. Someone has a recommendation."

"For you?"

"For Stevie. Any names you can get, I'd be most grateful."

"You will get out of my house."

I smiled. "Of course I will. But you're going to have to put out first."

CHAPTER FOURTEEN

GARY DISAPPEARED AFTER MY LITTLE interaction with him. Was he calling the police to have me removed? Or asking his friends for the name of a reputable psychologist? Did he have any friends?

I couldn't worry about our erstwhile host right now. My thoughts were about Stevie.

I had sent her off without much thinking about what she was probably going through. I'm not the most sensitive person in the world, but I try to make up for it by showing what concern I can feel.

In the guesthouse, Stevie was staring at a computer screen, her eyes focused really hard on the screen. Working hard was her version of counting backwards. I put my hands on her shoulders and pulled her away from the computer. "Hey," I said. "Do you want to talk?"

"Wikipedia is an extremely useful resource," she said.

I brought the laptop's screen down and the computer shut off.

Stevie stared somewhere over my shoulder.

"Can I do anything?" I asked.

She shook her head, still staring off at things that weren't there. "I'm fine."

You'd think having me around as a role model would have taught my sister better skills at lying. Or at least a few flashy head fakes.

"Why don't you take a break from this?" I said.

"Because I like keeping my mind occupied."

I brushed her bangs off her face. I needed to take her to get a haircut. I needed to take her clothes shopping. I needed to make everything all better. I couldn't do any of them. "This can wait. There's plenty of television that needs watching." I took her by the hand and led her out to the living room, where I sat her on the sofa and put the blue cashmere throw over her.

A quick sweep through the thousand channels brought up a direct feed from Sky TV. One of those detective shows set in the Lake Country. Starring a much younger Liam Bishop in some kind of cosmic coincidence. Aphrodite's hair, he was a good-looking bastard.

After a minute or so of the main character tramping around in the mud, my sister rested her head against my shoulder. "It doesn't really bother me," she said in a quiet voice.

"It doesn't?"

"Because I know I'm safe." She pulled back and looked up at me. "Sometimes I wonder if you ever feel safe."

I snorted. "I always feel safe, Stevie. The sharks and the polecats spend their time worrying about me."

She nodded, her eyes moving back and forth as she studied my face. Then she said, "This show was one of the only ones produced by Quaid/Hallett Television."

My jolt backward into the sofa was completely involuntary, I assure you. Quaid/Hallett Television was the initial joint venture, a small test. Before Quaid Media and the Hallett Group merged the companies entirely, creating a worldwide media conglomerate. Before I scotched that deal, and hard.

After I recovered my breathing, I said, "They kept the name?"

"This show's eight or nine years old. The company's been broken up since then. I'd like to watch something else, please."

I may have dropped the remote control once or twice while trying to figure out how to change the channel.

"Today upset you, too," Stevie said.

I shook my head. "It can upset me when I have time." I left the television tuned to some tennis match in Australia and grabbed my phone. "Until then, I have things to do."

The TV went off. "I'm going to go upstairs and lie down for a bit," she said.

Excellent idea.

Stevie was right: I was upset. Any thinking human being would have been upset, seeing what Penelope had gone through. In addition, I now had a better idea of what had gotten Colin killed.

Now my most pressing question was: what did I do with these pictures?

The obvious answer was that I should get them out of my house and into Nathaniel Ross's safekeeping. But I wondered if I should.

Yes, I knew they depicted a crime. Was there a statute of limitations on what Penelope had gone through? And yes, it was almost crystal clear that the pictures had to do with Colin's murder.

Almost, but not quite.

God only knew what would happen to me if the police found me with those things in my possession. I needed advice, and I needed it now.

I called his office and within a minute had him on the line. Roberto's money bought courtesy and promptness. I missed that part about having money. It would be oh-so-easy to get seduced back into it. Which is what Roberto was counting on, of course.

"We need to talk as soon as possible," he said.

"When will you be here?"

He hesitated a fraction of a second too long. "Look, Drusilla —"

I brought out my bitchiest Oxbridge. "*Mr. Ross*, you are not being paid a small fortune so that I can conform to your schedule." Shed-jewel. Two distinct words.

"Christ," he muttered. "Okay. I will be there in two hours."

"Make it ninety minutes." I hung up. Then I took the opportunity to nap, since at the rate things were going I had no idea when the next time I'd get sleep would be.

Nathaniel entered the estate two hours later. He could claim it was the traffic or last-minute business at the office, but we both knew better: he worked for me, and I was raised to be the one who ordered other people around. While I hadn't had much practice at it during the past eleven years, you don't forget that sort of attitude. It's bred in the bone.

Nathaniel walked into the guesthouse, and he moved straight to the sofa without so much as a hello or a handshake or whatever it was lawyers usually did to greet people. He hitched up the knees of his trousers and swung the briefcase up on the coffee table.

"Would you care for something to drink?" I asked. "It's cocktail hour already."

He ignored the pleasantries and snapped open the briefcase. "Here's a problem I've run into. You said you married Colin because he needed a green card and he was willing to pay?"

"And his visa was running out. Yes."

He tossed a packet of stapled papers at me. He wasn't being paid a fortune so that I'd have to start reading things. I tossed the papers back at him. "Summarize the issue."

Nathaniel grinned. "In LA it's, 'Give me the logline.' The short version is that Colin didn't need a green card. He had one already."

A herd of dancing goats could have wandered through that living room at that moment and I wouldn't have noticed. "That's insane."

He pointed to the photocopy of an ID card. "Permanent residency. He'd been here long enough."

"No." I shook my head. "He showed me the papers. They were expiring soon and he needed to get married."

"He got permanent residency in late June of last year." He put the papers down and folded his hands. "And you met him when, precisely?"

I felt as though I'd gotten a kick in the stomach. "Beginning of July. We got married two weeks later."

"And he got permanent residency before he met you, and he still paid you for it? The cops are going to have questions about that."

I had questions, too. Who were we going to ask? He was dead.

Nathaniel nodded, reaffirming what he'd just said. "You look like you could use that drink."

"I don't get it. This can't be true. Why would he pay me ten thousand dollars for a marriage he didn't need? Because he was a nice guy who wanted to help me out of some money troubles?"

Yeah, that sounded pretty unlikely to me, too. But Colin's weakness for women extended beyond his need to romance each and every one. When he was on an upswing in his mood, anything was possible and doing anything he could for a woman—saving each and every one—was perfectly reasonable. He knew I needed money. Did he think I wouldn't accept it without the marriage? The marriage worked well in his favor, too, of course. It was great publicity for the show. I wished he were there, so I could beat the answer out of him. After crying for joy that he was still alive, of course.

Hades. This wasn't even the worst development of the day.

The briefcase I'd taken out of Colin's apartment was lying on the ground by the coffee table, reminding me I had called Nathaniel for a reason. "Believe it or not, I can top your news," I said. "I don't want to talk to the police yet. And I don't think you're going to want me to talk to them after I tell you about this."

"That you couldn't tell me over the phone?"

"Yes."

Nathaniel picked up a pen and started clicking it. Click-click. Click-click. I wanted to rip it out of his hands and throw it across the room. Click-click.

"Tell me hypothetically." He gave me a thousand-mile stare, looking through me, rather than at me.

"This is a real problem."

"Give me the hypothetical version first."

Ah. I got it. If he knew about whatever I was going to tell him, then he had to do something about that information. If it were only a story, then he and I were having a simple chat and no one needed to do anything.

"Hypothetically speaking…Monday afternoon I arrived in Los Angeles and went to Colin's apartment. He wasn't there. I found a briefcase. That had money in it."

"How much money?" he asked.

"About fifty thousand. More or less."

Nathaniel closed his eyes and pinched the bridge of his nose.

I swung the briefcase up onto the sofa between us and opened it. "There was a false bottom." I showed him how it worked. Then I snapped the case shut and pushed it over to him.

He swore under his breath. "Any idea what this money's from?" he asked.

"None. I swear. The bills are non-sequential, though."

"This isn't good."

"What if there were something else?" I said. "More than likely related to his murder?"

Nathaniel tapped that damned annoying pen against the coffee table in a slow, irregular beat. He shrugged. "In this hypothetical situation, are you certain this evidence is important?"

"Ninety-nine percent sure." He glared at me, but I've been glared at by better. "How do I know? I'm not the one who did it. For the sake of this scenario, let's say it is."

He sighed. "What sort of evidence are you wondering about?"

"What if Colin had some photographs, let's say, of a famous or semi-famous young actress in compromising positions?"

Nathaniel looked unperturbed by the idea. "Then she gets her own TV show on FOX."

"What if they were taken when she was about thirteen years old?"

That earned a few taps of the pen against the table and a

thoughtful expression on his face. "That's bad."

"What's worse is who is—who might possibly be in the pictures with her."

He clicked the pen a few more times. I wondered how he'd react if I grabbed the pen out of his hand. He'd look surprised, momentarily taken aback, and then he'd playfully try to swipe it out of my hand and I'd pull away, smiling devilishly, of course, and he'd come over to take it from me, and he'd throw it over his shoulder and say, "To hell with the pen" and then—

"How would Colin have them?" He leaned back on the sofa.

It took me a second to snap out of my on-the-coffee-table fantasy to pay attention to what he was saying. Clearly I hadn't gotten enough sleep. "No idea yet."

He sat up straight. "Tell me you haven't been doing a little searching on your own."

I said nothing.

"You haven't, have you?"

"You told me not to tell you."

"Stay out of it. Let the police chase down what's going on. Jesus, interfering in an investigation will buy you so much trouble, you have no idea. Where are these pictures? Are they in here?"

That's when I realized: I couldn't do it. I couldn't hand the pictures over. I knew I would have to, eventually. I didn't want them anywhere near me, not just because they depicted a crime and a reputation-destroying crime at that, but because they had the stench of murder around them.

But once they were out of my hands, Zeus only knew where they'd end up.

And Penelope would get violated again.

I shook my head. "I don't know where they are."

His brown eyes stared right at me.

"The actress in question thinks I have them. She thinks Colin had them. She's very eager to get these photos back. She thinks I might have them, because…" I stood up and started to walk around, trying to work this out. "Penelope was at Colin's the night he died. He gives her the photos…but he must not have, because the next day she comes to me looking for them."

"He gave her fakes?"

I nodded. "He gives her photos, she tells him he's fucked, he's on the hook for blackmail, he calls me…and the next thing you know he's dead. The real photos can't be in Colin's apartment, because the police would have found them. I mean, I assume they would. She contacts me, offers me fifty thousand to give them up."

"If you don't have these photos, how do you know what's on them?"

I couldn't think of a reasonable explanation for that. "Let's call it a wild psychic hunch. Hypothetically."

Nathaniel shook his head. He ran his long, slender fingers through his blonde hair before lacing them together behind his head. "In this hypothetical situation, here's the problem. You have a briefcase full of money. That's probably evidence of a crime, but we don't know whether it is or not. You have this evidence. You say you got it from Colin before he was murdered, which might be true, might not. Everything else is conjecture. Where he got it, why he got it, who wants it, what anybody has done about it. Trust me, no one is going to admit to a goddamn thing, because we've already got you and Colin involved. Guess what? That's conspiracy."

"Conspiracy to do what?"

"Blackmail? What's the first thing anyone says when they're asked how you felt about him?" He waited for me to say something. "He ditched you in Vegas and he owed you money."

"If you're going to put it that way."

He laughed. "Yeah, I'm going to put it that way."

"Penelope Gurevich—"

"The one in the supposed pictures?"

I nodded. "She had a much better reason for killing my husband. Is she a suspect?"

"The cops are not happy with this case. They're afraid it's going to blow up in their face, like a few other high-profile ones have. You might have heard about one or two of them. If what you're telling me is true…"

"It is."

"How did Colin get these photos to begin with?"

I held my hands up. "I have no idea. Zero."

"In case you're interested, something like these pictures you described would be considered a reasonable motive for murder." He ran his hands through his dirty blonde hair. "I have to give the police the briefcase and the money. Do not say a goddamn word about those photographs unless you have them and you're prepared to say how you got them and when you got them. They're going to have lots of questions for you. You're not going to answer them. You don't say a word to them unless I say you can, do you understand me?"

I felt a shiver run through me. "I understand."

He tapped the envelope with his pen. "Give me everything. *Everything* you took out of his apartment."

I got him the briefcase and the money. He shook his head and put the plastic bag of money into Colin's briefcase, and then snapped both briefcases shut. "I'll set up an interview. I'll call you as soon as I hear anything."

"My schedule is open."

As it turned out, Nathaniel didn't have to go to the cops. When Nathaniel went out to the car to put the cases in the trunk, Gruen and Vilar were walking up the driveway, followed by a couple of uniforms. The detectives showed him the search warrant they'd brought.

I hoped to whatever deity might be watching over me—Zeus or whoever—their search warrant didn't cover the interior of the cabana by the pool.

Chapter Fifteen

NATHANIEL TOOK HIS SWEET TIME reading over the search warrant. I had the impression that cops as a general rule didn't wait for the searchee to figure out the warrant was good—they would start searching and you could complain about it later. But with Nathaniel, they waited. Nathaniel was a good attorney to have in my corner.

Made me very happy to have him on my side.

Made me resent Roberto knowing I'd need him.

While he read it, I said, "Can I go upstairs and talk to my sister?"

"Who?" He then quickly held up his hand, signaling he didn't want to know. "Yes. Does she have a lawyer?" Before I answered, he'd whipped out his cell phone. I hoped he was calling someone very expensive. And knew who to charge it to.

This had been a very bad day for Stevie. And now a house full of cops? Fuck. I ran upstairs and found her in the smaller bedroom, completely focused on her laptop. She hadn't even heard the cops arrive. I told her to grab the computer and come with me.

Vilar and Gruen stood near the front door. "May I ask what your name is?" Detective Vilar said.

"My sister never even met Colin Abbott," I told him. "She's going to go sit outside and wait for me there."

"Not with that, she's not," Gruen said, pointing to the computer.

Nathaniel held up the search warrant. "You can look for anything from the past year, solely related to Drusilla's marriage to Colin Abbott. And nothing else. Is that computer yours?" he asked me.

"I don't even know how to turn it on," I answered, completely truthfully.

"Get another warrant." He looked at me. "What do you have that pertains to you and Colin?"

I wasn't big on relationship souvenirs. I drew a blank.

Nathaniel pulled me into the corner of the living room. "Have you ever been through a house search before?"

I considered replying, "There's very little I haven't done before," but this wasn't the time. "No. I assume they're going to want to talk to me, too?" He nodded. "I've never had to talk to the police for something like this."

Mostly because I'd always managed to be elsewhere for something like this.

Also not something to mention at the moment.

"This is how it goes. They ask a question, you look at me. I either nod or I say you're not going to answer that. You don't say a damned thing without my say-so. Can you do that?"

"Yes."

"Don't believe anything they say. Cops can lie their asses off anywhere except under oath, and, frankly, they do it plenty then, too. Do not react to anything they pull out, because that's what they want, a reaction. Do you understand?"

I glared at him. "Yes. Understood."

He turned to look at me, his gaze focused on me. He had scary, intense eyes, dark brown under blonde eyebrows. The look was so intense I was glad I was on his side of the table. "You are number one on their hit parade. You answer wrong, you go home with them. Can you do this?"

I cracked a half-smile. "If I answer right, do I get to go home with you?"

Not so much as an eyebrow rose in response. He kept staring at me with those dark eyes. It was unnerving and I blinked first. I nodded.

"Get serious. And get focused," he said. He opened the door.

The uniformed cops, gloves on, started searching the kitchen. People often hide things in the kitchen—in the freezer, in the rubbish bin—in the mistaken belief that no one else in history has ever thought of hiding things in those places. One of them found our fireproof security box out of the hall closet. He brought it over to Gruen.

"What's that?" he asked.

"It's where we keep important papers," I told him.

"Open it."

"Do I have to?" I asked my lawyer.

"Let me look through it. If there's anything in there that relates to Colin Abbott, I'll remove it." Gruen started to object, but Nathaniel kept right on talking. "You're not going on a fishing expedition. Your warrant covers Mr. and Mrs. Abbott and that's it."

We took the box into the kitchen, because the uniforms had already left, and stood at the counter. I opened the box. Right on the top were five passports. For different nationalities. And different names. All of which had pictures of me in them at various ages over the past eleven years. "What the hell?" he muttered, as he flipped through them.

"You want me to explain?"

"No," he said. "These names—who picked them? A fourteen-year-old?"

Now, that wasn't fair. Some of them I picked when I was fifteen. If I had my druthers, I wouldn't be stuck right now with a moniker like Drusilla Thorne, but that was the name in the box in Chicago, and you dance with the one that you got. "Stevie's passport is in here, too."

"How many does she have?"

I pulled the red jacketed passport out. "Just the one. And I'd honestly prefer they not see it. She'll answer to Stevie Thorne."

Nathaniel glanced inside: the name meant nothing to him, although with a relatively easy web search and some guesses it wouldn't be hard to figure out who Stevie was.

He scanned through the rest of the papers: visas, birth certificates, and a few pictures of Stevie's mother. One paper was written in Hungarian. My first marriage certificate. I glanced at the date: it had been ten years.

He removed the only two papers in the box that might have any bearing on Colin's murder: my marriage certificate, and the naturalization form Colin had asked me to fill out. He'd never asked for it back. Now I knew why.

"We need to give them the briefcase," Nathaniel said.

"Do we?" I asked.

"Yes." He walked over to Gruen with the papers from the box. "Marriage certificate and proof that my client thought Colin Abbott needed a green card." Then he headed out the door, probably going to his car.

Gruen glanced at it before handing it back to me. "How long did you know Abbott before you married him?"

Couldn't be that hard for him to find out. "Two weeks," I said.

"You came to Los Angeles on Monday. Why?"

I said nothing, smiling placidly, until Nathaniel returned, Colin's briefcase in hand. Gruen repeated his question. Nathaniel nodded and pinched his fingers together. Keep it short. Got it. "I came to talk to my husband. He wasn't there. I did go into his apartment—"

"How?" Gruen asked.

"For the purposes of this conversation, the door was open," Nathaniel said. "She was married to the occupant."

"I found this briefcase. There was money and his passport in it. I wanted to talk to Colin about a divorce without him doing a runner on me again. I took the briefcase. Monday night I was going to give it back."

"Do you have any idea where this money might have come from?"

I shook my head. "I haven't any idea."

"Your husband paid you to marry him, didn't he?"

Nathaniel cut in. "Whatever arrangement my client might have had—"

Gruen pulled a sheet of paper out of his jacket. "How much money did he pay you?"

"Ten thousand," I said.

Gruen nodded. "Where did he get the money?" he asked.

"His piggy bank?" I shrugged. "I have no idea, Detective."

"You hadn't seen your husband in the past two months?" Detective Vilar asked.

I shook my head.

"You might be interested to learn where your husband did get the money he paid you." Gruen took out a couple of papers.

He handed one to Nathaniel, who scanned it without reaction before handing it to me. "This is an affidavit from Penelope saying she paid Colin Abbott fifty thousand dollars on July twenty-second." He handed another paper to Nathaniel. "Same day, he deposits fifteen thousand into his bank account. He paid you ten, you said? The day you got married. What day was that?"

His lips curled in a way that made me think of woodcuts depicting the Inquisition. He looked a hell of lot less attractive like that, for which I was utterly thankful: guys who are hot to do me violence turn off my libido, and I did not need to be attracted to a homicide detective.

When Nathaniel nodded, I said, "July twenty-third."

Colin got fifty thousand in July. Between the fifteen he put in his own bank and the ten he paid me, that accounted for half. What had he done with the other half?

"Penelope says that in January of this year, she paid him another fifty thousand dollars."

And then she paid him more money Monday night. And offered to pay me even more.

"What did you do with the money?" Gruen asked.

Nathaniel held up a hand, silently warning me not to say a goddamn thing. "Are you arresting my client today? No? This interview's over. The next time you talk to her, have an arrest warrant."

"We will." Gruen said that, of course. Staring at me. I stared at him right back. I didn't know what was wrong with me, either. I was going to have to go out and get laid. And fast, before I ended up in the women's penitentiary.

"Is your contact information up to date?" Vilar asked in that oh-so-mild voice.

I nodded. "By the way, Detective Gruen?"

He stopped in the doorway and looked back at me.

"If it turns out that cash from the briefcase isn't from a crime, do I inherit it?"

He stared at me for a second. Then he left without a word.

Nathaniel waited until the sound of the door closing had dissipated.

He gathered his notes and made ready to leave. At the door, he stopped. "You can expect to be arrested in the next day or so. I'd think about taking a plea. If they can't make the murder charge work, they're working on a blackmail angle. Which is a hell of a good motive."

"I should tell you right now I am not pleading anything except Not Guilty."

Then he turned and left. Story of my life.

Twenty-four hours. Well, one way or another it would be over soon.

CHAPTER SIXTEEN

"WHAT ARE YOU GOING TO do?" Stevie asked me.

I picked up my purse and checked to see if my keys were in it. "Go out, get drunk, pick up a good-looking male model, crawl home tomorrow morning. The usual."

She tilted her head to the side and pouted.

"Oh, stop moping." I dialed a number on my cell phone without looking. "I do want to get out of here, there will be little or no drunkenness involved, and I'll be home before bedtime, all right? If I can't find out what Colin was doing here in Los Angeles, maybe I can find out what he was doing back in Las Vegas."

"I don't want to go back to Las Vegas."

"Trust me, neither do I. Not that it's even possible at the moment." Roberto had made it clear I had better stay put. So, to play nicely, I was here. For now.

"What are you going to do?" Stevie was asking, but the phone picked up at the other end.

"Jenny?" I said. "Hi, it's Drusilla Thorne. Right, Colin's wife. Listen, is Kristin there? I need to speak with her. Okay, let me get a pencil." I put the phone on my shoulder for a second, counted to three, and then picked it up again. "Go ahead." Jenny told me Kristin's cell phone number, and I repeated it back. "Excellent. I was kind of hoping to see her in person, though. Can you tell me where she might be?"

When I threw the phone back in my purse, I looked at Stevie. "What's the best way for me to get to Sunset and Crescent Heights?"

She stopped wiggling her nose, and started talking.

⌘

Kristin had a job at a swanky health club called Medallion Health Club and Spa, teaching a class entitled "Strippercise." Better physique through the old bump-and-grind. Looking at the women milling about in the chi-chi juice bar, with its expensive lack of décor, I wondered why any of them thought they needed to work out ever again, as they'd already achieved physical perfection and probably were worshipped daily by multitudes. Then I chided myself for being unfair. For many of these women, maintaining the perfect body was not simple vanity: it was their job, whether they were actresses or trophy wives or keeping up with the Joneses. Where the Joneses were trophy wives.

Kristin bounced into the gym in a blue leotard and baggy sweatpants, an Adidas bag slung over her shoulder, her blonde hair up in a ponytail. She looked as stunning as ever. She said hi to everyone she saw, which reminded me so much of how she arrived at the casino stage every night. One guy in workout gear with a glowing sheen of sweat on him stopped her mid-aisle. She high-fived him and squealed, "That's absolutely brilliant, darling!" Then she continued on her bouncy way, heading toward the studio where her class was held.

I stepped into her path. When she looked up, she smiled at me automatically. And then her eyes narrowed, as though she were trying to place me, and widened again when she recognized me. Her mouth dropped open.

"Dru? Dru!" She dropped her bag and gave me a big girly hug, which is to say she pulled me close but not close enough for our breasts to meet, which would be much too icky. When she stepped back, she brushed her bangs out of her eyes and said, "What are you doing here in LA?"

"I need to talk to you. Jenny told me where you'd be."

"Are you taking my class today? I bet you'd be super. And we don't have any fancy dance moves."

I had to laugh at that. My unwillingness to do anything approximating a dance step in the show had been the cause of not a few arguments backstage. I might be lithe and fast and strong, but coordinated on the dance floor I am not. "This is what you're doing?"

She waved her hand in the air. *Comme çi comme ça.* "I teach a couple of times a week. Guess what my nighttime job is."

"You're a dancer?"

She giggled and nodded. "At the Canyon Coyote. You'll never believe who stuck twenty dollars in my waistband last night. Dean Oliphant. Oh, you don't watch the telly. Trust me, it was brilliant to get him. The Canyon Coyote is a top-notch place to work." She waved to a woman who came in, wearing pink spandex workout gear. "So, have you moved to LA? Do you need anything?

Everything all right?"

I shook my head. "Do you have anywhere we can talk?"

"I have to get the studio ready. Come on."

She took me into Studio C, a room with polished wooden floors and floor-to-ceiling mirrors with a barre running across them. There was a wooden pole in the center of the room, as glossy as the floors, with a stool next to it. Kristin dumped her bag on the ground and pulled out a pair of four-inch heels, an iPod, and several scarves. While she attached the iPod to the stereo, I closed the door. It didn't have a lock, which was annoying: I wanted us to have an uninterrupted conversation.

A few men started to mill around the windows into the studio, needing to take their water break and towel off the sweat right where they could see in. Kristin rolled her eyes and went over to the blinds, which she dropped in front of the windows. "They're always the same. Always hoping for a little look-see. So. What's up?"

"Have you heard about Colin?"

"That bastard. What's he up to these days?"

Best to get on with it. "He's dead."

She stared at me for a moment, like I'd switched to Chinese or something. After a second, she barked one forced laugh, without smiling. "You're joking. Please."

I shook my head. "No, I'm sorry."

She tottered over to the stool by the wooden pool and sat on it, her face blank. "How? When? What happened?"

"He was murdered."

"Murdered?" Her eyes got large and she put her hand in front of her mouth. She took a couple of deep breaths, gulping air. Then she leaned toward me, despite the fact that we were alone, and she whispered, "Was it Vin Behar?"

That was an interesting leap for logic for her to make. "What?"

"Was it Behar?"

"What makes you mention him?"

"Behar's paid a couple of visits to me here, in Los Angeles. He shows up out of the blue and says if I know anything about where Colin is, I'd better tell him. Because Colin is in big trouble."

"Why?"

She shrugged and shook her head. "If I knew anything about where Colin was, I sure as hell wouldn't tell that son of a bitch." She bit her lower lip, lipstick smearing her teeth, and her eyes widened as she fought not to cry, but it was a losing battle. She fell to the ground and the tears started coming. There was a tissue box by the stereo and I grabbed it for her. She took a handful of tissues and held them up to her face as she rocked back and forth. I watched her for a moment, envious that she was able to cry for Colin and I wasn't, not yet at least. Kristin and Colin had had a thing back when she first joined his show, three years ago, but they'd remained friends even after he'd moved on to others. Colin had been her main support system in the States, up until his disappearance two months ago.

I sat on the stool next to hers and put my arm around her shoulders. She leaned her head against me and we sat there for a moment; the only sound echoing through the room was her crying.

So Behar had been looking for Colin in Los Angeles. Interesting. How did he know Colin had come to Los Angeles? And if he knew that Colin was here, why didn't he know where Colin was?

The door opened and a couple of women, dressed for class, came rushing in, chatting away. When the one in front of the pack saw us sitting there on the floor, with Kristin sobbing and me doing my best to comfort her, she stopped dead and mimed her confusion as to what they should do. Good lord, the things you have to come right out and tell people. I waved my arm toward the door, indicating they should get the hell out.

They got.

After a minute or two, Kristin sat up and wiped her face. Her mascara was waterproof, at least. "Oh my God," she whispered. "I can't believe he's dead. Do the police know who killed him?"

I shook my head. "Did Behar say why Colin was in big trouble?"

She paused, for much too long, before she shook her head.

"Kristin. This is important. I need to know. Why was Behar looking for Colin?"

Her bouncy demeanor vanished. She was scared, and it wasn't too hard to guess that she was scared of me at that moment. Of my reaction to what she'd say.

Tough.

"Maybe you knew about this," she began.

Her voice trailed off, and I rolled my hand in the air. *Keep going.* When she didn't continue, I slammed my fist into one of the exercise mats. "Kristin. Please. Behar has basically been sitting on my ass for the past six weeks because of whatever this was. It has to be bad. Bad enough to make Colin jump ship on us in the middle of the damned show. What might he have done?"

"Colin would have told you if this were true, right?"

I don't like to judge people on their relative intelligence but Kristin could try the patience of the Dalai Lama. "Tell me what Behar told you."

"He said right before he disappeared, Colin suddenly had scads of money, and he must have stolen it from the casino."

Interesting. Because if that briefcase in Colin's apartment were any indication, that was true. No idea when that had shown up. Somehow Behar knew about it. And wanted some. I shook my head. "Oh, come on."

"That's what he said. Told him he was bonkers and fuck off. No way would Colin have done that."

She shook her head repeatedly, as if trying to get the ideas out of her head. Colin had been a big part of her life for a long time. Kristin never talked about her family or home life, other than her sister, Jenny, but the fact that she had never talked about them said almost as much as if she had. Colin had been family. And he was gone.

"I have another strange question about Colin. About some people he knew."

She turned around to look at herself in the wall mirror. "Go ahead. I can't promise I'll have the answer. You knew way more about him than I ever did."

And yet she had just told me something I hadn't known. I wanted to slap myself. "This is about last year. Before Colin disappeared."

She rummaged around in her Adidas bag and pulled out a sack full of makeup. I've never understood women who put on full makeup before exercising—makeup is wonderful, exercise is fantastic, but the two don't go very well together. But perhaps makeup was part of the full package of a class built around stripping. And more than likely Kristin wasn't in any position to cancel class on the fly.

"Colin knew a television actress by the name of Penelope Gurevich—"

She turned from the mirror, mascara wand forgotten. "The

siren?"

"Sorry?"

"From *The Night Glen*? The sex siren."

I needed to remind myself to never, ever watch that show. "Yes, her."

"He knew her? God, she's beautiful." She shook her head. "No. If he'd known her, he would have used that for promotion for the show."

"Trust me, I'm absolutely certain about this."

She shook her head. Then she stamped her foot and let out a yell of frustration. "No, I don't know anything about that. Listen, I've got to get started here." She shook her lithe arms out. "Can't believe I have to teach right now."

"It'll help take your mind off of it."

Kristin nodded. Then she gave me a quick hug and touched her forehead to mine. It was oddly endearing, given that we'd never been friends. As co-workers, we'd gotten along splendidly, but we had been at very, very different places in our lives when we worked together in Vegas. "Ring me about any funeral arrangements?"

"I will." I hadn't given a thought about what to do about burying Colin. What a To Do list I had stretching out in front of me. First, don't get arrested. Second, get my husband buried.

⁓

When I got home, Stevie told me what she'd found out while I was gone: Ian Jack Reynolds, president of Lang Studios and a major player in the world of movie and TV production, was married to former actress Amanda da Silva, who happened to have a brother named Benedict, who happened to have a daughter named Anne. Who, as it turned out, had gone to high school with Penelope

Gurevich. Who appeared in a number of photographs servicing the aforementioned Mr. Reynolds.

Which would have made for a nice big twist of fate, except for the fact that, as I may have mentioned, I don't believe that such things exist.

I told her what Kristin had told me: Behar had been after Colin for a while, arguing with Colin about money back in Las Vegas, continuing to harass her in Los Angeles while looking for him. And he'd been there the night Colin was murdered.

"Colin definitely had some money," Stevie said.

"He did. He got it from Penelope. Behar was all over it back in Las Vegas, according to Kristin. Why?"

"You're saying…what's the connection between Penelope, Colin, and Mr. Behar?" Stevie asked.

"Exactly. Except don't say 'Mr. Behar,' say 'Scumbag Behar.'"

She nodded, as if making a mental note of the proper honorific to use should she ever greet him in the future.

"We know how Colin and Vin knew each other. But that's it." I looked at my sister. "I should leave finding a connection between all them to the police, shouldn't I?"

"Yes. Yes, you should."

We both knew that wasn't going to happen.

"I'll keep at it," Stevie said.

"Go to bed, sweetie," I told her. "You'll do a better job in the morning with a proper amount of sleep."

She stared at me a moment, one of those "I know better than thou" stares my sister is so good at giving, and then she ruined the moment when her entire body shook with a tremendous yawn.

"Okay," she said. "A few hours' sleep."

She stood up and stared at me for a moment. Then she kissed

the top of my head, as I've done so many times for her, before slowly mounting the stairs up to the bedrooms.

I had too much residual adrenaline after the scene with Kristin, so rather than keep Stevie awake by pointlessly fidgeting upstairs, I sat on the sofa and closed my eyes. I expected that the image of Colin's dead body or worry about my own future, both legal and otherwise, was what would be flashing behind my eyelids.

Instead, I saw those goddamn photos we'd developed this afternoon.

And I imagined what Stevie must have gone through developing them.

I should have spent the afternoon comforting her, telling her everything was going to be okay, making plans to get her someone to talk to.

Most of the time, she seemed okay. I had spun out dealing with her problems for eleven years. Another day or so wasn't going to matter.

I closed my eyes again, and I saw the back of Peter Quaid's head. Or rather, what was left of it after I took a cricket bat to it. With the sound of Stevie's screams in the background.

I wasn't getting to sleep any time soon.

At a moment like that, two options were available: one, use the advanced meditation techniques Stevie had taught me to get control of my wandering mind, which almost always led to rest, if not outright sleep, or two, drink myself stupid.

I couldn't count backward from one thousand by ones, let alone thirteens, so I started checking every cupboard we had for alcohol.

We were out. Maybe Gary would have some. I could ask forgiveness later. This was an emergency.

The garden between the houses had low-level lamps dotted here and there, lighting trees from below and giving just enough illumination to prevent me from walking into a bed of azaleas or making full-body contact with a palm tree. The light pollution from Los Angeles gave me a good enough view of the ocean and the beach—really needed to make it to the beach before I was hauled off to the lockup. The dim blue underwater lights of the pool actually made the entire pool area glow like a radioactive site.

The only light anywhere near Gary's house was the glowing red ember of a cigar, hovering somewhere in the outdoors living room set up near the back entrance to the house.

Gary was sitting on the large overstuffed sofa, his feet up on a giant round table made out of cast concrete. It had a fire pit in the center, stacked with coals but not on. The cold and damp of the ocean breeze made sitting out here uncomfortable and bone-chilling.

I decided it was perfect.

I took a seat on the large wing chair near him and put my feet up on the fire pit near his. I wanted to start shivering or turn on one of the artfully placed heat lamps or drink a fifth of bourbon to warm myself up. I stayed put.

We sat in silence for several minutes as he puffed repeatedly on that cigar.

"What brings the helpless fly over to my web this evening?" he asked.

"Is that Cuban?"

I saw his silhouette nod once.

"You have any more?"

"Not for you."

"Have any really good liquor then?"

The cigar pointed over to the outdoors kitchen.

I headed over and looked in the bar cabinets. The interior lights flashed on, showing me what was available. Lord, here was the good stuff. And he didn't even keep a lock on it. I wondered how much of it I could drink by morning. "Can I make you anything? I'm a stellar bartender."

"No, thank you. I have been dry for thirteen years. And counting."

"And you keep a stocked bar?"

The silhouette turned toward me. "I'm a very good host."

I fixed a drink and came back over. "Can I turn on some of the heat lamps?"

"Only if we're going to have sex out here. Are we?"

Awkward. And refreshingly straightforward. I wondered how I'd feel about the matter if the events of the day hadn't happened and I wasn't more interested in liquid oblivion. "No, I wasn't planning on it."

"Oh, good, neither was I."

He puffed on his cigar. I enjoyed my drink.

"Were you envisioning sex happening?" I asked. "Not tonight, perhaps. But at some time?"

"Definitely not tonight."

"Because of this afternoon?"

He looked at me. "I actually vomited. After the two of you took those pictures away, I threw up. I haven't thrown up for ten years. And then the police arrived and I thought, What have I brought into my house?"

I decided to wait for him to finish that thought and not offer my own opinions.

"I knew, when I met you. I knew you were dangerous. You

didn't want your photo taken. In this town? Who doesn't want her photo taken? And then the way you handled Liam and Rachelle. And then the way you handled me. I thought, this is it, I've found her."

Sounded like he was getting romantic. "You'd found who?"

"The person to take care of me."

The way he said it didn't fill me with a lot of confidence that he meant "nurture." It definitely sounded more like he meant "murder."

I finished my drink and decided to make another one. Or three. On my way over to the bar area, I hit the buttons for the heat lamps to get them started up, and then I left my cocktail glass in the sink. I reached for the iced tea glass. "And you invited me into your house anyhow?"

"Different is always interesting. And you were so…coiled. Most women are like, well, *fine*, now we have to have sex. You wait like a cobra. It was terrifying."

"And even with that opinion you thought we would?"

He shrugged. "Everyone does in this town. It's a way to pass time."

"Don't lie. People do it everywhere. They just act like they don't."

He laughed. "True enough."

"You needn't worry. Your person is safe from me at the moment."

"After today, I admit I'm hoping it's safe from you for forever."

I sat back down with my triple rum and soda and mint garnish. "I may be out of your hair soon enough. One way or the other."

He rubbed his hand through the band of hair around the back

of his head. "What hair I have left."

"Gary, are you in the habit of bringing home people you're not especially certain of?"

He puffed in silence. The sound of the smoke expelling from his lungs seemed incredibly loud. That, and the machinery for the pool, buried somewhere off in the darkness.

"My father committed suicide."

Interesting change of subject. "I wish mine would have. Were you thinking of being like yours and committing suicide, too?" Then it dawned on me that was exactly what Gary had been doing. "You bring home scary women and hope one of them will do it."

He didn't argue with me.

"That's a stupid way to live. You're rationalizing insanity. You need to take your goddamn pills, Gary."

"How do you explain how you live? What's your rationale?"

Dammit, I had already finished my second drink, in a tall iced tea glass. I had to slow down. I put the glass on the fire pit table. "It's never dull, I'll tell you that."

My head flopped against the back of my extremely comfy wing chair, and I thought that with the heat lamps maybe it would be warm enough for me to sleep out here in the outdoor living room, staring out at the Pacific Ocean. "Don't get involved in murder. It's a terrible solution for things."

"Is it?"

"I've made a decision. I'm going to avoid murder from now on. I want you to vow you'll do the same."

He didn't say anything.

"What do you want, Gary?"

"From you?"

"No. In your life. Right now."

"I want to feel something."

I briefly reconsidered my decision not to have sex with him, and then decided I'd been right the first time. That wasn't the sort of feeling either of us needed at the moment. And I wasn't the slightest bit into him, which always portends boring sex, if not outright bad sex. "Tell you what, Gary. If I make it through the next several days alive and not the slightest bit incarcerated, I can make your life very interesting indeed, no sex involved at all. In return, you will stay alive and you will stop bringing home inappropriate girls your mother wouldn't approve of."

"Pray tell, how will you make my life interesting?"

"What can I say? I'm a magnet for trouble. You can live vicariously through me."

"What about your sister?"

My usual reaction to anyone, particularly a man, talking about Stevie flared up. I was drunk and needed to cool down. "She's fine. Don't worry about her."

"She's not fine. I saw her face today. I wouldn't be surprised if she threw up, too."

I had to agree with him there. "That's why I deal with these things, Gary. I can handle it. She can't. Let me deal with her. I can deal with you, too. You sit tight for the next couple of days and take your medications."

"What do you want in return?"

"For what?"

"Let's say wondering what in the hell you're going to do next is enough for me. And I stick around to see what fun and excitement you drag to my doorstep. What do you want?"

I thought about a million responses to that, most of them sarcastic and rude, some of them straightforward and complete lies.

I was drunk, but I've made plenty of bargains while completely toasted on any number of chemicals. Even followed through on some.

"You let us stay here," I said.

"You're a cheap date."

"I play nanny and make sure you're alive tomorrow, and you let us stay here for a while. Stevie is not doing well at the moment. I have more problems than you know about and I need to figure out what I'm going to do about all of them. Just let us stay here for a while." I banged my head against the soft leather backing of the chair. "Please."

We sat like that for quite a while. I don't know how long.

"What happens when I finally demand you sleep with me?" he said.

"Then maybe you get your wish and I kill you."

He stubbed his cigar out on the fire pit table. "Sounds fair enough," he said. "I'm in."

I wondered if by morning I would remember that Gary asking me to sleep with him was his version of a suicide note.

I made it back to the guesthouse and passed out on the living room sofa.

CHAPTER SEVENTEEN

I WOKE UP AT SIX, hung over and still mildly drunk and anxious to get to Anne's house.

I needed to know what Anne knew about Penelope and her Uncle Ian Jack.

Too early for that. Time to run. I set out down the hill.

Running on the beach in the early morning was a wonderful experience, much better than running in Vegas in the middle of the night or Firenze at any time of day. The chill of the Pacific Ocean air, the damp of the sand making each footstep that much harder to push off, the lack of sunbathers in my path. That run made me light-headed, I was so giddy.

Which is why I almost missed Detective Gruen standing at the wall separating the pedestrian/bike path from the beach. I stopped to do my mid-run stretches, which allowed me to survey the area: the other runners with fierce concentration or exhaustion on their faces, the homeless sitting on the benches, the coffee drinkers out for a walk and checking out the female runners in their tights. Even in the twilight of the morning, I could make out people's faces at forty, fifty meters away.

The woman in the shocking pink sprinter suit caught my attention first. For one thing, that much pink was hell on the eyeballs at this hour of the morning. For another thing, it wasn't keeping her warm enough, because her nipples were clearly outlined by the fabric. When she deliberately bumped into the man leaning on the wall, sipping his coffee, I was embarrassed for her. Touching a man is the clearest way to indicate interest in him, but there's such a thing as too obvious, which then becomes crass and desperate.

When the man stood up to brush off some of the spilled coffee and showed himself to be Detective Gruen, I forgot all about whatever her intentions might be and began to concentrate on his. I turned as if I meant to do another six-mile lap down the beach. He couldn't suspect I had recognized him from this distance. I had time to think. And calm myself down.

The likelihood that he happened to select this stretch of Santa Monica Beach at this hour of morning to drink his coffee was: nil. He was waiting for me. Or tailing me.

The best way of dealing with a surprise is to deal one in return. So a mile down the beach, I ran up to the pedestrian/bike path, crossed the boulevard, and headed back to the detective's perch. I came up behind him from the opposite direction he'd seen me go.

"Why, Detective, fancy meeting you here." I leaned up against the wall next to him. "See anything interesting?"

To his credit, he didn't startle. He turned his head slowly toward me. "Yup."

I sniffed the air over his cup of coffee. "Mind telling me where you got that? I've gone a good twelve hours without caffeine."

"I'll be happy to show you."

We'd gone about ten feet when I stopped dead and looked at him. "Wait a second. Are you even allowed to talk to me without my lawyer present?"

"The courts haven't ruled on the subject of getting coffee yet."

I grinned at him.

He took me to a local hole-in-the-wall coffee place staffed by a tall and lanky teenager named Mike and a purple-haired barista named Mo. I dug out the few crumpled bills I'd stashed in my tights' inner pocket for a large Americano, no cream and sugar thank you, and the detective and I sat on a concrete planter on the Third Street Promenade.

The coffee was not bad. I looked at Gruen over the edge of my cup. "Tell me, Detective, do you live in Santa Monica?"

"Couldn't afford it."

"I thought Santa Monica had rent control."

He shrugged.

I leaned back against the tree. "I haven't been here in Los Angeles long, but I'm certain Santa Monica is nowhere near Parker Center, which is where your police division is headquartered. So if it's not near your house, and not near your work, what brings you down here first thing in the morning?"

He stared right at me. I hadn't gotten to see his eyes up close. He had wonderful hazel eyes, large and with eyelashes any woman would envy. We stared at each other for three or four years. When I started to grin, he looked away. Ha! I won.

"What can I say? I like the ocean."

"Tell me, did that woman manage to get your phone number?

Offer to take your clothes to the dry cleaner's for that nasty coffee spill?"

That surprised him. "You saw her?"

"Does that sort of pick-up technique work in this city?"

He laughed. "I told her I was a cop. She moved on."

It was clear more than one woman had moved on when she'd found out he was a cop.

I, on the other hand, seemed to have something of a death wish. When it came to police officers, I couldn't stop myself. Everywhere Stevie and I moved to, the poster boys of local law enforcement tempted me into playing with fire.

My first husband had been a cop, as a matter of fact. An honest cop, a rarity amongst his compatriots in that overworked, understaffed rural force. I'd ended up a widow pretty damn fast for a reason. I've kept dating them, but I haven't made the mistake of getting serious with one of these boys again. Or with anyone, but definitely not cops.

I gave Gruen a sympathetic pat on the shoulder. "You must find surveillance taxing if you keep getting interrupted by overeager women. Which I'm sure you do, don't you?"

He didn't answer that. He also didn't deny he was watching me in a professional context. If anything, he seemed embarrassed by both the woman and my flirtations. It was time to take a ninety degree turn in our little chat. Keeping others off-balance is an excellent way to control a conversation. "You're right. Enough of this foreplay. Let's get right to why you're following me."

He went from self-conscious to all business. "You found Anne da Silva pretty fast. And you sure had some interesting information for us yesterday. I wonder what you'll get next."

"I can think lots of ways you can keep an eye on me,

Detective. And I'm sure you can think of a few that don't border on police harassment. Which this is, you know."

Wow. Was that the wrong thing for me to say. Nothing about his gaze was flirtatious any more. Without moving an inch, his body got rigid and he watched me like a specimen in a jar. He was sizing me up in some way. As he reached into his jacket, I half-expected him to pull out handcuffs or a gun and then read me my rights. Instead, he pulled out a single sheet of paper, unfolded it, and held it up. "I got a lot of questions about you. And every single thing you say or do makes me more curious. So I asked a friend of mine with the feds to run your prints through a couple of databases."

Did he? That was going to be interesting. My hand started shaking, so I concentrated on steadying the muscles holding my cup. "Can't imagine what you'd find in any of them. Not to mention use what you'd get out of any of them. Legally."

He shook his head. "Came up with nothing. Mostly."

I tensed up even harder. Because if it were a simple case of finding out my real name, he would have handled this whole conversation much differently.

I fought the urge to get up and run as fast as I could, away from him and away from that paper. Six-minute miles, I could make it back to Stevie in twelve, maybe fifteen minutes, tops. We could be gone before anyone arrived.

He smoothed the paper out over his thigh. "Kind of baffling what came back, though. Wanted to ask you about it." He handed it to me.

I didn't look down. "We probably need to do this with my lawyer present."

He shrugged. "Okay. You don't have to say anything."

Only then did I look down at the paper. The first thing I noticed was the empty gray box in the upper lefthand corner. Where a photo ought to go, but there was none there. Might be lots of reasons there might not be a photo. Then I glanced at the upper righthand corner, where I expected a name to be. Instead, I made out the words NAME WITHHELD.

Okay, that was interesting. My fingerprints connected to a nameless record.

Even more interesting, underneath the name said DECEASED.

"How long have you been dead?" Detective Gruen asked me. He took the paper from me, looked at it, and then handed it back. "I guess it says right there. You died seven years ago." He looked me up and down. "Have to say, you look great for a dead woman. All that running keeps you in shape."

Seven years ago. Which would make it four years after I disappeared.

Holy Zeus in a chariot, Mama and Roberto had wasted no time. Once I was out of the picture, they wanted to make it very hard for me to get back into it.

I concentrated on the flower arrangement in the concrete planter across the way from us. "You know what they say, Detective. Live fast, die young, leave a good-looking corpse. I'm doing my best."

"You're not in Witness Protection. You have no record. You're dead and you have no name. How did you manage that? Who are you?"

Whoever said you can't go home again had nothing on me. I couldn't go home, because I didn't fucking exist anymore. I'd been erased, quietly and officially. No wonder Stevie hadn't seen many stories online about me in the past few years. What was Stevie going to say when I told her about this? Had she known this already? No, I couldn't believe she would have seen something like this in the news and not told me.

Gruen studied me like we were in Interrogation Room One. Then he did something I didn't expect. He smiled. "You didn't know about this."

After a minute, I trusted myself enough to put the coffee down before I spilled it all over my lap. "You figured that out all on your own?"

"The badge says Detective."

Why would this federal database have a record for me that was, essentially, a non-record? It contained no useful information. Anyone running my prints wouldn't know anything more about me after getting this record than before.

I stood up and dusted myself off. "Lucky you, Detective Gruen. You will undoubtedly be getting a visit from Ed and Fred, your friendly neighborhood feds. Soon. Maybe this morning. What will you say when they ask where you got my fingerprints?"

"I'm going to tell them."

"I don't suppose you'd ring me when they showed up, would you?"

He grinned and shook his head. "I don't suppose I would." He finished his coffee and crumpled the cup. "You planning on leaving LA?"

"That's going to depend on Ed and Fred, isn't it?" I threw my cup at the nearest trash bin: a perfect shot, with a short wave of coffee cresting over the top. "Thanks for the chat, Detective. It's another work day. Why don't you find out who killed my husband?"

He tossed his cup, hit it off the rim, and watched it drop into the bin. "So what did you do?"

What the hell. If I was right about that record setting off any number of alarms, my time here was going to be very short, one way or the other. "I haven't done anything illegal in the city of Los Angeles or any of its environs."

"You sure about that?"

I shrugged. "The day is young yet." I gave him my standard flirtatious grin, but I sure wasn't feeling it. I was wondering why in the hell I'd ever left somewhere safe and homey and loving like Las Vegas to come here. "Let's talk again soon. I have to run." Before he said a word, I took off running down the Promenade, turning onto the sidewalk at Wilshire Avenue, heading toward the beach and then the guesthouse and maybe an FBI "Welcome Home!" party. Or worse.

I did not have much time left to find out what Colin had gotten me into.

When this was all over, I was changing my name for the last time, moving to New Zealand, and living out the rest of my life on a sheep farm. Alone.

Stevie was putting a tray of little somethings into the oven when I burst through the door into the guesthouse.

"Did you know I'm dead?"

"Again?"

"Legally dead. I'm serious. Gruen ran my fingerprints through the FBI. Or something. According to the federal government, I am deceased. I have been declared dead. I am an ex-parrot."

I put the paper he had given me on the kitchen counter, and

Stevie scanned it. Her brief but sharp intake of breath told me she hadn't known I'd been declared dead. If my family were like some others, my demise would have been pitched to the celeb magazines as a heart-wrenching story of a family's loss. But Mama kept things private, and with very few exceptions celebrity magazines don't go where they're not wanted. Whenever you see a magazine cover, it's almost guaranteed at least one PR person was involved in making that happen. No way would the media outlets risk incurring my family's wrath. Their publishers spent too much time at the same parties on Saint-Tropez as my mother did.

It was, after all, how my father had met her all those years ago. When she was seventeen and stupid and he was thirty-four and wily.

"When did Detective Gruen give this to you?"

"When he coincidentally ran into me during my morning run."

She tapped the kitchen counter. "You should call Mr. Ross about that."

"Stevie, let's focus on me being dead."

She folded the paper back up. "Dru, I had no idea. This hasn't been in the papers."

"That's how Roberto broke the trusts. Can't hold money in trust for a dead woman. So I have to do whatever it is he wants me to do to get that money back."

I couldn't look Stevie in the eye as I said that, because she had to guess what the deal was: her or the money. And better than that, she knew me better than anyone, and she'd know I hadn't fully made my decision yet.

"Or it's worse than that," she said. "This record is to notify someone else when your prints were run."

"Roberto."

She tilted her head to the side. "Maybe."

Oh God. Maybe that record was in the database so that my father could find me. If that were true, I had about twelve hours to live, tops.

Stevie sat at the kitchen table with her computer and said, "Hm," a lot.

The buzzer on the oven went off and Stevie didn't bat an eyelid, so I slipped on the silicone potholders to take out the tray of what turned out to be mini-quiches. I wondered why she needed to make mini-quiches at seven thirty in the morning, but I never ask that sort of thing out loud. She might become self-conscious about her cooking and then never make these little hors d'oeuvres again. And that would make me cry.

"Seven years ago," she said. "They did it on the QT too, it looks like. Someone would have had to go looking for the declaration using your formal name." The ugly full-length version of my birth name that nobody ever used. I think the only place it had ever been printed was on my birth certificate. The first time someone had laughed at my name was kindergarten, and that was the teacher.

I finished chewing the spinach mini-quiche I'd snagged. Stevie took the moment to count the remaining morsels and then glare at me. I drank some water. "Don't they have to wait seven years before declaring me dead?"

"It's only three in New York."

"Why?"

"I don't know," she said, her eyes darting around as she searched her data banks for the answer. "Do you think that's important? Should I research that?"

"No. No, don't. I'm dead? What happens to…everything I owned?"

"Gets divided up amongst family members, most likely." She shrugged. "Maybe Roberto did something else with it. Or your mother, perhaps."

"They have to give it back, right?"

She shook her head again. "If a person's dead…that's it. I guess you could try suing, but…"

Holy Zeus. I was disinherited. Unless I behaved myself. And even then it wasn't guaranteed, was it?

And if my father was looking for me, I was so screwed.

I picked up the nearest glass and threw it as hard as I could toward the kitchen door, where it shattered and flew in a million different directions. Stevie sat there and looked at me, while all I wanted to do was smash more and more things, as though that would make things all better. "I need to go shower," I said.

"I'll clean that up," Stevie replied.

I walked out of the kitchen before things started to get ugly. Roberto was right; I didn't want to live this way anymore. I didn't want to take care of Stevie, I didn't want to wonder where we were going next, I didn't want to spend one more second figuring out how to get us new identities and then burying the old ones six feet deep. I wanted to go home and live on Easy Street. Or, more specifically, Park Avenue in the 80s.

And if I hadn't fallen to the place in my life where ten thousand dollars became an absolute fortune instead of, well, nowhere near a fortune, I wouldn't be in this damned mess.

Of course, Stevie would have been long dead by this point, too.

There was a downside to damn near everything, wasn't there?

CHAPTER EIGHTEEN

EVERY HOUSE IN LA HAS a sign in the front telling you which security company they subscribe to and a sticker in the window warning would-be evildoers to stay the hell away. The problem for many people is, of course, nothing bad happens for the longest time, so they stop setting their alarms. Which makes it easy for someone like me to use the side gate to enter the cement-paved back garden, and once there, undo the latch on the sliding glass door into the kitchen. The broom handle that should have been wedged next to the door, preventing anyone from opening it, was up against the wall. Sloppy and dangerous. I decided I should have a chat with Anne about safety issues.

The coffee machine burbled and I was spreading the last of Anne's strawberry jam on a piece of toast when she walked down the stairs at nine a.m. She wore a pair of yellow-and-green striped flannel men's pajamas—men's pajamas are a fashion disaster that should die out for all women, right this minute—and had one finger under the rim of her glasses, rubbing the sleep out of one corner of her eye, when she walked into the kitchen. She stopped after passing the refrigerator and stared at me.

"Care for anything to eat, or will coffee be enough?" I asked.

"What the hell are you doing in my house?"

I tilted my head toward the sliding door. "It was open. Your side door was also unlocked, but I've since locked it and put on the deadbolt." I used my left foot to push one of the kitchen chairs out from the table and into her way. "Why don't you sit down and join me?"

She started to reach for the nearby phone. "I'm going to call the police, thanks."

I slid one of the pictures of Penelope and Anne's Uncle Ian Jack into my hand. Anne's voice trailed off. "Feel free to call after you and I have a bit of a chat."

Her face showed the progression from disgust at seeing some kind of pornography, to recognition that she knew one of the people in the photo, to horror that she knew both of the people.

Anne backed into in the chair I'd pushed at her and the phone stayed where it was. I put the photo in front of her and she pushed it away, not wanting to spend a second more looking at it. "Where did you get this?" she asked.

"I was hoping you could help me with that," I said.

The shock on her face was unmistakable. She'd never seen them before. She'd had no clue.

Perhaps prompting might help. "Turns out Colin had it."

She kept wrinkling her forehead, which was going to give her serious lines in a few years. "What?"

I picked up the picture, glanced at it, and then put it face-down on the pile. "You can understand my confusion."

She spread out the pile face-down. Maybe she was counting them. "There are others?"

I nodded and showed her. She glanced at the first few before covering her mouth. I turned the pictures back over.

"He had those?"

"He told me he was in trouble with Penelope. I think I now know why."

Anne looked at me as though I were deeply stupid. "Who are you?"

I shrugged. "You first. When did you meet Colin?"

"About two months ago," she said. "A little less."

I nodded. "Right after he disappeared from Vegas. He knew Penelope at least eight months ago. Before he knew me, in fact. She knew him well enough to give him fifty thousand dollars then, ten of which he then turned around and gave me. And in case you're wondering, that's not my story, that comes straight from the cops. How did you meet him?"

She ran a hand through her hair, which was barely mussed enough to be called bed head, her eyes focused on her memories. "We met...we met at a club one night."

"A club you usually go to?"

Her fingers pinched the bridge of her nose so hard she left fingernail impressions in the skin. "No. No, I was there to cover a band. I did a story on them for the *Weekly*."

"Did Penelope know you'd be there that night?"

"You think she sent him there to meet me?"

I nodded. "I think that's precisely what she did."

Anne snorted. "Right. Because it's so easy to guess how I'd react."

"He was gorgeous. He was charming. He was witty. Anne, I married him, and I may have bought myself an arrest because I was so taken in by how attractive he could be. You think you were set up? Trust me, I'm way ahead of you."

Her mouth opened and closed a couple of times. "Why would Penelope do that?"

If Anne didn't know, she wasn't going to like it. "If you helped him, she wasn't involved. You rented his apartment. You got him his cell phone. Your name is on his utilities. With your name on everything, Colin could disappear on the spur of the moment, with not many clues as to where he'd been." It was a good play. I knew how that trick worked. I'd done it enough times, to other people.

Anne looked as though she might throw up. Time to change the subject. I turned over a picture and covered everything but Penelope's face. "How old is Penelope here?" I asked.

Anne took a closer look. Then she stood up, putting her hand up to her face as though that could hide what she'd seen. "I'm not sure."

"Please. Take one little guess."

She kept her back to me as she fumbled through the cabinet for a mug. She spilled the milk the first time she tried to pour it into her cup. Her fingers couldn't get a good hold on the carafe. After a few seconds, she stood at the counter, not moving.

I said nothing and waited for her to get herself under control.

When she came back to the table, her cup of milky coffee in hand, I asked her again how old she thought Penelope was there.

Anne took a deep breath. "When we were in high school. Maybe eighth grade. Her hair was shorter then. Blonder. She said blonde hair would help her in auditions."

Auditions. I'd heard of the casting couch but this was insane. I looked at the expression on Penelope's face in the photo: complete boredom. Here she was, thirteen or fourteen, and she might have been doing math homework, if you didn't see what the other person in the picture was doing to her.

I was having sex when I was fourteen. I'd thought it was fun. (Well, not the part with my stepfather Patrick. But I hadn't thought about him in years.) Of course, I hadn't understood at the time that an older man like Peter Quaid didn't feel quite the same way about me as I felt about him. Even so, I couldn't imagine being bored with sex by that age.

I turned the picture over again. "Dammit."

Anne's jaw trembled. Then, surprisingly, she started to laugh.

"What's so funny?"

"Now I know why Penelope always had money in school. Her mom didn't work much. Penny wasn't getting any acting jobs and she wasn't working at Starbucks. She said it was residuals from the TV show. And since her family was limited to her and her mom, how much money would they need, right?" Her face got serious again. "My God, my uncle?"

"Are you close to him?"

"No. But…still."

"Were you and Penelope good friends in high school?"

Anne shrugged. "I thought we were."

"This isn't the kind of thing you can talk about, even with your best friend." I wondered for a second what best friends did talk about together.

Focus on the problem at hand, Dru.

"Do you have any guess who might have taken these pictures? Where Colin might have gotten them?"

She pushed her glasses up the bridge of her nose. "He didn't take them from Penny?"

I shook my head. "In fact, if I understand what Penelope was getting at yesterday—"

"You saw her?"

"Oh, yes. She said you were singing my praises."

Anne snorted. Not gently, either.

Points to her for honesty. "I thought as much. But that is what she said. She wanted to talk to me about Colin. Then it seemed she wanted to seduce me."

Anne's eyes widened. "Really?"

Discussion about Penelope's many and varied proclivities would have to wait until after I knew Anne a little better. "I'll tell you about our conversation in a second. When she wasn't trying to snog me, she told me Colin was supposed to get pictures for her. She thought he'd given them to her, and then discovered she'd been had. I found these yesterday."

Anne tilted backward in her chair, balancing on the two back legs and making me somewhat nervous. She studied me, her brown eyes seeming to examine every inch of my face. Then she stood, the chair dropping to the floor with a bang. Anne had come to some sort of decision.

"The night he…died, Colin called me. Late at night. Did I tell you that?"

"No, as a matter of fact you didn't. I told you he called me. You seemed devastated by that news."

She picked the chair up and righted it. "I was afraid he'd called you to say the same thing he'd said to me. He'd never said it before."

"Which was?"

"He told me he loved me."

She had my full attention. "He said what?"

"I thought it was one of those things people say, so I said, 'Oh, Colin, I love you, too,' something stupid like that, and he was quiet for a second, and then he said, 'No, I love you.' And then he said the two of us needed to talk, really talk, after he'd dealt with a couple of things." She pulled the chair out and sat down. "Guess it didn't go so good."

I have no idea how long I sat there, unable to speak. I could only stare at her, with her short brown hair and glasses and heart-shaped face and felt something, some knot of a feeling, unravel in my stomach. Was this jealousy? Was I jealous that Colin said that to her? No, I was certain it wasn't. There were any number of feelings I'd had about Colin, particularly in the last two days, but ownership had never been one of them. Maybe it was shock? That he'd said that?

Then it dawned on me. What I was feeling was sadness. For her. For him. Because right after they'd talked, everything had gone to hell.

I expect things to go to hell. Other people tend to be more resigned to it. But surprisingly, I had one ray of light to offer Anne on this.

"Anne, I'm going to tell you something, and you can believe it or not, it's up to you. But I knew Colin well enough. He never told anyone he loved them."

She shrugged. "Who knows why he said it."

I put my hand over hers and she stared at me, surprised at any sort of physical connection between us. "Anne, I don't know why he originally talked to you that night at the club, or what kind of plan he and Penelope cooked up between the two of them. But I saw Colin with a lot of women, and he never bothered saying he loved them. Ever. Why he said it to you then, that night, who knows. But it wasn't something he was in the habit of throwing out there, okay?"

It took a second for her to react, but when she did, it was total. She started crying, the kind of sobs where you can't breathe in between the waves. She rocked back and forth, keening in a way I'd never heard before. It sounded much more natural and true than the stoic, solemn bravery I had seen so much of. She moved to the floor, no longer worried about balancing on the chair, and she cried. As soon as one wave of sorrow broke, a wave of fury and frustration would build up.

I got down on the floor and put my arms around her. Whatever her relationship with Colin had been like, it had hit her harder than a span of two months would have indicated. Was that possible, to fall in love like that, so hard, so totally? And what did that feel like? It seemed so unlikely. Most people can't stop lying to themselves that long, let alone another person.

When she'd calmed down enough to cry quietly, I hunted down the nearest box of tissues and brought it back to the kitchen table. She took a few and blew her nose into them. She kept blowing and wiping until I was sure she must have been dehydrated.

When she gathered up the bushel of used tissues, I said, "I thought telling you would make you feel better."

"Don't you understand?" Her face still contorted from crying, but she was smiling nonetheless. "It does."

It took a few minutes more for her to gain control of herself. She washed her face in the kitchen sink and patted it dry with a dishtowel. She washed her glasses and wiped them with the same towel. Then she came back to the kitchen table and plopped down in her chair.

"Anyhow." Her attempt to change the subject made us both laugh. "The reason I was telling you that was, he called from a number I'd never seen before." She rattled it off. It had the Las Vegas 702 area code, but I didn't recognize it. I shrugged and shook my head. "Yesterday, after you came by, I got curious. So I looked at the phone's records."

"And how did you do that?"

She rolled her eyes. "I'm a journalist. I'm magic."

To be fair, getting a hold of a phone's records is one of the easier ways to gather information. I liked Anne.

"And?"

"The phone number's about eight months old. From last summer."

"When Penelope met him."

She licked a few drops of coffee off her lips. "Guess who the phone's registered to."

"Not Colin, I'll guess."

She shook her head.

After a few seconds, I gave up.

Anne leaned toward me. "You."

My mouth dropped open. "What?"

"You got a great calling plan on this phone."

"You're making this up."

She shook her head. "Almost all of the calls to or from that number came from one phone number, in Studio City. That is, up until about two months ago."

I sat back in my chair. "And the phone calls stop when he leaves Vegas." Anne nodded at me. "Perhaps he didn't need to call that number so often because he was talking to whoever he'd been calling in person."

Anne tapped the side of her nose. "Exactly."

"Who was he calling? Spit it out, Anne, or I'll throttle you."

"Guess. All right, fine. Here's a hint: Studio City."

"Where in the name of Zeus is Studio City?"

"Oh. It's on the other side of the hill. In the Valley? Lots of TV people live there."

"Penelope lives in Venice." Although she had just moved, hadn't she? Her big move out of the house.

She smiled. "But you're close. The number belongs to Eileen Gurevich."

"Penelope's..."

"Mother." Anne leaned back in her chair again. "Who, if you read magazines such as *People*, isn't getting along with her famous daughter so well at the moment."

There weren't many scenarios that would make this all better, but the one she was hinting at was awful. "He wasn't calling Penelope? Colin was helping Eileen blackmail her own daughter?"

Anne didn't like that idea any more than I did. "It might explain where those photos came from."

The mother having the pictures made sense. I mentally slapped myself for even thinking that, but it was true. Someone had had to take the pictures and then hold on to them for insurance. Or whatever they planned to do with them. Since Penelope only had her mother growing up, Eileen was the logical candidate.

Parents can do awful things sometimes.

"Maybe I should have a little chat with Eileen. And tell her I have the pictures. Find out what she knows."

"When?"

"No time like the present."

Anne stood up. "I'll go with you. For one thing, she's known me since I was in eighth grade. She's far more likely to talk to me than to you. And for another…" She looked at me. "I don't believe he'd do something like that. That he'd start blackmailing someone."

She must not have known anyone is capable of anything, if you push them hard enough. She'd learn.

That was not a fun line of thought to follow. So as I do with all unpleasant thoughts, I forced myself to think about other things. I stared at the crockery lining the counter under the glassware cabinet.

She picked up her phone and called that number in Studio City. After a few rings, she said, "Eileen? Hi, it's Anne da Silva… Hey, listen, would you mind doing a quickie interview with me?… Great. Is today good?…I'll be there at ten." She hung up. She shook her head. "Publicity gets them every time."

"But Penelope's mother isn't famous."

"Everyone's convinced they're really the famous ones. Have you hired your PR person yet?" Anne laughed. Then she looked thoughtful. "Do you really think Eileen knows something?"

I nodded. "How do we get there?"

"Take the 101 north."

"What is that? Everyone says 'the' 101."

She shrugged. "I don't know. Just how we do it in LA. Maybe saying 'the' alerts everyone that the conversation has turned to driving."

"As far as I can tell, most conversations in LA are about driving."

She nodded. "True enough. Whose car?"

So I ended up driving over to the Valley with my husband's girlfriend to find out if a TV star's mother had murdered him and maybe knew anything about the blackmail-worthy photos of her own daughter. I fit in so well with the vibe around here I began to wonder if I'd been an Angeleno in a previous life.

CHAPTER NINETEEN

WE HEADED "OVER THE HILL" to the San Fernando Valley. Anne told me about how Los Angeles was divided up: movie people lived in the Basin, on the West Side (Beverly Hills, Bel Air, Westwood, Brentwood, Pacific Palisades), and TV people, who had less prestige than movie people, lived on the other side of the Mulholland ridge, in Studio City or Sherman Oaks or Encino.

Growing up, Anne's family had been movie people and lived in Westwood. Penelope was TV and lived in Sherman Oaks. The girls had attended the same school, the exclusive and expensive Hargreaves Prep. The kind of school that would mold the girls into high-achieving, well-educated members of society.

I attended schools like that. Didn't help develop me into a better person than I was turning out to be anyway. I doubt it did with any of the other girls, either.

Penelope's mother Eileen now lived in Studio City, in a ranch-style house south of Ventura Boulevard. That was the cushier area, so Eileen was doing well. On the Basin side of town, the important address was "north of Sunset Boulevard." Everything I heard about this place told me living in Los Angeles seemed to be all about 1) where you lived and 2) what you drove.

The house wasn't anything fancy. Every house on the block looked almost exactly like it, except for the new McMansion at the end of the block, rising from the ashes of a previous ranch house. Eileen's house was a pale yellow, with giant rocks forming the exterior shell of the fireplace. The front lawn was neatly mowed, and there were fences marking each side of the property, as there were between every two houses on the block.

I wondered what Penelope's mother would be like. If Anne's guess was right—and she seemed right enough I had gone along with her on this expedition—Eileen had participated in pimping her own daughter out for the low, low price of her daughter getting a few guest shots on crime dramas and some material for blackmail at the same time. Those pictures were in focus, with the participants' features and what they were doing clearly visible. As any photographer will tell you, getting that kind of photo right once is a miracle—getting them right every time takes careful, meticulous planning. Or a massive coincidence.

And we all know how I feel about those.

It's easy to assume that a parent who would exploit their own kid in this way or in any way is some kind of obvious monster. It would be so nice if we could easily spot them. Maybe they'd have slavering jaws. Or clawed hands. Definitely a hunchback. But the thing about monsters is they look like you and me. That's how they move among us for years, continuing the evil they do. They always have really good reasons for what they've done, of course, because everyone is always the hero of their own story.

Hey, my father is extraordinarily wealthy and wears really nice suits and gets thousand-dollar haircuts. Most people want to get to know him, not throw him in a maximum security hellhole, which is exactly where he belongs, for reasons other than what he did to his own kids. For what he let happen to Stevie, he deserves nothing less than being tortured repeatedly, and revived immediately when he passes out so that he can be tortured again.

I'll be happy to help with the torturing. You just have to ask. I'll keep my schedule open.

I'm not very "turn the other cheek" about my father.

Between Anne's first speculation that Penelope's mother was involved and Eileen opening the door, my imagination had gone crazy picturing her as some demented lowlife with morning whiskey breath and a cigarette dangling on her lower lip. Or maybe some evil dominatrix, ready to hurt and use any innocent that crossed her path.

The woman who opened the door, however, was someone you might see at any supermarket. Mid-forties, very pretty, with long blonde hair, crow's feet setting in but makeup expertly applied, still in shape. She wore capri pants and a plaid shirt with three-quarter sleeves. Her toenails were painted purple. You could definitely see the resemblance between her and her daughter.

Anne smiled. "Hi, Mrs. Gurevich, I don't know if you remember me—"

"Anne da Silva! Of course I remember you! Come on in, please."

"This is my associate, Dru," Anne said.

"Hi there," Eileen said. She didn't pay me much attention, as I wasn't the one with the byline.

She led us into the living room, where Anne and I sat on one sofa, which sat catty-cornered to the sofa Eileen sat on. The house was neat and tidy, with no clutter visible and knickknacks expertly arranged on the side tables. Eileen offered us Diet Cokes, which both Anne and I passed on. Then she asked, "What exactly is this article about?"

Anne leaned forward as she set up her recorder on the coffee table. "I did an article on Penelope about a year ago, when the show started, and I was struck at the time about how she talked about you."

"Oh?" Eileen said, puffing up a bit.

"She didn't mention you at all," Anne said.

Nice one, I thought, as Eileen deflated.

"When Penelope and I were in school together, the two of you were the closest mother-daughter pair ever. So I'll come right out with it: I want to do a story on how parents and children become estranged when the children become famous. One of the interesting aspects is how Penelope's been famous twice in her life, and why things are different this time around."

Wow. Anne won points for creativity. Coming up with story angles was her forte, I suppose.

Eileen nodded. "It's gotten a lot more difficult since she became an adult."

"You and Penelope's dad divorced when she was three?"

"Two."

"And the two of you lived together until Penelope turned twenty-one."

The older woman shook her head. "Until a few months ago, actually."

Aha. Penelope had moved out on her own, and she'd moved

about as far as she could within the same geographic region.

"Were you involved in Penelope's career when she was a kid? I mean, besides being her mom."

"I was her manager," Eileen said. She looked around the house with pride. "My money bought us this house."

"What happened to all of her money she earned as a kid?"

"There are really strict laws about that. You know the Jackie Coogan laws, of course. Everything she earned was put into a trust. She got everything when she was twenty-one."

"You're not involved with anything she's doing now, though."

Eileen tapped the top of her can of soda idly. "Penny won't even talk to me anymore. She said she wanted to work things out a couple of months ago, so we took a vacation to Las Vegas together, but it was terrible."

"Whose idea was it to go there?" Anne asked.

"Mine," Eileen said, which knocked one theory of mine dead. "Well…it was my suggestion that we go away somewhere. She suggested Vegas."

And just like that, my theory revived on the spot: Penelope had set all of the pieces in motion.

"When were you there?" I asked.

"Excuse me, who are you again?" Eileen asked.

"She's with me," Anne said. "That is an interesting angle. When did you go to Vegas?"

"We went there for Labor Day weekend. She was supposed to appear at a nightclub. It was a promotion thing."

"At the Marrakesh?" I asked.

She nodded. "You look familiar."

"I recently lived in Las Vegas myself. I worked at the Marrakesh."

She smiled. She had beautiful teeth. Then the corners of her mouth dipped a little and she sat back. "What did you say your name was?"

"I didn't. Drusilla Thorne."

It took her a few seconds, and then the look of recognition entered her eyes. "Oh my God." Eileen looked at Anne. "What's this all about?"

"It's about Penelope," Anne said.

"And a few other things," I added.

Eileen stared at me. "Is this about Colin? You're his wife, right?"

"Yes. Did you know Colin?" My voice stayed theatrically mild.

Eileen smiled again, this time a nervous, embarrassed smile. Amazing how few of her teeth were on display that time. "Um, I'm not really sure—"

"Don't be embarrassed. I'm sure Colin told you that we had married for practical reasons."

"Yes, he said you needed a green card."

I blinked. "More or less. So, should I assume you were one of his many girlfriends?"

At those words, Anne, next to me, tensed. I put my hand on her forearm, briefly: don't freak out about this, not now.

"We had a relationship, yes." Eileen couldn't decide whether she was annoyed or embarrassed to talk about this. "Is it important? I haven't heard from him for a while."

"When?" I asked.

"Is that important?"

"It might be," Anne said.

"Did you know that Colin knew Penelope?" I asked.

Eileen laughed, embarrassed. "No, Penny never met him. I

mentioned him, but she never met him."

I looked at Anne. "I have a theory about this." To Eileen I said, "When did you meet Colin?"

Eileen was about to argue with me again, but then she gave up and thought about it. "Labor Day weekend. I saw his show, and I met him afterward, and we had drinks."

Anne looked at me. I shrugged. "Colin had drinks with a *lot* of women, if you know what I mean. How did you end up at the show?"

Eileen rolled her eyes as she nodded, and then she laughed. "We were at the hotel. They comped us rooms."

"And you went to Colin's magic show."

"I had free tickets, why not? Look, what is this about?"

"Have you seen Colin since then? Since that weekend in Vegas?"

"Yes. Look, I don't want to get in the middle of a problem between the two of you."

"Believe me, Colin and I don't have any problems between us. Did you see him here, in Los Angeles?" I asked her.

She nodded. "He stayed with me a couple of times, okay? He was doing some consulting work on a show about a magician."

Anne leaned back on the sofa, her entire body sagging more than relaxing. "No, he wasn't," she said softly.

I reached over and patted her hand. "It's not what you think, sweetheart. I've figured out what he was doing."

Eileen looked from me to Anne and back. "This isn't about an article, is it? Look, if you're upset about Colin seeing other women —" Eileen's voice was rising in pitch. She was starting to get nervous. Good.

"If a little thing like that upset me, I wouldn't be hanging around with her." I tilted my head toward Anne. As my meaning finally dawned on Eileen, I said, "So we all have something in common, okay? Let's move on. There's really no pleasant way to say this, so I'll just tell you. Are you aware that Colin died the other day?"

Eileen's hand flew to her mouth as her eyes widened. Comically, her forehead didn't move, reducing the surprise somewhat. "Are you kidding? Oh my God, what happened?"

"While going through some of Colin's things, we found some photos of Penelope. Bad photos," Anne said.

Eileen stood up. "I want you to leave now. I don't know what kind of sick game you're playing."

Anne had laid the manila envelope between us on the sofa. Her hand kept reaching for it, and then backing away. I made it easier on her by sliding one of the photos out. "This is the game, Eileen."

Eileen stared at the photo for a moment, and then she became enraged. "Jesus Christ! Where did you get those?"

She lunged for the photo. I yanked it out of her way and she grabbed my arm in the process. I grabbed hers in return and pushed out of my seat, forcing her backwards, forcing her up against the wall.

I leaned in close. "Don't do that." Then I let go, stepping backwards. I waggled my index finger at her. "That's rude."

Eileen looked at Anne, her eyes wide. "Call the police!"

Anne still sat on the sofa, stunned—whether by Eileen's outburst or by mine I couldn't tell. She didn't move and she didn't call anyone. I sat back down beside her and slid the photo back in the envelope.

Most middle-class people's first reaction is to call the police, like it's a magical incantation. Too many television shows telling them the police can and will solve all problems, I suppose. "Excellent idea. As I told Anne this morning, please call Detective Samuel Gruen. He's really dishy, Eileen. Seriously, I look at him, and I have visions about doing nasty things in dark alleys. Also, he works Robbery-Homicide and he would love to talk to you about your photographic works of art here."

"I've never seen that garbage before in my life! Why are you doing this to me?" Eileen yelled.

"Do shut up," I told her. "Your phone's over there. By the way, Gruen is a homicide detective."

All the air got sucked out of the room in a hurry. Eileen's head tilted. "Homicide?" she said.

"So instead of calling the police, you should possibly consider finding yourself a good lawyer instead." I looked at Anne. "Today's been a raging success. We've accomplished one major goal."

Anne looked at me. "What's that?"

"You guessed correctly, she's the photographer." I looked up at our erstwhile hostess. "Why don't you sit the fuck down now and shut it?"

"How do you know?" Anne asked.

"Well, I could get technical and say, her body language or she has some sort of tell or something. But all it was is that I showed her photos of her daughter being raped and her first concern was for herself." I glared at Eileen. "So sit down and shut up."

Eileen shook her head. "You said homicide."

"When's the last time you talked to Colin?" Anne said.

The woman froze. Her mouth opened and closed once. She was more shaken by Colin's death than she was by these photos.

Maybe I should set her up on a blind date with my father.

I held up my hand out as a stop sign toward Eileen. "Wait! I love guessing games. About a month ago."

She looked at me, all the fight draining out of her now. "How did you know?"

"Because that's when he managed to finally steal the negatives from you."

People can't help automatic reactions to things. If you're secretly pleased by something you should be angry about, you smile, maybe only for a second but you do it. If you hate an idea, you can't keep your forehead muscles from bunching enough to signal your displeasure, even if you're in the middle of saying, "I love it!"

And if you feel confident of something in the face of evidence otherwise, you smirk.

Eileen fucking smirked.

"How did I get these photos, Eileen, if you still have the negatives?"

"I love my daughter. I will protect her."

I looked at Anne. "Why did Penelope bring Colin into this? Why not just steal them herself?"

Eileen flinched, and an idea occurred to me.

"You had a burglary here, didn't you? Maybe a year ago?"

The look on Eileen's face was priceless. Bingo; one more point to Drusilla. "In May," she said.

"May." Ten months ago. Right before the phone calls started between Las Vegas and Studio City. "I can guess this one. The place was torn apart but nothing got stolen. Because they didn't find what they were looking for."

"Colin didn't do that," Anne said.

"No, of course not. He wasn't even needed until—"

Suddenly it was so clear and I laughed. I had to.

"He was needed because Colin had a certain talent. In addition to all of the other talents the three of us are so familiar with." I looked at Eileen. "You showed him the negatives at some point, didn't you? You were infatuated with him, you told him about the photos, maybe that you were planning on blackmailing Penelope—"

"I love my daughter!" Eileen said.

"Tomato, tomahto. If they're not here, you keep them in a safety deposit box, perhaps? At a bank?"

Her mouth twitched. Hit.

"You told him about the photos, he said he didn't believe you, you took him to the bank, he looked at them, he handed them back."

"Oh my God," Anne said.

"Yeah. Colin was extremely good at something called close-up magic, Eileen. Do you know what that is? Close-up magic is when the magician has his hands right in front of your face and you still can't see him do the trick. He switched the photos on you in front of your eyes."

Eileen gave a delicate little snort. Clearly she didn't believe me. Who cared. I was done talking to Eileen Gurevich.

I stood up and grabbed the envelope with the pictures in it. "Why don't you prove I'm a liar, love? Go to the bank. Find the negatives. Reassure yourself they're still there."

Anne grabbed her bag. "We're done?"

"Do let's get out of here before we vomit," I said.

"Wait!" Eileen said. "What are you going to do now?"

I opened the front door for Anne. "Well, of course, we'll have to give the pictures to that police you're so eager to call." I shrugged. "Perhaps they'll draw the same conclusions I did about who was behind the lens."

"Oh God. Please don't."

I looked at her. If she thought she was suffering now, she had no idea what lay in store for her, no matter who the agent of her destruction was: me, Penelope, or LAPD's finest. "I'd avoid Penelope. For a while, at least."

Anne and I left.

Once we were in the car, Anne turned and stared at me. "How can you be so cavalier about this?"

I shook my head. "Because I have little choice in the matter." When she tilted her head at me in surprise, I added, "It's better than losing my composure altogether. I like to save that for the big moments."

She slumped back in the driver's seat, trying to make the words come out. "How can everything I knew be wrong?"

I started to reassure her, because of course everything she knew wasn't... Except who was I to say whether it was or wasn't? She'd had a rough morning: Her best friend from high school had had a whole different life that Anne hadn't the first clue about. The best friend's mom was a piece of work on her own. Her boyfriend had been married and had been up to some kind of nefarious dealing with said best friend. And maybe even worst of all, her uncle had been screwing her friend while they were in high school.

The uncle. A man who was involved in all these goings-on. We had pictures, we had nefarious doings—but did we have any blackmail going on?

Maybe Anne needed some rage therapy. And I could get some more answers.

"There's someone else we could talk to," I said. "Someone who might be able to explain some of this to us."

Her teeth were chewing her lower lip, perhaps in an attempt to stave off another round of crying. "Who?"

"Think you can get us in to see your uncle?" I asked.

CHAPTER TWENTY

YOU'D THINK THAT THE PRESIDENT of a major motion pictures studio would be really, really hard to get a hold of. And maybe other days he was, but this day he was in the office.

Anne called his assistant, Peter, to see if we could get fifteen minutes with the prez.

"Is this an interview with *People* magazine?" Peter asked.

"No, this isn't business. This is family stuff."

"Is it about your screenplay? Because he hasn't read it yet."

Anne assured him it was not about the screenplay.

"He's very busy today, so if you could arrange to see him on a weekend—"

"Peter? Shut up and pencil me in. We'll be there in forty-five minutes." Anne snapped her phone shut.

Anne hadn't struck me as the kind of person who told other people what to do. She was losing her patience.

"Think that's going to work?" I asked her.

"It's the only kind of attitude these guys recognize," Anne said. Then she shivered, as if she couldn't believe she'd done that.

Lang was one of the newer, smaller studios. They didn't have the gigantic lots of Warner Brothers or Paramount. They leased everything as they needed it from Warners and Paramount, instead of sticking themselves with the overhead.

And until the second we drove on to the lot and I saw the actual studio sign—mentioning they were a division of the Hallett Group, Inc.—I hadn't realized that I was actually connected to Lang, and therefore to Ian Jack Reynolds. What I would give to be able to fire this son of a bitch.

I shook my head. No matter what, HG was never going to be my company. After all, the CEO would rather see me dead than let me inherit.

"Are you okay?" Anne asked.

"Air quality's crap today," I said. "Having a bit of an asthmatic thing."

Anne drove up to the security guard, who motioned for her to roll down her window. "I'm here to see Ian Jack Reynolds."

The guard checked his list. He shook his head.

Anne put the car into park. "Call Peter Hill-Pender. We have an appointment."

The guard called, and then he waved us onto the lot, such as it was. It was more like an industrial park, several buildings grouped around a common area. We parked and walked toward the newest-looking two-story building.

Peter Hill-Pender was an officious looking twenty-five-year old, all bespoke suit and natty haircut. Anne had told me during the drive that he was a JD/MBA from Northwestern who'd fought to get this low-paying job over a whole rodeo of other overqualified, over-lettered applicants. Everyone had to start somewhere, and Ian Jack Reynolds himself had gotten his first job in Hollywood as a producer's receptionist.

Peter steered us toward the leather director's chairs in the waiting area. "He's busy." When Anne flashed him a look of complete disbelief, Peter held up his hands in surrender. "Seriously. He's on a phone call with two of the producers of an action movie. He'll be with you as soon as it's done."

Anne nodded. "Stars or budget?"

"What?"

"What's the problem? The stars or the budget?"

Peter stared at her for a moment. Then he shrugged. "You can replace actors."

I was reminded of Gary's comment about Liam Bishop the night we'd met. *No matter how big you get, it ends.* You had to throw the tantrums while you could, because one day no one is going to give a damn. I picked up the *Variety* sitting on the table and started flipping through it. Even if I could read some quickly, I had the feeling it was boring.

Twenty minutes later, Ian Jack Reynolds opened the door to his office and gave a curt wave to Anne. *Come in.* A plain, unassuming guy with good threads and gold cufflinks. He wore a beige phone headset, the kind with the microphone arm lining his cheek. He was behind his desk by the time Anne got to her feet. As I followed her in, I took my time to get a good look at this man. A man who had a thing for underage former TV stars. He seemed like the kind of energetic, fast-paced business type who was so busy talking on his phone he wouldn't have time for anything so mundane as touching another person.

He pushed one cuff back past his flashy gold watch as he sat behind his wide but empty desk. Empty except for that phone. "What is it, Annie? Who's this?"

I introduced myself. "My husband was murdered Monday night."

"I'm sorry to hear that—"

"His name was Colin Abbott."

He scrunched up his eyebrows like he was thinking hard, but he didn't need to bother with answering. He'd already done so physically. When I said Colin's name, Reynolds' left hand—he was right-handed, so like most people he didn't have as much control over the non-dominant hand—jerked. Maybe a fraction of an inch.

Damn it. That was not the answer I wanted to that question. There were few reasons Reynolds would have heard Colin's name, none of them good.

He gave me a perfunctory apologetic smile. "Sorry to hear about your husband." He pulled himself toward his desk, ready to get back to his day. We didn't move, and he looked at us with annoyance. He asked Anne, "Is that it? C'mon."

Anne's face was mixture of deference and anger. She might not be able to do this, but I was more than willing.

"No, that is not it." I pulled one of the photos out of the yellow envelope and slammed it down on the desk in front of him. "Look familiar, Ian?"

"What the hell is this—" And then, none too soon, the answer dawned on him. The left hand twitched again and his mouth opened. He was trying to come up with some kind of response, some way to attack his way out of this.

Been there, done that, not interested.

"Don't worry, Ian." I slapped three more pictures in front of him. "There's lots of different angles."

He looked up at me. Not at Anne. He didn't want to face her. "What's this about?"

"Besides your taste in sex partners?"

"Who in the hell do you think you are?"

I started to circle his desk. There would be no hiding from me, not back there. "Colin had these photos. He stole them and hid them. Awfully nice of him. How did you know him?"

"I don't know—"

"Yes. You did. You knew him, or you knew his name. How?"

He looked at Anne, pleading for help. "I swear I have no idea what you mean."

She shook her head. "This isn't a joke. *Any* of it."

A long row of thigh-height cabinets lined the wall behind Reynolds's desk, and one of the few decorations on them was a crystal vase with three blooming orchids in it. I picked up the vase in one hand and threw it at the opposite wall. It hit high and splintered with a beautiful ringing tone. Crystal rained all over the carpeting by that wall.

Reynolds was out of his chair and backing away from me.

I put my hand on his phone. "This goes next. Somebody murdered my husband. I think they murdered him over these photos."

The door opened and Peter the Flunkie came running in. "What's going on?"

"Call the police!" Reynolds barked.

Once again, the magical invocation of the police. I smiled at Peter. "Please do." I gave the same recitation of Detective Gruen's phone number I'd given Eileen Gurevich. And I reached for the photos on the desk.

What a dilemma he had: a crazy woman in his office versus those photos. Reynolds's sense of self-preservation showed up at last. "Wait."

Peter stopped in the doorway. "What?"

"Give me a second to talk to her."

"Ian, you can't stay—"

Anne stepped in front of him. "Get out until we call you, okay?"

This new assertiveness of hers was refreshing. "Sit down, Ian. We aren't done talking."

Peter waited to get the okay from Reynolds, who nodded. "I'm leaving the door open."

I didn't have to say anything to Anne. She shut the door as soon as Peter was gone.

Reynolds sat. Not behind his desk. That was too close to me. No, he sat on the lovely butter-yellow butter-smooth leather sofa by the as-yet-unmarked wall. "What do you want?"

"How did you hear Colin's name? Did he contact you?"

Reynolds shook his head.

I wrapped my hands around the phone, preparing to yank it out of the wall.

"I overheard his name. That was it."

"You never talked to him, he never called you?"

The left hand remained silent. "No."

"Penelope came to you about this."

"No." That was a lie. Darling Penelope.

"What does she want, Ian? She wants something from you. Money? Better parts?"

"You can take this crazy shit somewhere else. Because I've had enough."

"Really? One teenager was enough for you, is that it?"

He moved in, index finger pointed at me, trying to physically intimidate me. "What do you want? I don't have it. That bitch is taking everything."

Maybe physical intimidation works on people who are afraid to push back. The first time someone hit me I was nine years old and I didn't know how to defend myself. I learned.

I elbowed him in the stomach, which knocked the wind out of him. Then I wrenched his arm up behind him and pushed him face-down on his desk. Must have hurt, his cheek up against the mahogany veneer like that. "You're a very bad man, Mr. Reynolds. That means you don't get to make judgments about other people."

He grunted once or twice as I pushed upwards before Anne laid a hand on my arm. "Stop," she said.

Until she touched me, I hadn't realized how hard I was trembling. With rage. I was about twenty seconds from hurting this guy in a way that couldn't be dealt with or explained. I sent the message to my fingers: *Let go.* It took a few seconds to release my grip on his wrist and the back of his neck. I backed up.

Ian sprang off the desk and whirled around as though he were going to take me on. Anne stepped in front of him, calm and unthreatening. She put a hand on his chest, lightly, barely touching, enough to serve as a barrier. "Don't. Leave it. You're in the wrong here, Uncle Ian. No matter what happened to Colin or what he did, you've done something terrible."

"You have no idea!" Ian shouted.

I pulled the door open. "Let's go, Anne. This man wouldn't know the truth if it came up and bit his arse."

She shook her head and followed me through the doorway.

"You got bad friends, Annie," he said.

She gazed at him for a second, and then shook her head. We left.

⁂

As we walked back to the car, we stepped lively and said nothing to each other. Anne got behind the wheel and I put on my seatbelt. We sat there, both of us staring off into our own worlds. She had her hands on the steering wheel, and then dropped them into her lap. "What happened?" Anne asked.

That made me smile. "What, did you miss all that then? Penelope's blackmailing your uncle. That's why she needs those photos. As proof."

She shook her head. "No. To you. What happened to you?"

"I apologize. I shouldn't have reacted so strongly. My temper can be frightening."

"I don't care about him. He can drive into a tree for all I care. What happened to you to make you react that way?"

"Aren't you furious to find out what he did?"

"As a child, Dru? What happened to you as a child?"

A million deflections sprang to mind, but that display of rage couldn't be so easily dismissed. "Nothing happened to me." Which was true, or mostly true, depending on how you looked at it. Some people might even say it was completely false, but it wasn't, not really. Anything that happened to me I signed up for. Sure, I might not have realized what I was signing up for, with my father's furious approval, but I hadn't been starry eyed at the time. I shook my head, but I had to give her something. "People who abuse children make me furious."

She kept staring at me. "Oh my God."

"Like Penelope and her mother. The whole setup might have

been sweet little Penny's idea—"

"Jesus Christ. She was a kid. It wasn't her idea. It couldn't have been."

Kids can be so damned gullible sometimes. Like if you tell them you love them, right up until they hit a delayed puberty, so you get disgusted and turn to their little sister. "Could have been made to think it was her idea."

"What is wrong with you?"

"Anne, Eileen's job was to say, no, that's a terrible, horrible, no-good idea. And she didn't. She failed as a parent. She failed as a human being. Makes me furious."

"I'm sure it does," Anne said quietly.

"Annie, this is not about me." Her question made me think about the other avenue of this murder I had been avoiding. Mostly because all hell would break loose if there was anything to my suspicions.

Penelope did make an excellent suspect. In fact, in my heart of hearts I wanted her to have done it. But I had another suspect in mind, too, someone who would have been very, very unhappy to find out a minor Vegas magician was married to his stepdaughter.

I needed more information. And I couldn't ask Anne for help. All I had to do was mention the name "Roberto Montesinos" and she was going to be painted on that story like a bikini on a supermodel.

"I need to get my car at your house."

"Have you talked to anyone about this?"

I looked at her. "Will I need to get a taxi?"

She drove.

Chapter Twenty-One

HOW IN THE HELL HAD my savior, Nathaniel Ross, showed up right when I needed him? The only reason Roberto would have hired him was because he already knew about the murder, and he could only have known about the murder if he had had a part in it. Thinking of Roberto as a suspect didn't fill me with glee. It made me angry. Because if it were true, he'd get away with it.

Penelope was going to get away with it.

My father was going to get away with it.

Hell, even *I* was going to get away with what I'd done.

Everyone was going to walk away scot-free.

First, I checked the phone calls I'd made from my phone that night. I must have found Colin's body around midnight, judging by when I called Stevie.

Then I called Nathaniel from my car. "I have a quick

question."

"Tell me you are not investigating Colin's murder."

"No, not about that. I'm wondering about Monday night. When you…got hired."

"What about it?"

"How did that happen? You get a phone call to the Batcave or something? Because you were at Colin's apartment awfully quickly."

"My service got a call from our mutual friend and they told me to get the hell out to Hollywood."

"What time did *they* get that call?" I asked.

"What? Who cares?"

"Can you check, please? It's actually important."

"Go home and drink a margarita or something, would you?"

I did the next best thing. I started my long return drive to Pacific Palisades. There is no quick way to cross the west side of Los Angeles, so I had plenty of time to think. An hour into the traffic, Nathaniel called me.

"You first," he said. "Why do you want to know?"

"I found Colin's body at midnight. I called Stevie a few minutes later."

"The service called me at twelve thirty-eight. I'm sure they'd gotten the call no more than five minutes before that. It was top priority."

After I'd found Colin's body. Not before.

Not a chance would Roberto have cut it that close if there was a remote possibility I was going to be found with the body. He was much too savvy for that. He would have kept me away from Colin's apartment. Or had Nathaniel on standby.

Roberto hadn't killed Colin, and he hadn't subcontracted the job.

"If I don't talk to you in an hour, come on out to Sir Gareth's house."

"Why?" Nathaniel asked.

"Because I might be about to commit a murder," I said, and I hung up.

CHAPTER TWENTY-TWO

STEVIE LOOKED UP FROM HER book when I walked in. She marked her page with her finger and smiled. "You're back! You're never going to believe what I've found out!"

I leaned against the doorframe between the living room and kitchen and didn't say anything.

The enthusiasm drained off her face. "What is it?"

When was the last time I had seen my sister? Seen the person she'd grown into over the past eleven years? Stevie was small and girlish, but it was time to stop thinking of her as my eleven-year-old sister. She hadn't been that girl for, well, eleven years. She'd been my auxiliary, the person who did stuff because I told her to. But you couldn't have a brain like the one she did and keep being a child. You'd explode or something. So at least I'd taught her something.

I folded my arms across my chest. "How did you start off the conversation with Roberto? 'The good news is, you don't have to worry about your son-in-law causing a public relations hassle. The bad news is, you still have to worry about you-know-who causing one.'"

She put the book down beside her, page forgotten. She didn't fool me, though. We'd been together too long, and I knew her tells. She was about to deflect. Stevie doesn't lie so much as she skirts around the issue. "What are you talking about?"

"Don't do this. Please don't do this, Stevie. I'm trying to talk to you and not...lose my temper."

Her only response was to pinch her lips more.

"You called Roberto, didn't you? You're the one who told him where we are. Say it! How could you do that?"

She curled up further into herself and leaned a little away from me. After a few seconds, she nodded.

What the hell did she have to look so miserable about? She wasn't the one Roberto and Jane were going to happen to.

She had made that call. I couldn't let myself believe it for certain until I saw her face. She had told him where we were and made sure that I was going back to...well, to whatever it was they had lined up for me. After all of these years together, she was the one who said, that's it, game over, we're done.

"How could you not have told me you did that?"

"You'd be angry," she whispered.

"You got that right." I ran my hands through my hair, pulling it, messing it up. "Why? Why did you do it?"

The tears in her eyes were making the dark blue irises even larger than normal. "I was afraid you were in serious trouble this time."

"You thought I'd killed him."

"No. I didn't, Drusilla, honest and truly. But I couldn't go through it again. I can't lie and run and hide and start all over again. Not anymore."

I dug my toes into the carpeting, pushing them against the floor until they started to hurt and at last I felt something. We had been on the run for eleven years, me because of what I'd done, her because I was her only family in the world. And she didn't know any other way of living, but she knew she didn't want to do this anymore. Maybe it was this house. The power of having a soft bed at long last.

What the hell. Tell her everything. "Roberto gave me an ultimatum. I will go home to New York, get all my money, and live really, really well. You, on the other hand, have to go away somewhere, far away, and I have to agree to never see you again."

"Why?"

I had been asking myself that question over and over since Roberto had laid the situation out for me. My first explanation was that my mother hated Stevie. And while that was still true, that wasn't the reason. Not deep down. No, my family's much more pragmatic than letting a little thing like emotions rule their behavior. They're playing a bigger game than that.

"They'd have a hostage to ensure my good behavior."

Stevie nodded. Of course.

"You'd be very comfortable. Probably be able to get anything you could want."

"Except see you."

I nodded. "So that's where I am, Stevie. I don't want to do this anymore, either. I want to go back to New York and do piles of cocaine and party every night and not give a good goddamn about anything. I can't do that here. I can't do that—"

"With me."

My toes dug into the flooring again.

"And what if you don't agree?"

"Roberto kidnaps me and takes me back, I suppose. Or worse, he simply reveals who I am. Without the family's resources to protect me. And when Daddy finds me, I'm dead."

"They wouldn't do that to you." She sighed and pulled on her ponytail. "It's much more psychologically effective to have you make the decision. And alive."

That's my sister. Analytic to a fault.

"I can't believe you called him."

She glared at me. When had Stevie learned to start glaring? "You'd be in jail, Dru. If you rang me right now, I'd do it again."

I nodded. We were screwed, no matter how we looked at it.

We sat in silence for a while. Half an hour. An hour. I wasn't sure. My mobile phone rang. Nathaniel asked if I had, in fact, killed anyone. "No, not yet. Sit tight, though. The night is young." I hung up. "You were going to tell me good news when I walked through the door. What was it?"

"Guess what the name of the security coordinator on *The Night Glen* is."

Twenty questions. My least favorite game. I shrugged.

"Mike Behar."

I sat up straight. "Would he happen to be Vin's brother?"

She nodded. "He would."

"Jesus—" Stevie's grunt of annoyance shut me up. I invoked some other deity and then told her what had happened that day, with Anne, with Eileen, with Ian Jack.

Stevie got that heavy-duty look on her face that meant her brain was analyzing. "So, after a break-in at her mother's house last May, she needs someone with a very specific skill set to help her.

She definitely wants someone to…"

"Seduce her mother and steal the photos," I added, trying to be helpful. "She talks to her security guy, who calls his brother in Las Vegas, who says, 'I know somebody.'" A huge rush of tension left my body, now that we had found that association. Everybody is connected to everyone else on this planet, some more than others. "Although why Colin would have done any kind of deal with Vin Behar, I have no idea."

She shrugged. "Perhaps there was the money? By the way, Mike Behar has a juvenile record for violence. Amateur boxing gone wrong. Sealed, but…"

Mike Behar wailing on Colin could fit, but I had the same problem with that scenario as I did with his older brother Vin killing Colin: there was no way in hell Colin would have turned his back on either of them that night in his apartment. I shook my head. "Penelope gets her photos, or at least she thinks she does. She gets the photos from Colin and then wants to shut him up. So why doesn't she just take out a gun and shoot him?"

Stevie raised an eyebrow at me.

"Come on. It's the American way. But she doesn't do that. She says she's going to tie him in with the blackmail, only she doesn't have the right photos."

My sister shook her head. "What I've wondered is, why did Colin give her the wrong pictures? You said he sounded scared on the phone. Why would he be scared if he'd done that? He would know he had her over a barrel. He would have all the power."

The answer was obvious. "Because Colin didn't know he had the wrong pictures."

"Someone switched the pictures on him." Stevie leaned toward me. "You know what you should find out?"

"When did Penelope find out the pictures were fakes?"

Stevie nodded.

If Penelope found out before midnight, most likely she killed him in a rage. If it was after midnight, she had the wrong photos and Colin was already dead.

My lawyer was going to kill me for investigating, but I simply had to know.

CHAPTER TWENTY-THREE

I CALLED PENELOPE AND LEFT a message saying I had her lost items. She called me back within twenty minutes and said she was still on set, in some hellhole called Reseda, but she would meet me at her condo at ten p.m. I told her that Pacific Palisades was closer and she should come to me. I didn't fancy being cornered in her condo if things went south.

"Where do I go hide?" Stevie asked.

I waggled a thumb over my shoulder. "There's space under the kitchen sink."

She snorted and flushed a little.

"Is there a football match on anywhere in the world that you might want to watch?" When she nodded, I asked, "Would you feel okay watching it in Gary's house? Without me? He might or might not be there while you are."

After a second's hesitation, she nodded. But it was the least sincere nod I'd ever seen. She wasn't that thrilled by the idea. I considered calling Anne, but by the time we parted that afternoon, it had finally dawned on me that getting cozy with a journalist who might be very interested in my past could prove detrimental to my health. So I called the only other person who had a vested interest in me and Stevie walking away from this in one piece. Or rather, in two separate yet still alive pieces.

"Are you kidding me?" Nathaniel said.

"The beautiful thing is, you get to charge your hourly rate and all you have to do is drink beer."

The noise he made indicated the money was the least of his problems with this plan. "Why are you talking to Penelope at all?" he said.

"You make an excellent point. You should come here and stop me." I hung up on him and looked at Stevie. "Let's go see how Gary is with this plan."

We walked from the guesthouse, passed the tennis court and the pool cabana, and walked through the outdoor living room to the French doors into the back of the house. Inside, the only lights on were the low-level mood lighting that was probably controlled by a computer somewhere.

"He's not home," Stevie said.

I took out my set of lock picks. "That's not a problem."

Stevie reached out and turned one of the antique pewter handles on the door. It was unlocked.

"You're good," I said.

"You never start with the simplest possibilities," she told me.

We walked into the house and I called out, "Gary!"

My voice bounced off the grand marble staircase and echoed throughout the mansion. There was no response.

"He likes you, Stevie. He won't mind if he finds you here."

"He will mind the intrusion. He will."

We started walking up the giant staircase. I squeezed her shoulder. "He'll forgive you a lot faster than he's going to forgive me."

"For what?"

In case things went south with Penelope, of course. Every aspect of this goddamned mess pointed right back to her. "Remember, if Gary finds you here and he gets angry, cry. Actually, no matter what happens, I want you to cry, make those big puppy dog eyes, and then run as fast as you can."

She gave me a thumbs-up.

The door to the media room was closed. I knocked on it, on the off-chance he was in there. No answer. I swung the door open and Stevie went in. Then I went back to the giant window that faced out toward the driveway and courtyard and waited.

Penelope's white BMW pulled into the driveway of Gary's estate and parked in the front courtyard area, near the fountain, exactly as I'd instructed Penelope to when we spoke. I watched as she got out and walked down the stone path that led around the house to the garden area. I watched her totter on her five-inch high sandals on the uneven stones and wondered why she didn't keep a pair of flats in her car.

I'd left the large gate on the side of the house unlocked, but she'd still have to fiddle with opening it, which gave me the time to walk downstairs and wait for her in the outdoors living room. I turned on the fire in the freshly restocked cast concrete fire pit table and made myself comfortable on the sofa. She came through the grove of trees, clutching her thin, fashionable purse to her side. So, she didn't come bearing the extra money she promised me. That's okay, I wasn't going to give her the photos. This way, no one was happy, which was fine.

"Do you have them?" she asked.

"There's wine and beer if you need anything."

"Just give them to me."

"I have a question for you first."

"Do you even have them?" she said.

I pulled out the well-worn envelope of proofs and slapped a couple on the edge of the table in front of her. She sat down on the sofa catty-cornered to me and looked at them. She stared at them, her eyes completely without feeling for what the girl in the pictures was doing. She might have been looking at ads for refrigerators.

"I'm sorry," I said.

"Do you have the negatives?"

"For what happened to you."

She wrinkled her nose at that, although there wasn't too much wrinkle. Already using Botox, perhaps. "I'm fine."

"Have you talked to someone? Some kind of psychiatrist?"

That question genuinely confused her. "Why?"

"Because what happened wasn't normal. And neither is what you're doing about it."

She looked at me, a slight smile on her lips, and then she laughed. It was a weird, high-pitched laugh, completely out of character. "Everything's going to be okay now."

"Let me guess. You're blackmailing Ian Jack Reynolds."

"I'm going to be a very big star. He can make me a movie star. And he will."

Something was very wrong with Penelope. Something I couldn't fix. She was just damaged enough that yes, just maybe, she could have murdered Colin for standing in her way.

"I have one question," I repeated.

"I've paid. Give me the negatives."

"I will. Tell me one thing first. When did you find out you didn't have the right negatives before?"

"Why?"

"It's a simple question. Did you find out before midnight, or after midnight?"

"Yeah, don't answer that," said a male voice behind me.

Fuck.

I started to turn around.

"Slow down there," said Vin Behar. Who was standing about five meters behind me. And holding a gun.

Hearing Vin Behar's voice over the open phone line from the phone I'd stashed in the cushions of the sofa should be all the prompting Stevie would need to call the police. Because if she didn't, the next ten minutes were about to get very, very difficult.

I turned back around to Penelope. "You invited Vin to join us? I thought you were close with his brother, Mike."

Penelope simpered. "Mike said Vin would be better at handling this. So I told him to meet me here."

There was only reason she would need Vin Behar with her: to do the dirty work.

"Let's see your hands," Behar said, closer now. "Come on, hold 'em up."

I flopped my hands upwards. "So you own a gun." Behar used guns—undoubtedly without serial numbers; hello, Las Vegas—and yet Colin hadn't been shot.

"Vin, that's kind of scary. Put it away."

The older man's hand didn't move. "Give me the photos," he said.

"Before midnight or after?" I asked Penelope.

She grunted. "The next morning. Mike had this viewer to look at them."

The next morning. Penelope had sauntered away from Colin's apartment, absolutely sure she was large and in charge, and the next morning discovered she'd been played. When it was too late for Penelope to do anything about it.

She hadn't murdered Colin.

"Now you got it," Behar said. "I'm not going to let you hurt her."

"No, he's not," Penelope said.

"Shut up," he said.

Penelope looked up at him, sharply. Perhaps that was her first clue that Behar wasn't here to protect her. She thought he was on her side, but he wasn't. When he said, "I'm not going to let you hurt her," there was only one person he could mean. Of course.

"Kristin," I said.

"Who's Kristin?" Penelope asked.

"The person who murdered Colin," I said.

"Where are the goddamned photos?" His voice was gravelly and his hand shook, just a little. I was right with my guess. Kristin had murdered Colin, and Behar had helped in whatever capacity he could.

A shaky gun hand is a scary sight. A guy who's already party to one murder and might have nothing to lose is a scarier one.

A ball of energy swirled in my solar plexus. Nervous energy. Anticipation. And fear. Most of it was fear that something would go wrong and I was about to get hurt. I don't enjoy pain, not even a little bit. Fear that I would get myself killed and leave Stevie alone. Fear that I would blow my one shot at getting out of this hellish mess. Fear that more than one of the three of us here needed to die. "They're not here."

Penelope shrieked with frustration. Should I tell her that we had much, much bigger problems on our hands? No. Let her find out the hard way.

"I'm deeply moved that you're so chivalrous. Who knew down deep Vin Behar was such a romantic?"

"Shut up and give 'em," he said.

His trigger finger was getting itchy.

So was mine.

Ten years ago, after we'd been in hiding for a year, I made Stevie a promise. Three promises, to be exact. Three things I would never do.

One: despite how badly we needed money, I would never get involved in illegal operations, like selling drugs.

Two: despite my penchant for using men to find places to live when we first moved anywhere, I wouldn't turn pro at it.

And three: I would never ever kill someone again. No matter what the circumstances.

"*There is always a better way*," she had said to me. "*Look at what it's done to you.*"

But promises were made to be broken, and ten years of keeping my promises to her was not too shabby. That was ten years longer than I'd kept a promise to anyone else.

Right now, I could not hesitate. I could not bargain. It was going to be him or me, and right now my only goal was to be the one to walk away.

I shook my head slowly. "I won't tell you where they are if you shoot me."

"Yeah? Well, I can shoot her." He swung the gun toward

Penelope.

Which is when I grabbed the small fire pit shovel and hurled a scoopful of coals toward him.

He ducked and pointed the gun downward, which was all I could have hoped for with that maneuver. I leapt up before he could right himself, and I slammed my foot into the side of his knee at the same time I struck the underside of his nose. He grabbed me as he fell, pulling me after him. We seemed to fall in slow motion. Everything goes a lot slower when you're in the middle of things. Even with Penelope screaming in the background.

"Stupid bitch!" he yelled.

I landed on top of him and took advantage of the moment to drive my elbow into his throat. I then took the fire pit shovel and jammed it into the wrist of the hand holding the gun, hard. Not hard enough, dammit: I didn't cut the skin. But he let go of the gun.

The second I reared back, preparing to drive the shovel where it would do the most harm—his face—Behar roared up, pushing me off and to the side. He socked me pretty good in the stomach, which felt like a boulder smashed into me and got worse from there, spreading a flood of fire. Holy Olympus, that hurt. I spit up bile as he pulled me behind him and reached for the gun. I'd failed. I'd had my shot. And he was going to get his.

"Bitch," he said.

The command "Freeze" from somewhere near the door into the house was quite easy to notice, despite the blood rushing through my ears. I froze.

Behar seemed not to hear it. He kept moving.

"Hey, idiot," Detective Gruen said. "Freeze."

Only then did Vin Behar look up.

I dropped the fire pit shovel and stayed mostly frozen, moving only enough to look back at the detective. Penelope was cowering behind him, safe from the Big Bad World.

As Gruen cuffed Behar, I sat up. The detective didn't seem to be swinging two pairs of handcuffs, so maybe I was safe for now.

Penelope was standing off to the side, her jaw opening and closing, but no sounds came out. She had managed to scoop up the photographs and stick them back into the envelope, though. She was definitely focused on her number-one priority.

Four uniformed police officers ran into the yard. Gruen waved at Behar, telling them to take out the trash. Then Gruen looked at me. "You got anything you want to say?"

I shook my head. "My lawyer should be here soon. You'll want to have a chat with Kristin Blake, though."

"Why's that?"

"She murdered Colin. She worked with us in Las Vegas. This bloke was helping her."

The French door opened and Nathaniel walked out. "I made it here ahead of about four thousand cop cars. What the hell happened? Are you okay?"

"Mr. Behar and I had a disagreement as to whether I should be alive or not." I looked up at the detective. "How did you get here so fast?"

"Already on my way, and I got a call from your sister. You need a doctor?" Gruen asked.

I shook my head. I glanced up at Nathaniel and tilted my head toward Gruen.

"You were already on your way?" Nathaniel asked.

"Yeah, some friends of your client are in town."

Ed and Fred, the feds. Why hadn't they come with Gruen? I

shook my head. This was a bad night.

"Where can I find Kristin Blake?" Gruen asked.

"I have her number in my phone. She teaches aerobics at the Medallion Health Club and Spa, and at night she dances," I said.

"Exotic dancing?" Nathaniel said.

I nodded. "It's amazingly good money. Honestly, if I had the sort of coordination required—"

"Where?" Gruen asked.

I looked at Nathaniel. When he nodded, I said, "The Canyon Jackal."

After a moment's pause, the detective said, "What?"

My nerves were shot, my stomach hurt like hell, and now I was drawing a blank on the name of the place. I never draw blanks. "Is that not a place? She said it was very upscale. The Canyon... some kind of animal."

"The Canyon Coyote?" Nathaniel said.

I snapped my fingers. "That's it!" I looked at him. "Please tell me you've heard of it because you have clients who work there."

"I take the Fifth," he said.

"Yeah, I know it," Gruen said, as he took out his radio. Then he walked away.

"Men," I muttered. "Are we all done here?"

"We need to talk," Nathaniel said.

"We will," I said. "Penelope?"

Penelope Gurevich, looking lost and alone and like a little girl, looked up at me. "What is it?"

I tilted my head off to the side. "I need to talk to you."

The police officer who'd been standing with her fell into step alongside her.

I held up my hand. "Alone."

Penelope stumbled, following me down the concrete path toward the pool area.

In the door of the cabana, I turned and looked at her. Her face was blue from the reflection of the underwater pool lights. "Don't do what you're going to do, Penelope. It's a bad idea."

"I deserve to get something for it," she said.

I reached up to the edge of the overhanging canopy and wedged my fingers into the little slit I'd made in the fabric. My fingers hit the edge of the cellophane envelope and I pulled it out.

"Burn them. You have a good career."

"What would you do?" she asked.

"Me?" I said. "I'd kill the son of a bitch so he couldn't hurt anyone else."

She tucked the package of negatives into her tiny purse. "You have your way, and I have mine."

As I watched her walk away, I hoped I'd done the right thing. The photos most definitely belonged to her, after all. She'd paid the most heavily for them.

Nathaniel was waiting for me inside Gary's house. Gary, I noticed, was at the top of the grand staircase, watching the goings-on downstairs.

"I got a call," Nathaniel said.

"Let me guess from whom."

"He requests the pleasure of your company at the Peninsula Hotel."

I nodded. "If what the good detective Gruen just told me is true, then yes, I very definitely agree I should be there." Ed and Fred might risk going after me there, but Roberto's guards would run excellent interference. "I need you to take care of Stevie. My New York friend will take her off your hands as soon as he can."

"Get whatever you need to bring with you, and I'll take the both of you myself," Nathaniel said.

I looked up the staircase again, and this time Nathaniel followed my gaze. Stevie was standing there now, too, next to Gary, both of them watching me. I shook my head at her. "She can't come with me. I can't explain why."

"What do you need to bring with you?"

What did I need out of the guesthouse? Nothing. Not one damned thing, really. Well, except for our metal box full of documents. Everything else was replaceable. "My box of documents. Best not left here."

He nodded and turned to talk to one of the uniformed officers.

I walked across the gardens to the front door of the guesthouse and entered. The first thing I noticed was that the living room was a bloody mess—the pillows were everywhere.

Then I noticed our jackets and sweaters strewn on the ground.

And then I discovered that Vin Behar hadn't come to visit me by himself.

"Hello, Kristin," I said.

CHAPTER TWENTY-FOUR

KRISTIN WAS HOLDING A GUN. She wasn't a trained shooter, which meant she was in danger of killing both of us. I had a problem with half of that equation. I held my hands up and started moving, slowly, to my right, through the living room. Into the shadows. A moving target's a great deal harder to hit.

"Hi Kristin."

"Shut up." Her voice was nasally. She'd been crying. Angry, crying, and armed. A fabulous combination.

"Talk to me," I said softly.

"I hate you," she said. "I hate you so much. I wish you were dead."

The gun pointed my direction made that clear. "Everything's going to be okay, Kristin." I had to keep her talking. I also had to keep reminding her who she was, make sure she was aware that this was real life. It's easy to dissociate when things are getting out of hand.

"You've ruined everything. Everything."

"Just relax. Take a deep breath, and relax."

"Stop!"

I didn't stop. "Relax, and breathe. Everything will be fine. Just slow down and talk to me."

"None of this would have happened except for you!"

"I don't understand what you mean. Can you tell me what you mean, Kristin?"

"I was so *thrilled* when Vince told me you were at Colin's apartment that night. Finally we were done with you but no!"

My peripheral vision showed me movement through the living room window. Gruen was walking up to the front door. I kept moving, to turn Kristin's focus totally away from that area.

"You had the bracelet. He called you and asked you to bring it back."

"He starts telling me that things have gone wrong with Penelope but oh no, everything is all right, because Drusilla will figure it out!"

She was screeching. She was definitely on the verge of pulling that trigger. And I know from personal experience that if you've killed once, the second one gets that much easier.

"Kristin, think about this. There's no going back after killing someone."

"Don't you think I know that?" she screamed. "I loved him."

Gruen opened the front door, quietly, gun drawn. Somewhere to my right, I saw movement in the kitchen. Someone was coming in the back door.

"Yes, you were angry that night. But you don't have to be angry now."

"He'd left me."

He'd left all of us, but this probably wasn't a good time to recap my darling late husband's foibles.

"Why?" I asked her. "Why did you kill him?"

Kristin's mouth trembled. "I didn't—"

"Kristin, you need to tell someone. Confession really is good for the soul."

She shook her head.

"The photos? He double-crossed you? He wanted all the money?"

She said nothing as she stared at me, her lips growing whiter and whiter as she clenched her mouth shut.

She was staring at me.

I was her reason?

She'd done it because of me?

"You killed him because of me?" I asked.

"After everything we'd been through," she yelled, "after everything we'd done and planned, he says he's in love with you."

Laughing would be the wrong response. "Kristin—"

But my words couldn't stop her. She was letting out the rage she'd been holding in. "All the time we'd spent together and worked together and you show up and take everything away from me!"

Gruen rolled his hand in the air. *Keep her talking.*

"What did I take, Kristin?" I said.

"Shut up!"

"I have a right to know why you want to kill me."

"You took my job. You took Colin. You took my life! You show up in Las Vegas, and he says we're done. You show up in Los Angeles, and suddenly now we're through with Penelope, too. And oh no, no, we weren't."

"I didn't know anything that was going on with Penelope."

"On top of everything else, right in front of me he tells you he loves you!"

What was she talking about? And then, suddenly, I knew. "You mean, he said it when he was on the phone."

"Yes."

"Think, Kristin. Did he say my name?"

"He didn't have to."

"He didn't say my name, because he wasn't talking to me when he said it."

I only knew she'd heard me because she blinked and then adjusted her stance.

"It wasn't over with you because of me. He was on the phone with Annie, Kristin. Anne da Silva."

Kristin's face screwed up, as though I'd told her a very funny joke. "Oh fuck off," she said. "Please. Don't insult me."

"You killed him for the wrong girl. Think about that for the rest of your miserable life."

"Her?"

The way she dismissed Annie made me want to slap her.

"She's a better person than you are, Kristin. And that's even before we consider that you're a stupid, selfish, murdering bitch."

Gruen grabbed Kristin's hand. "Put the gun down," he said.

Kristin shrieked, but she was no match for him. And after a second, he had the gun and she was sobbing against the pile of coats and sweaters.

Gruen's partner, Detective Vilar, walked in from the kitchen, gun drawn. He pulled a white card out of his pocket. "Kristin Blake?" he asked in a tone so polite I could barely hear him.

Everything happened extremely fast after that, or at least it seemed to. Kristin was arrested and taken by somebody. Penelope gave her statement to someone. The police swept through both houses to make sure we didn't have anyone else lying in wait with heavy artillery.

Gruen wanted a statement and Nathaniel okayed it. So I recapped everything that had happened that night, even the parts he knew. After we were done, I looked at Nathaniel. "Can I have a second with him?" I asked.

Nathaniel didn't say anything.

"It's not anything to do with Colin's murder," I said.

My lawyer held up a hand: I had five minutes. Then he wandered over to the outdoor living room, where Stevie was pouring glasses of water for the people who were still here.

"You didn't bring your close personal law enforcement friends with you?"

"They're waiting for me to give them a call back."

"They might frown on locals withholding evidence."

"I called my friend in Washington," he said. "The one who ran your name for me? I asked him to run these guys."

"And...they're not actually FBI," I guessed.

He nodded. "Something wrong there."

"If it bothers you, I'm certain they're legitimate government employees. They're probably just doing someone a favor."

"What did you do? Why are they looking for you?"

I smiled. As I'd said to Kristin, confession is good. The human need to confess is strong and universal. Every authoritarian organization has played on this trait for thousands of years. You just don't feel the need to confess if you honestly believe you did the right thing. And besides which, I'd gotten absolution a thousand times over from the one person who could give it to me, Stevie.

I shook my head. "It's not your problem."

"Why are they here?"

"To put a bullet in my frontal lobes."

He did that squinting thing, as if trying to figure out if I was kidding or not. Then he nodded and reached into his pocket. To get his handcuffs? To get his phone to call Ed and Fred?

Stress was making me a moron, saying something like that to him. So I did my usual flirtatious grin, as if to say, *Just kidding.* "Don't worry about me. I'll be fine. What are you going to tell them?"

He held up a baggie, and I blinked at a sudden reflection of light.

My bracelet.

He was going to show them my bracelet?

Then I got it.

"That's where you got my fingerprints."

"The bracelet belonged to an Australian magician who worked in Las Vegas, pawn shop capital of the world. Who's to say where he got it?"

The magnitude of the lie he was about to tell floored me. I don't like being in debt to people, for any reason, for any amount. "Well played, Detective. What's the price? Don't be shy, I'm willing to pay it. Whatever it is."

"If they do any further digging, it's your problem." He put the baggie away. "You won't be getting this back."

"No, they'll take that off your hands." I wasn't upset to see it go. It was time to begin a new phase of my life. I hadn't realized the weight of the stress I'd been under until that moment, when it lifted. "So. What now?"

"You owe me. I have the feeling this is an investment that will pay off."

"I have a list of things I'm quite talented at."

"I'm sure." He wrote something in his notebook and put it away without looking over at me again.

Nathaniel wandered over and handed me a cup of water, which I drank without even thinking about it.

"What was that about?" he asked.

"Kristin's confessed to killing Colin. Vin's confessed to being an accessory. The LAPD has no further interest in me. Oh, and the detective's offering not to turn me over to the feds. In my wildest dreams this involves sexual blackmail of some sort. That about covers it. You?"

"You're in good spirits," Nathaniel said.

"They've arrested Colin's murderer. What's not to like?"

True, I still felt like hell, I was somewhat responsible for Colin's death, and none of this had brought him back from the dead. But at least this part of the night was over.

Nathaniel and I walked back out to the pool area without speaking. I thought about Colin and the more I thought about him and how he lived and why he died, the sadder I became. And then, with no warning, I burst into tears. Hysterical tears. Unstoppable tears. For Colin, for the mess Kristin had made, for what could have been. For what I did to Peter Quaid eleven years ago. For what was.

Everything that I hadn't felt over the past two days or the past decade came pouring out in a rush, and I had to stop moving because my legs wouldn't hold me anymore. Nathaniel gently guided me onto a chaise longue, his arm around my shoulders. I must have destroyed the fabric of his suit, wiping my eyes and nose on his shoulder. Who cared. He could buy another suit. I could not buy another Colin, and I could not buy back what I had done eleven years ago. There is never any going back. However much you might want to.

CHAPTER TWENTY-FIVE

MORNING AT GARY'S ESTATE WAS simply glorious, no matter the weather. Because we were right on the ocean, it could be warm and sunny, or it could be cold and overcast.

Despite the time of year, today was one of the warm and sunny ones.

Cooking always calmed Stevie's nerves. After the crazy night we'd had, she was ready for some cooking. So first thing in the morning, she baked up a storm in the kitchen, and then she returned upstairs to lie down for a while. And hide.

I arranged a small repast on the French cafe table on the veranda, set the three chairs in place, and then sat down to wait for Roberto's arrival.

Stevie and I didn't retreat to the Peninsula after the police left. After I collected myself, Nathaniel argued with me about staying versus leaving. We settled it by my calling Roberto and telling him I would see him in the morning. And neither the time nor the place was negotiable.

I handed Nathaniel's phone back to him. "He'll pay you in full, no matter what, don't worry."

He just shook his head at me.

Stevie and I walked back to the guesthouse, and we talked. A short talk. But one we'd avoided for so long.

"It's time to get help," I said.

"You mean a psychologist, for me?" she said.

I nodded. "And me."

She had a quick in-draw of breath, and then she gave me a big hug, not one of her usual little-sister hugs, but one of a friend who actually gave a good goddamn whether I lived or died.

I thought about that, as I sat at the French table and waited.

Roberto's car arrived precisely at eleven a.m. The limousine parked halfway down the driveway that led around to the guesthouse. The chauffeur hopped to open the back door and Roberto glided out. He strode across the lawn without noticing any of it—as fantastic estates went, for Roberto this one probably rated as someplace the help might be stashed.

I glanced up at the balcony outside Gary's master bedroom. He was in the window, watching. He'd said we could stay. For a bit, but only if things were exciting in a safe, not-too-exciting way. I compromised with him and said I wouldn't bring home any more psychotic killers. Unless it couldn't be helped.

Roberto stopped at the edge of the black stone walkway that ringed the guesthouse. "Why aren't you ready to leave?"

"Won't you sit down and join me?" I said.

"Your game playing is tiresome."

I poured two coffees from the carafe. "Good. I think so, too.

So here it is. I'm not going back to New York with you."

"Why not?"

"Because Stevie is here. Until she comes with me or she's all right staying on her own, I belong with her."

He hitched up the knees of his trousers as he sat on the chair opposite me. "You are prepared to live this way for the rest of your natural life?"

I smiled. And nodded.

Roberto shook his head. "You can't do this. Living on people's charity. Or worse."

"I'll make do, as always."

"You belong back in New York."

"Change the terms and we're both on that flight with you."

He took his glasses off and rubbed them with his pocket handkerchief. "What makes you think I won't simply take you with me?"

I looked at the limo, taking my own sweet time, and then back at Roberto. "Because we're missing a player. There's you, and there's me, and there's..." I pointed to the empty chair.

It took him a mite longer to figure out what I was hinting at than I expected. He narrowed his eyes and shook his head, confused. "Jane's waiting for you in New York."

"No, she isn't. I mean, yes, she is, but she doesn't know she's waiting for me, does she? If she knew, she would have been here with you. Or flown out the next day. But she's not here. She hasn't called. Not once. You've been here for almost a week and she's back there. How on earth have you explained to her what you're doing here? Work? Hm. Well, I'm sure I could come up with a way to explain it to her."

The dawning realization of where I was going with this

bloomed on Roberto's face and I almost laughed right then. "My God, Trudy—"

"Drusilla," I reminded him. "It's Drusilla, until such time as, well, it isn't. What do you think Mumsy is going to say when I tell her you found me about a week ago? And you never mentioned a word to her? I think she's not going to like that."

He was disgusted with me, and he didn't bother to hide it. "You would tell her such a lie."

"Oh, no. No no. I would tell her the truth. I would tell her what had happened. Thing is, Roberto, I'm very, very good at making the truth sound like a lie. And I've had problems with stepfathers and other men in the past. She'd hear the story of how and when you found me from you, and then she'd hear it from me, and my story would be just this much different." I squeezed my thumb and index fingers together. "And your marriage will be over so fast you won't believe it."

"You would do that to your mother?"

"To protect Stevie? Absolutely. I have done worse, after all. Speaking of whom. You need to find out what my father is up to. I don't fancy waking up dead any time soon. If I have another problem with him, I'll go public. With everything. Ask me if Mama is going to survive some of those revelations."

We sat there for a few moments in silence. I sipped my coffee while Roberto stared at me in shock.

"You're playing with fire."

"It's my favorite form of exercise."

"You belong back in New York," he said, repeating himself.

That quaver in his voice was a wonderful thing to hear. I'd won.

"Now's not a good time, but—" I glanced down at my watch.

"—I can make it in, oh, two and a half years. In court, if necessary. Or any time before then. Your call."

He sat back, his head hitting the exterior of the guesthouse, and we sat there in silence together for a few moments. "You will stay in Los Angeles."

"Maybe I like moving every two months or so."

He glared at me. "Find something you like about this place and stay put."

His real message wasn't very subtle. I knew what he was telling me. He had a handle on where I was and I wouldn't be off his radar screen ever again. So if Los Angeles was all right, I might as well get comfortable.

"You'll remain here? With that actor?"

I glanced up at the window again. Gary was gone. "He's not my boyfriend, Roberto. As long as he'll put up with us, I'm perfectly fine. He seems quite fond of Stevie. And she's—" I wanted to say *happy* or *secure* or *steady*, but please: I was hopeful, not deluded. "She seems to like Los Angeles as much as anywhere."

Roberto seemed like he had a million things he wanted to tell me, or dictate to me, but instead he shot his cuffs and stared out the window for a minute. "Well. Is there anything I can do for you before I leave? At least let me give you some money."

I shook my head. "You have stringy money. I've held out for eleven years. A few more is not a long time at this point. Then we'll have a real talk, all of us. And Roberto?"

"What?"

"Look into how you're going to raise me from the dead, would you? I have an awful lot of money coming my way on my thirtieth. I plan on getting it."

"Drusilla, listen—"

"We do things my way, or we do them the hard way. Your choice."

He left. I watched him go with something approaching sadness. I actually liked Roberto, as much as I liked anyone. He saved me once, he did, I am happy to say that. Now I need to save myself and not rely on anyone.

Most people would take the easy road. Most people go along to get along, and live a life of quiet desperation, and all that crap. Most people don't go out of their way to make their lives that much harder.

And if I'd learned nothing else from the past few months, it was that most people don't really have the stomach to use blackmail to get what they want.

I, on the other hand, have no such qualms.

About The Author

Diane Patterson has an MFA in Film from the University of Southern California and a BA in Linguistics from Stanford University. She's been a shill in a magic act, a production assistant on a science-fiction TV show, and a tech writer at Apple. She lives with her family in the San Francisco Bay Area.

Want to get an email when my next book is released? Sign up here: http://eepurl.com/uP4yD

Books By Diane Patterson

The Sound Of Footsteps

You Know Who I Am

Everybody Takes The Money

Visit DianePatterson.com for up-to-date information.

For news about new releases, join the mailing list: http://eepurl.com/uP4yD

Follow Diane on Twitter: https://twitter.com/dianepatterson

Diane's Author page on Facebook: http://www.facebook.com/pages/Diane-Patterson/331432836956998